Counting Sleeping Beauties

By the same author

Drawing from Memory
Letters from Africa: A goldmine of Creative Calligraphy
Memoirs: Our Stories, Our Lives

Counting Sleeping Beauties

Hazel Frankel

First published by Jacana Media (Pty) Ltd in 2009

10 Orange Street
Sunnyside
Auckland Park 2092
South Africa
+2711 628 3200
www.jacana.co.za

ISBN 978-1-77009-544-1

Set in Caslon 10.5/13.5
Printed by CTP Book Printers, Cape Town
Job No. 000984

See a complete list of Jacana titles at www.jacana.co.za

Dedication
For E. E.

Acknowledgements

I would like to thank Joy Orlek, Stella Granville, Avril Rubenstein and Judy Shear who read early drafts of the manuscript and believed in its worth; Stella Kane who gave so generously of her time, skills and insights to bring the novel to its current form; the judges of the EU award for their favour; Bridget and Maggie at Jacana for their infectious enthusiasm.

My husband Lester and my children Ilan, Daniella, Gabriel and Jonathan have been an ongoing source of encouragement, support and love: thank you all so much.

Prologue
2000

In my mother's things after she dies, I find an old shoebox. It is labelled in her convent cursive Hannah's Box and has painted flowers and butterflies all the way around the sides. On the lid is a park with a lake, the sun's rays extending across the whole length and breadth as if to obliterate the shadows thrown by the tall, green trees. Bright silver stars are scattered over the black background inside. I feel the weight of the thick wax crayons as I run my fingers over my childhood.

In the box, bundled and tied together with still-shiny ribbons are the letters that I wrote in broad print during the time when my voice was silenced, in the time of the disappearance of colour. Gently I separate the pages, some have torn on the fold lines as if they have been looked at and replaced many times. They are undated but the order in which they were written has been preserved.

I read:

Dear Isabelle,
Please will you bring me a music box like Elise's?
With love from Hannah.

Dear Fairy Isabelle,
We are having a ballet concert with fairies and elves
and birds and butterflies. I want to be the Blue Rose.
With love from Hannah.

Dear Fairy Queen Isabelle,
Can you tell Zeida and Bobba to come home, please?
The house is so empty and I miss them.
With love from Hannah.

Each letter starts at the top edge of the page. There are no ruled lines so the writing slopes upwards and there is a large space underneath each body of writing. The lead of the pencil is smudged and the words are uneven, though each is separated from the next by the measured space of a small forefinger.

I don't want to go back to that place but, as if transfixed by the headlights of a motorcar, I can't stop myself. I open one letter after another.

I wrote them to my Fairy Queen, Isabelle. My mother preserved each one.

The route of the driveway to the Sanctuary has not been altered, although it is no longer rough gravel but neat, grey brick. At the top, outside Stone House, I park and get out of the car, the late afternoon sun glowing through the jacaranda trees where I once hid away in the mass of lilac florets.

I stop walking and stare down, transfixed to the place just as I was then. My cheeks are wet as a breath of wind brushes my cheek.

The children gather around me. They babble and giggle, following me onto the lawn where we sit in a circle, Marina and Xhosi, James and Tuli, Lily and Enrico. Inside, the babies are fast asleep in their cots, watched over by Sister Sula. My own daughters, Tanya and Ella are at home. I will see them soon, after these little ones are safely tucked up in their beds.

Across the orange rooftops of Johannesburg, the shadows fall as the bright red sun ball sink towards the horizon. There isn't a sound as I clear my throat and begin to read,

"In the high and far-off times, O Best Beloved, when the world was very young...."

Part 1
1953-1955

Rock, Paper, Scissors

A children's game in which the hand represents either paper, rock or scissors. Paper beats rock, rock breaks scissors and scissors cuts paper. The game is similar to Eenie, Meeny, Mynie, Mo, throwing a dice, flipping a coin or drawing straws, and results in the random selection of winner or victim.

The Stone House smells of cinnamon and nutmeg and spices.

"Nearly ready, Clementine," I say, "then we will have tea with Bobba and Zeida. You'll see." I am resting with my dolls until we can eat our warm gingerbread. I stare at the squares on the ceiling where light and shadow dance on the pressed flowers in the corners.

When Mommy bakes, she looks up Mrs Beeton's recipe and then spreads newspapers over the kitchen table. I sift the flour and baking powder into the ceramic bowl. Sometimes the handle of the sifter sticks and the flour flies out and I cough. The eggs and sugar whip together in the mixing bowl and change colour from dark yellow to light. The mixture whooshes all the way up the sides of the bowl and Mommy says,

"I think that's enough now, Hannah." She stops the machine and scoops down the batter with her bendy spatula. "Do you want to lick off the beaters?" The runny mixture is sweet and delicious. I curl my tongue round the cold metal and slurp off the last drops. "Here, use the spatula." She gives it to me and I clean the bowl so Violet won't have to wash it. When the cake is ready, I have a slice, steaming and crumbly and the butter melts down my chin.

Zeida drinks his tea from a glass, sucking a sugar lump. He always says, "*Ay a maichl.*" He tells me it means a miracle and when I say, "Zeida, what's a miracle?" he smiles at Bobba and Mommy as we sit together in the kitchen and says, "This."

Violet takes away our cups and plates. I sit in the scullery as she washes up and then go with her into the yard to take down the washing. She always clicks her tongue if it's drizzling or if the dogs come near the clean sheets.

3

I get up and close the door to preserve a few more peaceful moments so I can finish the seam I'm working on. Hannah is in her room giving her dolls a tea party as usual. Clementine, her favourite, has a new cape that my mother knitted. My mother is having her afternoon nap.

Carefully, I feed the satin under the foot, the only sound in the house the clacking treadle of my sewing machine. If I make a mistake, I will have to pull the stitching out and this will ruin the patina. At least Hannah isn't in here pleading for a chance to press the pedal and then racing the foot across the fabric.

A sharp kick below my ribcage makes me catch my breath. The swell of my stomach is obvious now. I will be most disappointed if the dress doesn't fit me for Nathan's function, the lawyers' ball and highlight of our social calendar. There will be a five-piece band this year and we are all looking forward to dressing up for the occasion and dancing after the presentations have been made. Madge, Beatrice and I practise the waltz and quickstep moves together in the lounge, playing *Fascination* and *Some Enchanted Evening* on our gramophone. At first we dance on the carpet but trip over our own feet. Now when they come over, we roll back the carpet and dance on the wooden floor. We put on our new high-heel shoes, and giggle at our antics as we try to keep our balance. There will be more decorum when I waltz with Nathan, his hand in the small of my back as he reaches down, his height a striking contrast to my small frame.

Reluctantly, I fold up the dress panels, some of which are still pinned to the paper pattern, and place them on top of my wardrobe. I call Hannah and she follows me down the long passage with its pressed ceiling and shiny wooden floor, past the stained glass window, down the stone stairs and into the glorious summer sunshine. We meet Nathan striding up the driveway, debonair in his new pin stripe suit, having given his old one away so as not to clutter his wardrobe. His hair is smartly slicked back despite a long day at the office.

Hannah runs.

"Daddy, Daddy! Come see. I can do cartwheels. Come to the front lawn."

"Careful my spectacles, Hannah." He takes them out of his pocket and hands them to me, then lifts her high on his shoulders and carries her off.

"Nathan, you do know Frans has a shebeen in the back garden?"

"Susan, the last thing I can face now is a domestic drama. I've had a difficult day with that Supreme Court case pending and the advocate querying the finer details. In any event, how can you be so sure?"

"I smelt beer on his breath while we were planting the pansies and violets. Then I saw him skulking by the compost heap. I went to check and found my freesia and hyacinth bulbs next to buckets of fermenting sugar and bread!"

"Oh, it's skokiaan, I suppose."

"It's no wonder it's so busy in the lane on Thursday afternoons and no wonder he's around then, even though it is his day off. How could he have deceived me for so long? He has to be discharged, Nathan."

"Pity to let him go, though. The garden is looking glorious with the pink and lilac of the sweet peas and the yellow and orange of the Barberton daisies. He's a good worker – you've always said so."

"You sound as if you condone his behaviour but really...."

"I suppose it could become quite ugly if he is drunk on the job."

"He needs a warning at the very least. Tell him to get rid of his brew today!"

"I'll chat to him about it. I'd hate for Hannah to find the stuff."

As Hannah finishes her cartwheels, Nathan shows her how to swing an old golf club of his that he has cut down for her. They stand on the lawn and aim towards the front door.

"Do be careful of the flowerbed, Hannah. And that stained

5

glass is the focus of the façade. It's a hundred years old so please watch what you're doing."

"Don't worry, Sue. It's the perfect putting distance for Hannah. And it is only a plastic ball." Nathan turns to Hannah and I suspect he winks at her as she swipes again. The ball flies through the air and lands at my feet. "And she's improving all the time. Aren't you, Hannah?" I hand the ball back to her as a car revs up the driveway. My father has returned from having his hearing aid checked.

"Zeida, Zeida! Is it fixed now?"

"I hope so." He steps out of the car, slams the door and straightens his braces.

"Here, Hannahle, a Nestlé for you." He gives her the one-penny chocolate in its red wrapper and she puts it in her pocket. He pushes up his sleeves where the silver elasticised bands hold up the white material. "Come to my arms, you bundle of charms." Grabbing her, he swings her round and round so that her arms stretch wide towards me. "My little Blackie! How was your day?" He ruffles her dark shiny curls and puts her down so that she is standing on his shoes.

As he moves, the hearing aid gives a piercing whistle. He sighs and fiddles to adjust it where it is clipped to the front of his shirt. The screech intensifies.

"Daddy's going to read to me, Zeida. Come with, come with!" They do the quick step into the cool house and I drift in behind them, imagining the perfect satin of my seams.

In the breakfast room, Nathan takes her on his lap and rocks in the old chair. Once more he begins the Kipling tale,

"…Then at last the Elephant's Child came to the great, grey, green, greasy Limpopo River all set around with fever trees," and Hannah shrieks, "great! grey! green! greasy! Again, Daddy. Read more!"

Nathan hugs her tight.

Sometimes I take my lunch in my bedroom. I blow my soup cool and offer Hannah the spoon.

"It's delicious," I say, as is all the food in my daughter's house.

"No thank you, Bobba," she says. "You eat. I'll have mine now-now."

Day after day, *tog-tegelach*, I am in bed, unable to get up. I wait for Susan to sit beside me. If Hannahle is back from school she stays with me.

If you can't do as you wish, do as you can – *az men ken nit vi men vil, tut men vi men ken.*

I put the cards onto the *perena*.

"*Lomir shpielen*. Let's play." I deal to the side of my legs where the bed is flat. I try not to bump and mix them up.

"*Tsvei far dir un tsvei far mir*. Two for you. Two for me."

"Can I take *these* cards together?" She points to the three and four of spades, then the seven of clubs.

"*Gut, gut.*"

"Bobba, you must say, good, good. Can I take the queen and the king together? They both have a heart!"

"No, no. Queens go with queens. Like this." My brother David taught me *Cassino*. So many years ago. Struggled to teach me tactics. I never cared about the game. All I wanted was to spend time with him. Have his full attention.

"You must watch the cards and count what's gone out." The words I hear are still in his voice.

"Are the kings and queens married, Bobba?" We laugh and go on playing. Hannah's tongue sticks out from between her teeth as she concentrates. She clears the deck.

"Bobba, *I'm* winning this time!" So she has her chance to deal. She places the cards down in twos, holding the full pack tightly. No cards fall.

I lean back against the pillows and close my eyes. A poem starts in my head:

Fire in the stove.

Burning wood.

Chattering teeth.

"Bobba, what's the matter?" Hannah stands beside me.

"It's nothing, Hannahle." I know I cannot explain my memories to her. But how content we are, Hannah and I, together, counting our points.

From my wardrobe I fetch down a small wooden box with my special trinkets.

"Look, Hannahle, on the ship I kept this under my head every night when I slept."

"Oh, like your pillow!"

"When Zeida and I stepped out together for the first time, I wore this." I take out the round brooch, framed with a circle of silver. She holds it carefully, shining the grey stone on her jersey. Then I take out the necklace of bright beads, from my parents on my twelfth birthday, my *Bat Mitzvah* day. Special even without a party. Also in the box are tiny pieces of brown wrapping paper. My poems. About Morris. About David. About Cossacks, *a cholerye af zei*, may the cholera be upon them. Perhaps I will read them again later.

Ice over the lake.

Laughter echoes.

Birds stitch the bloody sky.

So long since I was well enough to write. But I must try again.

"Bobba, please can I wear it?" Hannah wants the brooch on her nightdress. I carefully pin it onto her peter pan collar.

I point at the brass samovar. The copper platters. My silver candlesticks. "I brought these on the ship from Litte, wrapped in the *perena* from my bed. To keep them safe. All the things from *my* Bobba. Your great-great-grandmother. One day they will be yours."

"What's great-great?" I try to explain. "And where's Litte, Bobba?"

"Lithuania is far away. Over the sea. In Russia. I lived in a *shtetl* called Yaneshik. Zeida came from another shtetl called Kurshan. Such small towns with streets full of *blotte*, full of mud. *Blotte* when it rained. *Blotte* when it didn't. Sometimes the wooden houses caught fire and we ran with buckets. No Jews live there anymore." I am sorry I say this but she doesn't ask me anything. "We came here by cart, then train, then boat. We were herrings in a barrel at the bottom of the boat. How the babies cried. How the animals moaned in steerage. No fresh air. Vomiting as the ship rocked in the storms. We had hard-boiled eggs, cold potatoes, dried biscuit, dried fish. It took five months to get here. *Eints, tsvei, drei, fier, finf menaten.*" I show her the numbers with my fingers. The noise, the stink, the fear all come back to me.

Afterwards we landed at Cape Town, passed through immigration. My friends were given new surnames, names not their own. Because the boere couldn't understand their Yiddish. I was lucky. The official said, "*Ag ja, Leah, een van die moeders van die Bybel*, one of the great mothers of the Bible." I even kept my own maiden name, Weinstein. Maybe because it is like his language, Afrikaans.

"We came to Johannesburg. Lived in Wynberg. After a time, my twin sisters Betty and Rosie also came looking for husbands. They stayed with us and the *shadchen* fixed them up." I can see that Hannah doesn't understand. Not the ideas. Not my mixture of Yiddish and English. Still she listens, looking at my face. "Then they moved to their own homes but we always spent *Shabbos* and *Yom Tov* together." I go on, "When your Mommy married your Daddy, they lived in a one bedroom flat in Clarendon Circle. We wrapped you up tightly in your blanket when you were born. You slept in a drawer." I show her with my hands. "You were this small."

"Like the cat's cradle Zeida makes with string, Bobba."

"Then, you all moved here to Parktown so you could have a garden to play in." Morris gave Nathan and Susan the down payment for this house. He had made a profit in the share market and didn't have to work anymore. How proud we were then. As they say, *ver es hot gelt hot di gantse velt* – he who has money has the whole world.

"You know, Hannahle, the first thing I bought was our own

9

dinner service. With *twenty-four* of each kind of plate. Side, soup, fish and meat. Royal Doulton. Fine English crockery."

"Is it the special dishes for *Shabbos* with the green leaves and red flowers, Bobba?"

"Yes, that's right, darling. And on *Pesach* we use different crockery. And kings' pattern cutlery for everyone. At home, we had to *kasher* the same plates we used every day to have enough at our *seder.*"

A man's voice comes over on the wireless. Iron, steel, engineering and electrical. The stock exchange report. We hear it every day. Morris stops his game of Patience. He puts his head close to the loudspeaker. Hannah stands behind him. Afterwards comes the weather report. There is no gale warning.

"Bobba, what's gale warning?"

"*Ich veis nit.* I don't know." In such things I am as ignorant as she. Morris takes her on his lap,

"Look, Hannahle, my game is nearly over. I can put the ten and eleven of hearts here, then the *yas*, that's the jack, then queen, king, ace! And I win." She turns over his cards and shows me the bicycles, the same as on the red and blue packs she uses with me.

Salt on the challah, salt on my cheeks,
wine in the silver cup, wine in my veins.
Spilt salt. Spilt blood. Empty sky.

Through the open window David crawled and ran. The Cossacks, *a cholerye af zei*, may the cholera be upon them, shot him anyway. My tears run. The child's eyes are on me. She jumps off Morris's lap, comes up to my pillow. She strokes my arm, her hand under the *perena*. I say the *Shema Yisrael* and Hannahle copies me, *kein ainhora*. She skips out of the room and comes back dragging her old carrycot.

"Bobba, this is for my new baby! What do you think?"

10

Ma and I look at each other. We grind mieliemeal in Ma's *tshetlo* and *lekwala*. Boil, then stir. We dip the pap in the tomato and onion on a separate wooden plate, so we know each food is good even when eaten on its own. Afterwards, we drink sour milk that the donkey man gave us for our dried beans. Ma sweeps our room, the packed *boloko* floor with two sleeping mats and Matlina's wooden cradle. I unpin my *kobo*, blue and orange, then fetch cool water in Ma's pot from the great clay drum in the shade of the tree. The cold wind blows, but we keep warm by the side of the mountain from the fire next to our round hut. And always I wait for Jack.

Maybe I could still be at school, leaving at cock-crow and – then back at sunset, summer and winter, had Pa not left us here in Pietersburg. My reading and writing were getting better and the teacher told me that I would be teacher, one day. But Pa hit Ma and she fell to the ground. Stop! Stop! Stop! I hid away, too scared to breathe.

"*Ek is weg! Nou is ek weg.*" He threw the sjambok on the sand and left. There was nothing that I could do to stop him. Now though, I must look out for Ma and she for me. I cook *stywe* pap, or sometimes mielierys for my brothers. They keep watch over the cows and sheep on van Rooyen's farm, and come home tired and cold at the end of the day.

"Supper," I shout. Then they drink their beer and go to visit their women. If Jack is around, we eat meat.

"Ready, Ma," I say and we sit outside on the green grass under the edge of the grass roof to keep the sun from our eyes and suck on the oranges from the valley. I squeeze juice into Matlina's mouth and she drinks it up like a baby sparrow. She's so pretty with her dark skin and bright black eyes. She walks now and speaks a little. When she calls me, she laughs and I take her *pepa*. I do everything for her and I must do everything right. I love her and I tell her this. It is different from how I love Jack.

Today is the first time that I leave my home. Ma cries and

11

lifts Matlina's hand in a wave. When I come back, I will make some small oxen of river clay for her to play with. Like the ones Pa made for me when I was a small girl. This is what I think as I sit at the back of the train.

They say Jack went to Egoli, Johannesburg, so I must go there too. This is the only way. There is nobody to look after us. My uncle is the leader of our Zion Christian Church. He drives a big black car when he comes to see us, but he has his own wives and children. The money he gives is little and Ma does not want to ask for more. She still works but she is too old to go far from home, so now I must. Ma will look after Matlina and visit me when I am in job with good money. I want Matlina to have books and clothes for school.

Why did Jack leave me? He's not a tsotsi but he forgot to say goodbye. I know that he's a good man but now I am alone and I must look after our baby, his baby, made next to the fire on the night of my sixteenth birthday, under the moon. Yes, he is my husband in the true way because he lay with me many nights, and afterwards, he held me.

I sing *Tula tu tula baba tula summa* for myself and for Matlina, our daughter. How I love to hold her in my arms to suck my breasts and sleep on my back or on the grass mat by the doorway. Always I can hear her if she cries while I am at the fire. The singing fills my heart.

A woman needs only three things: the love of her mother, the love of her husband and the love of his seed. So always I am hoping for one thing. That when I get to Egoli, the man I see when I get off the train will be Jack. That he will come behind me and put his hands over my eyes, pick me up and take me to a place where I'm safe, where I won't have to worry.

Today I'm wearing my church dress, dark green, with buttons in front. My other clothes are in my brown packet, which is tied with string. The skin under my feet is hard from hopping with no shoes in the sand and Ma's shoes pinch me. It is a long journey and I have cold, stiff pap for my lunch and for my supper. The train moves from the platform. I stand to see my Matlina from the window and she calls "Ma!" to me.

12

I laugh and send kisses to them with both my hands from my mouth. Then I can't see them anymore with all the people around me trekking to Egoli in the hot train. I sit in my small place. If I go to the lavatory I will lose this place but already my bladder is pressing. I must not make a fool of myself in front of these strangers. Softly I say to the woman sitting next to me,

"Please, I must go. Can you hold my seat?" I see that she can understand Sesotho because she nods her head. I take my bundle with me and make my way in the passage, past all the people and say, "*Skusie. Skusie.*" The train rocks. I look for the latrine. There is a sign *Nie-Blankes Alleenlik/Non-Whites Only.* English, Afrikaans. No Sesotho, no Xhosa yet so many black people are here. I wait in a line. I think I will burst. I go in the small room and close the door. The lock is broken so I put my packet in front of it. Also my foot, just to be safe. But I don't feel safe. I sit on the closed lid, stand up, open it and sit down on the cold seat of wood. At last I let go of my bladder but there is nothing to dry myself with. There is a long chain with a handle. I pull it quickly and there is a grumbling noise when the water comes down. I am surprised but there is nobody to laugh with me. I wonder where the water goes. At home, we dig a hole in the ground at the back of the hut and cover it with soil.

I wash my hands under the drips from the tap and splash my face. I take off my doek, smooth down my hair and cover my head again. I go back to my seat and thank the old woman. Her mouth moves as if to smile at me. Then her tears come. Her chest shakes in her blue dress with white on the sleeves and collar for the religious society of her family. She is not from Z C C and at home I must not talk to these people. Here I think it does not matter, we are far from her church and mine. We are nowhere.

So Gertrude tells me her sorrow, takes a cloth from her pocket and blows her nose.

"My sister has died. There is no money for the coffin, or to slaughter a cow to feed everyone, or for beer and *puttu* pap." I know the shame for the family if the funeral is not done right.

"We sent my brother a telegram at the mines. No reply. I must go to the compound to look for him. The life is hard for woman alone," she says.

Maybe the one she seeks will be the first one she sees when she gets off the train, I think. Her hope is my hope. Our bodies sway and touch each other and I feel comfort from this stranger.

"Matlina looks like Jack. Just the same," I tell Gertrude.

I think about that night under the moon. By the fire. Jack put his arms around me to kiss me to show me what's what. With us Sotho, only when the woman carries his child and our man sees we are strong enough to carry his seed, will he give lobola and stay with us. But then he leaves to be with another woman and forgets his firstborn. Ma told me this – because of Pa. But nothing could put out our fire, not Ma's words for sure, my heart drumming with so much wanting. I think about Jack's flat belly and muscles from carrying wood and coal for the fires on the trains. He is my Jack and he is my song.

At last we are at Park Station in the city of gold. We are tired and hungry. We step down the narrow stairs of the carriage onto the platform, with the railway line dark under us. It is so strange, the smell of the train and the city, the noise of the engine with smoke coming from the chimney. Gertrude has a torn paper like mine with an address on it. We must both find a place to stay and a place to work.

When we come out into the street, there are people everywhere, more than I have ever seen together, even at Sunday church. Fruit sellers calling, men selling pap and wors, children eating monkey nuts and spitting out the shells, running with bare feet, women shouting, *Mielies! Mielies*! Everyone pushing and bumping. The streets are full of cars but none with black people. Only some buses. Also separate buses for whites. I am afraid that I might get on the wrong one. I don't know how much to pay for the ticket. My food packet is empty and I haven't eaten since the train.

I bid farewell to Gertrude. She wishes me the same and goes on her way. How we will find each other again? I wish I were at home with Ma on the green hill, me singing to Matlina and suckling her. What now? I look at Ma's paper. Again I must talk to strangers. Suddenly a man's voice is next to my ear.

"*Ousi.*" I stand stiff. I am not "*Ousi.*" I am young and full of life. I don't know if he is crook but I must ask. I take in my breath and show my paper.

"Jan Smuts Avenue. *Kom, ek sal dit vir jou wys. Kom, kom.*" I keep myself straight and my parcel of clothes tight to my chest. He grabs my arm.

"*Loop regs daar.* Go right at the corner, then straight. After three blocks, *gaan links*, go left. Then you can't go anymore. It's like this." He makes his one hand touch the other on the palm like a T. I know my letters well from school, so does he think I'm a *setlatla*? "So then you must go right again." He checks the house number.

"It's far. *Sal ek met jou loop?* Want me to walk with you?"

"No. Thank you. *Baie dankie.*"

I begin. The streets are wide and of black, hard stone. My legs are tired and it is dark already. My stomach feels like string inside but I must walk up straight. Behind the high buildings I see the same stars that are at my home. I cross the bridge over the railway. More buildings. Then the houses start. I want to sit down on the side of the road. I have nothing left to drink. My face is wet and the perspiration drips between my breasts. My feet are so swollen. Ma's shoes are tight with one lace broken. I think I can take them off but then I won't be able to put them back.

The night is black when I find my number. There are big wooden gates that stand open and a steep hill with so many trees I can't see where the house is. I pull in my breath. I must walk up and round, round and up, up and up over lots of small, loose stones. At last, at the top, Stone House. I fix my doek, smooth my dress and brush the dust off my shoes with a cloth. Then I see my Auntie Violet in the light of a window. Her head is down and she is washing dishes. I hear dogs barking and then something heavy hits my chest, knocking me down. I can't breathe.

"*Voetsek! Voetsek!*" The dog is so big and he bites and tears my dress. Then another one comes. I am on the ground. I try to kick them away.

"*Owa! Owa!* Help! Violet!"

"Sheriff! Major! Down, boys! Down!" A voice comes out of the dark.

The dogs jump off me and run away. I stand. I worry how I look. Lucky there is no blood but my dress is torn. I wobble to my feet and my chest shakes.

"Sorry, baas. So sorry, Master! Thank you." I bob, clasp my hands together in front of me. Violet is next to me, wiping her hands on her apron. At first she doesn't know me but then she put out her arms.

"Sina! Is it Sina?" She hugs me to her breast.

"Violet, who is this woman?"

"It is my cousin's child, come from home. All the way from Pietersburg. Sorry, Master." The man smiles a bit.

"It's alright, Violet. Never mind. Give her some sugar water and something to eat. She's had a bad fright. She can sleep in your room tonight. Goodnight." He walks back into the house and Violet turns back to me.

"*Haai*! Sina, I'm so glad to see you. Let me give you some tea. You must be tired from the train. Look at you! We must clean you up. Did those *blerry* dogs hurt you?" Violet chatters as she walks me to the outside lavatory that is a hole in the cement floor with a chain to bring the water. She shows me where to shower. Then she takes me to her room and I sit on a wooden orange box. She brings me a big tin of rooibos tea and leaves me as she goes and finishes in the kitchen.

16

Early in the morning, *morgen in der frie*. Hannahle creeps into my room, a little shy. Her mother still sleeps. The child plays with my silver hairbrushes at my dressing table. She puts my tortoiseshell combs into her curls but they fall out and clatter onto the glass top. She peeps at me. I quickly shut my eyes. As they say, *az zei zoggen*, the treasure of children is greater than the dividends from money – *protsent fun kinder iz teierer vi fun gelt*.

"Bobba, are you awake?" She comes and sits on my bed. How we talk, she and me. Her voice is sweet. Like Dora, my sister in Lithuania who remained there with Miriam and with my *Tate-Mame*, my parents. "My teacher showed me how to do my name, Bobba, look." Hannah goes to the kindergarten and on a piece of paper she shows me her writing in red crayon. Always I tell her,

"Hannahle, no one can take away your education – *zei kennen fun dier nit aveknemen daine dertsiung*." I see her eyes grow big so I try to explain. "You must always learn well at school, Hannahle."

"You mustn't say lerren, Bobba. You must say learn!" Here in Johannesburg I am ashamed of my *tsebrochene Aingels*, my broken English. So I try again,

"You must always learn well at school, Hannahle," and she claps her hands together.

"Don't worry, Bobba. I will, you'll see." She sneezes and her little face crinkles. I think, *genossen af der emes*. It means to sneeze on the truth. I say,

"*In der heim*, in Russia, my brothers went to *cheder* until *Bar Mitzvah* age. But after that there was a quota for Jews in government school. None of us girls went. We helped in the house and also with our little shop in the front room. Our *shopkele*. We were so close to one another, Miriam, Betty, Rosie, Dora, Dina and I. We looked after the hens and chickens and eggs in the cellar. We collected the grapes in barrels for *Kiddush* wine and stored herring in vats. When the fish ran out, there was always the brine." Hannah doesn't know what I mean so I say, "It's salty water, like water from the sea, to keep the herring fresh," and she nods. "And we also helped others. We took *matza* at *Pesach* time to the families even more poor than ourselves and wine so that everyone could drink four cups and have enough to pour out enough for the ten plagues." I start the traditional refrain, "*dam, tzivardea, kinim, arov, dever ...*," and Hannah shouts

"I know, I know! Blood, frogs, lice, flies, murrain, boils, hail, locusts, darkness, killing of the first-born! See how well I learn my lessons, Bobba!"

Yes, she knows the words, may there be a blessing on her head – *a gezunt af ir keppele*. But she does not know how sometimes we had only one chicken – one between all of us. And meat only if a neighbour killed a cow. If we invited guests and strangers, only they would eat meat – we might get one bite. I think of the suppers of herring brine and rough black bread. Or a potato. If we were lucky we would exchange some eggs for a little flank, or some turnips for a few chops. Sometimes Mama sewed up a dress for Mrs Kuperowitz, or Tati helped Mr Rubinstein fix the wheel of his cart. Then they would give us a little butter for the rye bread or a drop of cream for the *burikes* soup. On *Shabbos* we ate *cholent* and *perogen* and sometimes a carp on *Yom Tov*. As they say, only in our dreams are there carrots as big as bears – *nor in cholem zainen meren vi beren*.

Yet we tried to make special times special. Believed completely that our divine Creator, blessed be He, had His reasons. That though He did not provide for us in this world He would provide for us in the next. Because we did not want to upset our parents, we said nothing. We consoled ourselves with our forefathers' wisdom: from overeating one suffers more than from not eating enough – *fun iberessen cholyet men mer vi fun nit deressen*.

"Mama used to say, 'Leah, the cart is coming. What a *tumel*. So much noise. Go with Betty and Dora please and bring some coal from the road.' So we collected the broken pieces from between the stones, put them in our aprons. Then we lit the *pripertchile*, fetched water in a bucket from the well in the market place, heated it.

"'We all learnt arithmetic too, Hannahle, so we could give the customers the right number of *zlotys* and *groschen*. Spoke our *Mame-Loshen*, Yiddish, and also a little Russian. Tati, our father, may he rest in peace, *zol er liegen in zain ru*, also showed us *Tate-Loshen*, Hebrew. How clearly I remember his words,

"'Leahle, Dorale, Mirala, this is the language of the scriptures and of our forefathers,' he said. 'Here is the *alef-beis*. They are the same characters as Yiddish but the sounds are different. Listen.' He read from the *siddur* and instructed us, 'when you pray, this is where you must bow and this is when you must stand up straight.' And still, before sleep, with my head on my pillow, his voices *davens*, *Shema Yisrael*...." I see Hannah put her hands over her eyes and whisper the same words to herself.

Winter was bitter. The wind howled around the privy. The trees were bare. But. Not only the weather, or the black spiders, or the hunger frightened us. There were also the laws of the Czar of all Russias, *zol er brennen afn fyer*, may he burn in the fire of hell. Laws for all the Jews that he forced into the Pale of settlement.

"Why did you come here, Bobba?" Hannah's voice interrupts my memories.

"Because we were almost starving in Yaneshik, Hannahle. Because here in Africa the summer is broiling but the law does us no harm. Because this is a land of milk and honey – *a land fun milch oen honik*." I don't mention Cossacks.

"I'm so glad you came here, Bobba, otherwise I wouldn't have known you." I can't help laughing. She puts up her fingers. One by one, I take them and we play the well-loved counting game, "*kleine yidderle, maise fiddele, holtshaker, shmantleker, grobbe poyer*."

"Bobba, please can I brush your hair?"

"Of course. And you can put in my tortoiseshell combs for me." I push back the goose-down *perena* and lift myself off the bed. My crocheted shawl is wrapped around my shoulders, the shawl given to me by Mama. With all her hopes for warmth in my marriage. I sit in front of the dressing table in my white flannel nightgown. Hannahle cuddles next to me on the stool. I put on my round spectacles and untie my headscarf. My hair falls to my shoulders and down my back, soft gold like the wheat in Russia. My eyes are like the lake near Yaneshik. Blue-grey.

I shake out the knots with my fingers and give Hannah my silver-backed brush. She pulls it through the hair. Scalp to end, scalp to end, softly stroking, never jerking.

"Bobba, look at your hair. It's fairy gold." I take the strands from her hand and wind them around my fingers. We watch them float down into the dustbin. I sing to her the words my mother sang to me, *Oifn pripertchile brent a fyerel*.

But suddenly I feel ill. My head is full of terrible noises. The memories come marching.

Four in the bed. Head to foot.
Bare window. Moonless sky.
Wolf at the door. Out! Out!

There is a choking feeling in my chest. The old feeling of rage and pain. I put my hand on Hannah's arm.

"Sorry Bobba, am I hurting you?" I twist my hair roughly on top of my head and jab in the pins. My plait is a crown but when I see my face in the looking glass it is white like snow, *vais vi shnei*. Hannah chatters,

"Bobba, I want my hair to be like yours. I'm going to tell Mommy not to cut it anymore." She grabs a towel from the drying rack and holds it over her short curls so it hangs down her back. She spins. The towel spins too.

"How do I look?" She takes my face in her hands. "Am I beautiful like you, Bobba?" She is so happy. I try to calm myself.

"Beautiful, Hannahle, *kein ainhora*. Now tell me the story of *Sleeping Beauty*." I listen carefully to each word and copy the sounds.

"You know I'm the princess waiting for my prince? It's in the fairy story Daddy reads to me, Bobba. Now *you* must tell

20

me one!" she laughs. I begin,

"In a forest far away there was a very poor old woman who had many, many children …. *Iz geven amol a babetska, on zie hot gehat a sach, a sach kinderlach.* One day she went away and the bad, big wolf came…."

As much as I try to think in English, it is the Yiddish words of my Tati that I hear inside me, "*oen er hot oefgegessen alle kleine kinderlach* and he ate up all the children. When the old woman came home, she cut the wolf open and they all jumped out. Then she filled up his stomach with stones and sewed him closed. All the children ran around shouting, "*Shteiner, beiner boich! Shteiner, beiner boich!* Now you have stones in your belly, Mr Wolf!"

Hannah helps me to put on my clothes. Her little fingers struggle with the cloth buttons down the back of my dress. Growing up, I was lucky to have Miriam's hand-me-downs. Too tight. Torn rags. *Tsurrissene shmattes.* Here, Morris drives me to the dressmaker who measures my body for the shirtwaist dresses I like, with the starched belts and wide buckles. I choose my own material. Pretty buttons, down the front, down the back; puffed sleeves in summer and tight long sleeves in winter. Whatever I want. I hear Morris talking to Nathan about a good business deal so I know there is money enough. And he is happy when he sees that I am feeling better.

"Pass to me my shoes Hannahle, please. Yes, that's right, the black ones with the laces." How my bunions ache. These shoes are too tight. I will ask Morris for new ones.

"Hannahle, I think we should make *latkes*, yes?"

"What's *latkes*, Bobba?"

"Grated, fried potato. Much better than boiled!" I sing to her, "*Zuntik bulves, Montik bulves, Dienstik bulves*…." Sunday, Monday, every single day in Litte, we ate potatoes. We made a joke of it, but it was no joke. "Come, you can help me grate them, Hannahle, but you must be careful of your fingers." She looks up to me,

"Say careful, Bobba, not kerreful!" I take her small hand in mine and slowly we walk to the kitchen.

21

"Here's the chicken, Zeida brought from the *shochet*. We must prepare everything today because we mustn't cook tomorrow, you know." *Shabbos* and holidays are celebrated in Johannesburg the same as back at home when the siren blew at the flourmill and we knew it was time to light candles, *bensh licht*. On *Yom Tov*, walkers came from other *shtetlach* to us to tell us it was time.

"Look, Bobba! Look at my face in the candlestick, all bent and shiny!" We polish the candlesticks together, me and Hannahle. She laughs, *zol zi gezunt zain*, may she stay well. I join in. As children my sisters and I did the same. Same candlesticks. Different kitchen. But here we also have decanters of home made wine and flowers in cut glass vases with a rose pattern. We are short of nothing.

Morris. Short like his brothers. Not very handsome. A square face. Eyes too close together and nose too big. There is a big dent on his forehead and he is deaf in his right ear. But he is a fine man, a *mentsh*. Gentle always, even though I have been a burden to him. After Susan, they told me no more babies, but he never speaks of it, only tells me I am the perfect wife and that he loves me still.

In the beginning, when he came to South Africa, Morris, Moshe we called him then, was a smous, a *tryer*. He travelled from farm to farm and into the towns hawking pots and pans, buttons and trinkets. He used a borrowed wagon, then got his own. He was away for many weeks and when he came home he was dirty and exhausted, *shmutsik* and *farmatert*. Afterwards he worked in the butchery with Charlie, his *landsman*, also born in Kurshan. Morris learned to cut and trim the meat. He also learnt to handle money.

Only then, at last, did he send for me, five years after our promise to be together. I was so afraid to leave my family behind. What would I find in the new country? But he was waiting for me, my Moshe, and we married and boarded with Charlie. When Charlie died, Moshe ran the business on his own.

We bought a house in Wynberg and also our own shop –

Gersons, General Dealers. Together we weighed out small packets – sugar, tea, butter, sold tinned food, jam, soap, Milk of Magnesia and Vaseline. The shop did well and Moshe made enough money to buy boat tickets for my family. Ita Liefsa, my dear sister, *zol zi liegen in ir ru*, may her soul rest peacefully, had already passed away and David, Dora and Miriam stayed with our parents. But Betty, Rosie and Dina came.

I am not sure if I am talking to myself or to Hannah. I peel the potatoes, cut up the chicken into pieces and sing,

"*In dem beis hamikdash, in a vinkele cheder, zietst die almone Bas-Tsion alein….*" With her tongue Hannahle makes the lullaby, "lalalala…," and we go on together, "*rozinkes mit mandlen….*"

When Morris comes home, our cooking is done. Hannah puts her hand into his pocket for her Nestlé. There she also finds a piece of string knotted into a circle.

"Blackie," he says, "let's try to get Cat's Cradle right." He holds her hands up and winds the string around them. Puts his own fingers through and changes the string into a pattern. A cradle. But when Hannah tries to lift it off with her small fingers, the pattern breaks.

"Dox!" says Nathan as he comes home. It is their joke word for Out!

The light from the bare globe shines in my eyes. In Violet's small room, the feet of her iron bed are on bricks to save us from the *tokoloshe* in the night. Over the mattress is a white cloth with red flowers and blue butterflies.

I lie on cardboard pieces on the stone floor and rest my head on my arm.

Suddenly Violet shakes me.

"Sina! Wake up. Here's some food for you."

I am thankful for the thick slices of bread and jam and also the sour porridge she brings me. I finish every bite.

"Look at you, Sina! Same eyes as your mother. Same smile. So good to have you here. Welcome."

I laugh. Violet looks very smart in her overall and apron. Her skin looks more black than mine. And her eyes.

"Sina, tell me, how is Tuli, my sister? And your brother, Temba? He always brought my pot of water from the river and carried my firewood."

"Yes, Violet, they are well. My brothers work on the farm in the valley now, Mr van Rooyen's, you know? And Temba married last summer. His wife is pregnant." We talk late into the night. "Uncle Mpo died. TB." She shakes her head and puts her hand on my shoulder.

"And Jack? And Matlina?"

"The baby is with Ma in Pietersburg. Jack is somewhere here in the city. I have come to look for him…."

"In this big city maybe you'll never find him, you know."

"I know."

"Sina, your dompas? Is it in order?"

"Yes, Violet."

"You must always keep it with you. If you go to jail who will pay to get you out?" She clicks her tongue, "My friend Maria left it at her home one night when she came to visit me. When she walked back the police arrested her. Next thing, her madam had to pay bail and then she took the money from Maria's wages. And the money for the lawyer. Whites are

24

okay as long you do the job, don't make trouble, don't ask for something extra." She breathes deeply. "And you don't want jail. It's bad. But if your book is okay, you can get work."

"I hope so. Because I must send money home."

I go to wash. At home I fetch water in the pot and share it with someone else or with the cooking. Here, water pours from a metal container over my head and my body. Very cold. I shake while I dry myself, rub my skin roughly with Violet's towel. I put on clean clothes and run back to Violet's room.

There are voices inside. Maybe it is wrong to be sleeping in the room with this woman? She is from my same church but still she is a stranger to me. I don't know what I should do. I knock softly.

"Come."

Inside, Violet says,

"Sina, this is Frans. He is the gardener here. He's my …." She looks at him. "We're lucky. The Master doesn't mind that we are together as long we don't make noise and we are not drunk." She shows her white teeth. Like always when she came to visit Ma when I was small. She smiles at me like her life is good.

"He makes his own beer but he only drinks on the weekend." Frans's fingers are like wors and his arms are like Pa's. His hairy chest shows where his blue boiler suit is open and his skin shines. He takes a hot ball of pap from the pot on the table, throws it from hand to hand to cool it, then he squashes it and pushes it into the gravy. He opens his mouth wide and bites. After he finishes chewing, he licks his lips and wipes them with his hands. Then he takes more.

"Sina, sit. Eat with us." Soon my lips are burning with the chilli and pepper and onions. When we finish, Violet pulls a thin curtain on a string across from one wall to the other. She and Frans go behind it. I will sleep on the cardboard on the floor with my *kobo*. I use my arms as a cushion and cover my ears with my hands.

I wake in the night and I need the lavatory. I want to hold on until morning but I just have to go. The metal door squeaks as I slip through. The moon gives me a clear path just as at home. Afterwards I return to Violet's room and lie down, trying not to make any sound. Violet and Frans are fast asleep, bound together. The night is long.

I cry for myself and for Jack, thinking he will come back to me. Hoping to find him. He's just like Frans. Using his woman to warm him in the cold nights. Only that. It is always so.

"Sina! Time to get up." Violet stands over me. "I put a bucket outside for you. Wash your face and brush your teeth." I dress and fix my hair, damp from sweat. On the wall next to a picture of yellow flowers is small glass on a string. I look at my face and put Vaseline on my skin.

"Come, we need to speak to my Madam. Maybe you can work here with me. It would be good for you and for me. What do you think, Sina?"

We go into the kitchen.

"When Madam comes in you must curtsey," Violet smiles, "but I know I don't have to tell you. You have good manners. I can see that."

She straightens her starched white apron and leaves me in the scullery. The floor is made of square stones next to each other, yellow and cold.

Madam wears a long red dressing gown and slippers. Her belly is big and her hair short and curly-brown. She smiles at me but what I think is she very tired. Or sad.

"Good morning. Zina, is it?" Sina, I want to say and my heart beats hard.

"Morning, Ma'am."

"Violet tells me you have come to look for work. I was thinking...would you like to help us here?" She looks at both of us. "It's a big house and also now another baby is coming. I have spoken to the Master. He says it's fine because Violet knows you and your family." I look at the floor and bob.

"Thank you, Ma'am."

"Good. That's settled then. The Master will decide about your wages. Violet, Zina can help you make the beds and do the washing and ironing, don't you think? You must take

26

Thursdays off and every second Sunday, Zina. I want you here on the days that Violet is off, please. You can sleep in the second servant's room. Will that be alright?"

What would she say if I say, no? Or if I speak about my baby and no husband? But I say nothing and she will never ask. Violet begins teaching me the kitchen work straight away.

"There are strict rules because these people are Jewish. We never cook their meat in milk and they never eat pig." There is a big sink with two basins, a rack full of potatoes, squash, pumpkin and onions. There are apples and oranges in a glass bowl on the table, clean pots upside downside on the draining board and dishcloths folded and also hanging on hooks. Plates for meat and plates for any food cooked with butter or cream. Such a lot of food. So many dishes, plates, forks and knives, cups and saucers in this one kitchen. So many things, so difficult to learn.

"There are also separate plates for the week when no bread is eaten. It is called *Pesach* and it is at the same time as our Easter." Violet says I must wait and see how it is done.

Every week when Madam brings meat from the butcher, we soak it in huge square tins and then pour coarse salt over it. It takes out the blood. Then the red water runs off onto wooden boards. We have to rinse the meat three times and it takes all the morning. One drop of blood left and it is forbidden to eat it. Then Zeida chops and slices the meat with his butcher's knife. He uses a small axe for the chops and ribs.

"We grill the liver with salt in a special pan to drain the blood out. Then we mince it with fried onions and push out every drop of meat in the mincing machine using pieces of bread." Violet shows me to do this for Friday night. "There are never any leftovers, they like it too much." When there is chicken, we pull out feathers and burn off the hard ends with matches.

A small girl runs in and holds her nose. "It's smelly. It's smelly. Oh, who's this, Violet?" And Violet says,

"Hannah, this is your new nanny, Sina." The girl smiles at me and I know it is alright.

27

Friday nights are special. The Madam and Bobba and Hannah put candles into the silver candlesticks. I must set the table right with two plaited breads and also wine. We use the good cutlery and dishes and white tablecloth. I check with Violet all the time so as not to make mistakes, not to break anything or put things in the wrong place. We could both lose our jobs. Violet is kind to me when she sees that I am afraid and she takes care of me, like Ma. She trusts me to do it right.

The Sabbath meal takes a long time to prepare. First chopped liver, then soup with *perogen,* that is meat pies. After, we serve meat and chicken. Violet and I go to our rooms until the eating is finished and we hear their blessings.

Sometime they give us the left over roast potatoes or chicken and the Master cuts slices of watermelon or spanspek for us. Zeida gives me 1/- and Violet 2/6. If Frans helps to clear the table, he gets 1/-. I am pleased for this extra money to send home. We three eat together and Violet and I take turns to cook our own meat and gravy and *stywe* pap on our hotplate in the garage. Then we eat in Violet's room on a wooden crate covered with a pretty cloth, but first we thank the Lord.

Saturday is the family's Sabbath. *Shabbos.* They have a cold lunch and Hannie helps me to take off the table. We sprinkle the breadcrumbs from the tablecloth onto the back lawn and watch the sparrows eat. One Sunday, Violet goes to our church meeting, the next week it is my turn. We walk, then take the bus, then walk again. The prayers are the same as in Pietersburg. I look at all the faces, one by one. Each time, I am hoping. Each time it is some other man, never my Jack.

When we come home, we sit outside Violet's room in the shade, and stitch her cloth by hand, me on one side, Violet on the other. It is very hot and we sweat a lot and wipe our hands on our overalls. We listen to her wireless and sing the Our Father hymns together. At teatime we go back inside.

For sure this is good place to work.

Daddy sprays the fruit trees at the bottom of the garden. He mixes and pumps the poison mixture from a metal tank and it stinks. He says it's called pesticide. Then we walk down the drive together. He won't let me carry the tube for the pump because it is lethal. He climbs to the very tops of the trees and sprays them with a long rubber hose and nozzle.

"This is where the best fruit will be. If I don't spray, the aphids will ruin the leaves or the birds will steal the fruit and there will be none left for us."

When the plums and apricots are ripe, Frans picks them and fills the baskets. He is taller and fatter than Daddy. And pitch black. He doesn't talk to me but grunts as he climbs. He gets caught in the branches. Sometimes he calls me and throws me a peach or a loquat and I take it to Zinkie to wash.

Mommy makes jam and chutney in huge metal pots. She takes the pips out and boils the fruit with mountains of sugar. When the jam bubbles the fruit skins rise to the top. She takes them out with a slatted spoon and also the pips that were left in by mistake. She checks the temperature of the jam with a special thermometer. She blows, holding the spoon over her hand not to spill, and gives me a taste. Mommy wipes the sweat off her neck and face with her apron.

We have to sterilise the Ball jars in another big pot of boiling water but I can't understand where the balls are. Mommy knows exactly when the jam is ready because the mixture gets thick. She ladles the jam into each jar and I whiz the red rubber rings up and down on her wooden spoon, until I miss and they fall on the floor and Mommy has to sterilise them again. When the jam is cool she closes each jar with the red seals and glass covers. Then I put on the metal screw tops, except I can't screw them tightly enough so Mommy checks. She writes labels for the bottles and puts on the date, 1954. We store the jars in the cool pantry next to the kitchen and we use the jam for sandwiches, for Swiss roll and for Sunday scones. There is also enough to give away for presents. I can't tell Mommy but

I only really like it when we cook the jam and I lick it warm from the spoon. Otherwise I like Marmite and peanut butter better, especially Black Cat.

Mommy and Daddy go out with their friends and I stay with Zinkie. She brings her plate of food and sits with me outside the kitchen. She puts the plate inside the flower circle of the carpet and I kneel over it. Then she shows me how to roll the white mielie pap into little balls, dropping it from one hand to the other because it is very hot. I blow on it and push handfuls into the tomato gravy and slurp it into my mouth. My fingers are burning and messy. I ate roast potatoes and chops with Mommy and Daddy first, but Zinkie's brown onions are delicious. I dip and dip.

Zinkie knows all the people in my family and talks to them when they come to visit. I know about her baby girl, Matlina and her mother, Ma. They stay in Pietersburg in a hut on a high hill like our house. There are lots of trees and flowers there and they have to walk to fetch water in a bucket. To show me how she does it, Zinkie stands up and puts the empty pot of pap on her head. She walks to the end of the passage without dropping it. I try but the pot is too heavy and crashes off straight away. Lucky it's empty.

Sometimes Zinkie sings softly about someone who has died and tells me what the words mean. Also, she sings me a song with the names of Mommy's cousin and her boyfriend, Beatrice and Isaac, wishing them good luck for when they get married.

Aboetie Isaakie, *wanawa-di-tchaba*
Gwantenu-thetiele
Mosadikiwa-ghagho
Kwenene Kwenene Kwenene Kwenene Kwenene Kwenene
Mosadikiwa-ghagho

The next verse is the same, except Zinkie changes the first line to "Beatrisie" and she sings it again and again so I learn the words. I am going to be a flower girl and Zinkie is allowed to come. My dress will be white satin with a stiff net petticoat that stands out and I'm going to wear a tiara. It's diamante. I know Beatrice will look beautiful. Mommy has already told me I have to go to bed early the night before because it will be a long day. I want to ask how it can be longer than any other day but I don't. I know Zinkie's husband is Jack so I say,

"Zinkie, where is he? Why isn't he here with you, like my Daddy and Mommy?" But she shakes her head,

"Don'chew worry, Hannie. Come lie down now." I fall asleep on her pillow-legs and when I wake up in the morning tucked in my own bed, I can't remember how I got there.

Daddy promised me a chocolate, and I find it under my cushion.

Violet and I are in the kitchen washing up. The Master is reading his newspaper and eating Jungle Oats. Then he walks to work in town. He takes his lunch packet under his arm and uses his closed umbrella as a walking stick. He wishes us good morning and good night but he doesn't talk to us, the servants.

"Why doesn't he take the car or the bus to town?" I ask Violet. "It's far." I know because town is near Park Station.

"He tells the Madam that he needs to walk and think."

When he comes home he plays with Hannah and reads to her. I hear them laughing in her room when I close all the curtains and take off the bedspreads and fold them away. Then, after supper he works in his study.

"Violet, I need to find Jack. Please, will you help me?" Before she answers, the Madam comes back. My Madam likes to shop a lot. Every day she takes the car out until lunchtime. And brings back lots of parcels.

"What's John Orr's?" I ask Violet as we carry in the green packets with black writing and purple flowers and leaves. They are tied with string.

"*Haai*, it's Madam's best shop for clothes. Just now she'll open everything and try the dresses on. Also she buys shirts and ties for the Master. Sometimes everything sells for cheaper and the clothes are in big boxes and everyone grabs. I saw it once when I went with her to help carry."

Madam is tired and breathing hard.

"Is Madam altogether well with the baby?" I ask Violet. I turn the handle of the washing machine and the rollers squeeze out the water from the sheets. I think she will say that it's not my business. That I am nothing to the Madam.

"She runs around too much. She wants to be busy all the time. When Hannah was born she had two babies at once. But one died. Now Madam doesn't want to stay at home but the Master never lets her work. He told me I must look after her. That's why he's happy that you can help me. You came at a

32

good time, Sina."

I nod and go back to my washing. I am waiting for the end of the month to send my first postal order home. How I want to hold Matlina so that she falls asleep on my breast.

I care for Hannah with her black eyes and smooth skin. I make the beds and she follows me around. She talks to her doll and also to me.

"Zinkie, you must call her Clementine."

Hannah sings some of my songs now too. I hear her whispering "*Tula tu tula baba…*" and then some English. I try to learn her songs. And I hear new words from Violet and the Madam so my English gets better.

Hannah shows me her tricks on the front lawn.

"Look, Zinkie, cartwheels," and she make her legs go round and round like the wagon wheels on our sand roads. Then she stands on her hands and walks. And she stands on her head until her face is red hot. When her father comes home he laughs.

"Well, I can do that too!" And in his smart trousers, he stands on his hands next to her and looks in her face.

On Friday afternoons when I polish the silver, Hannah stands on the kitchen chair next to the table polishing candlesticks, big plates, spoons and forks. She has her own *lappie* for the Silvo and she dabs it onto the wine cup for the special *Shabbos* blessing. She calls Bobba to help and smiles when she sees her face in the silver. She shows me how her fingers are black. When Zeida gives her a shilling she polishes it too.

"Here, Zinkie, it's for you," but I don't take it. Sometimes Violet asks me to bring the very big brass and copper pots from Bobba's room out on the grass in the sun. We use Brasso to polish and it has a strong smell. Hannah likes it. She runs around on the lawn playing with the dogs and throwing Clementine up in the air. Then she comes back to help me.

"My turn, my turn, Zinkie."

Violet is her first nanny and must bath her and make sure she eats her food but Hannie and I spend more time together

33

now so Violet cook and set the table and do everything exactly as Madam likes it. And now that Madam is heavy she leaves Hannie for me.

So the days pass, each one like the one before, until the new baby arrives. She is called Elise. Visitors bring presents of clothes for both little girls. Every day I dress Hannie neatly and roll her hair in thick curls around my fingers as I brush it. I put in a starched ribbon.

"Zinkie, please fix my bow. Can you make each side exactly the same, please?" Then I fetch the baby to change her. I take the big blanket and tie her *pepa* on my back. "Can I have Jungle Oats, Zinkie?" I mix Hannah's porridge while Elise sleeps on my back and Madam rests.

Hannah takes her milk with a teaspoon of sugar in a plastic drinking bottle in her little brown suitcase to school. Also a towel and clean clothes for in case. Madam gives the towel to Violet and asks her to stitch a flower onto it. Violet says,

"Sina, why you don't do it?"

"I don't know how. At school I didn't have the money for needle and cotton."

So Violet teaches me.

"See, first you must separate the strings of filosheen to get to the right thickness. You need more for flowers than for stems." She shows me satin stitch for leaves and petals and chain stitches for stems. Also feather stitch and blanket stitch for edges. I sometimes prick myself or the cotton pulls out if I don't make a strong knot. Still, Madam is pleased with my small red daisies. Hannah too.

"Will you help me make Ma a beautiful present for Christmas?" I ask Violet. "When I have money I will buy cottons, needles and plain white sheeting." I sit with Hannie and sew in my lunchtime while Madam sleeps. How I love to watch the needle go in and out, holding the colours as the pattern grows.

We sing and Hannie says,

"Where is your mother, Zinkie? Where is your baby?" chattering on and on. Working on Violet's cloth we make the sheet into the field and the cotton into flowers, very bright and different on the material from how the colours look on the wooden reels.

I think the sewing is talking to me, plain Sina from Plot 23b, PO Pietersburg. I think, this is me making this magic. Sina Salamina. My name that means 'so much, so much.' *Haai*.

I can't wait for another minute even though it is still dark grey outside. I crawl out of bed. I have a new box of paints with seventy-two colours and three new brushes of different sizes. Daddy told me they are hog hair and when I'm bigger he will buy me brushes made from the tail of the sable antelope. I also have a new painting book with lots of pages.

I don't put on my gown or slippers. There's no time. I carry the paint box and book in my arms and hold the brushes tightly in my hand. I tiptoe down the long passage but I mustn't stand on the creaky bits outside Mommy and Daddy's room. In the kitchen, the stone floor is icy. I put everything down on the floor, pull out the wooden chair, stand on it, cover the wooden table with lots of newspaper and fill a fish paste jar with water. Then I put out all my artist's stuff and climb onto the chair.

I dip my new brush into the water and start with the green paint. I lift some colour off the little block and put it into the metal pans in the lid. I keep adding until it is as dark as the leaves on the oak tree outside my window. I brush the colour down onto the paper and the picture starts growing under my brush. I mix dark red with dark blue and use this purple for flowers in the grass. Yellow and red together make bright rays for my sun. I try each brush, the tiny one for the veins in the leaves and for the flower petals, the bigger ones for the trunks of the trees and for the background.

I forget the ticking of the big, round clock on the wall. The wet, pretty colours fill one sheet after the other with patterns and zigzags. Miss Levine showed us at school how to stop the paint from smudging, so as I finish each page I put it down on the floor, careful not to tilt it. The floor is covered with my pictures and I can't wait to show Mommy and Daddy.

The kitchen door shoots open.

"Hannah?" Suddenly Mommy is there in her long maroon dressing gown.

"Mommy? What's wrong?"

"It's *Shabbos*. Did you forget?"

36

"I just wanted…. Oh Mommy. Sorry, Mommy."

"Pack up quickly, before Daddy comes down the passage and sees what you've been doing. Hurry up." I lean over to pick up the water jar and knock it onto the floor. The water goes everywhere.

"Oh Hannah! Don't you look?" She picks up the still-wet pages from the floor. I try to help her but she pushes my hand away.

"Let me do it please. It's quicker."

Some of the paintings stick together. When I try to separate them the next day they tear at the edges.

My photographs. I dust them and straighten the dressing table doilies. Photographs of Morris and me and our families in our *shtetlach*. Yaneshik. Kurshan. I walk around my room. Back and forth, back and forth. Perhaps I will write down the new poems I have had in my mind for the last few days. Perhaps.

I lie down on my *perena*. I think of my first walk alone with Morris. The grass field. The look in his eyes as he asks me to step out with him. His voice full of longing. His laugh as I beam, thank you. I am smaller than him and my long golden-blonde hair falls down my back with a ribbon behind each ear. My skin is pale. Seldom am I in the sun – I work indoors most days, sweeping, cooking, making the beds. Helping Mama.

"Oh Leah," Morris says, "How much I enjoy all the holy days we are all together, the whole *mishpochah*. And it's good to be here with you."

We spend time together, get to know each other, find that we have the same values within big families who never enough food, who make a living from bone-dry ground, half-starved cows and skinny hens. Who have no time for play. We both enjoy the *Yom Teivim*, times we can relax. It is true what they say, troubles are as plentiful as firewood but we can't heat the oven with them – *tsores vi holts, ober men ken nit dem oiven ainhitsen dermit*.

We walk towards the stream at the far end of the field, find a shady spot to sit down. From my skirt pocket I take a twist of paper filled with fat apple slices.

"Have some."

"Thanks. Were you expecting to walk out with me?" Morris teases and watches me chew. My cheeks grow hot. The field is dotted with blue cornflowers, daisies and nasturtiums, wild strawberries and gooseberries for jam and *compôte*. My skin itches from the dry grass. Maybe I should get up and run. I pick a few flowers for something to do with my hands then put the bunch down next to me. He tells me one of his father's jokes in Hebrew and I share a Yiddish fable from the *Tsena Rena* with him. I say,

"Would you like a few more?"

What I really want is for him to kiss me. Then and there. But I am afraid. I take a deep breath and turn to him. He tilts his head. I am flustered. My hands are sticky so I put them into my pockets. Morris seems relaxed.

"Strange they let us come out together like this, don't you think?" he says. "Mama usually forbids me to go anywhere alone with a girl."

"Does it mean she thinks I am good enough for you? And your father? What does he think?" Morris grins broadly and shows strong bright teeth.

"Mama makes the decisions, but she lets Tati think he's in control."

"My Mama always seems to agree with my father."

I feel more confident now. I know for sure that I want to be there. With him. He looks into my eyes. I can smell his skin, like fresh grass. I take my hands out of my pockets. As his face comes nearer to me, my eyes cross. I feel awkward and anxious that I will do the wrong thing at the wrong moment and spoil everything.

I move towards him to make it easy for him to reach my mouth with his.

I could never picture how this could work. Now I am surprised it is so simple. And fine because it is what we both want. Within seconds his arms are around me and he draws me up to him. We are bound in an embrace that carries our whole life forward.

I get out of bed.

From the top of my wardrobe I take more photographs, my notebooks, bundles of letters, letters about everything that happened in our *shtetl*, letters from Dora and Miriam, may G-d help them, about who went away, who had babies, who died. *Az zei zogt men* – as they say, the road to the cemetery is paved with suffering – *oisbrukirt mit tsores iz der veg tsum bais-hakvores*.

I put on my spectacles and smooth out the papers. I read,

39

1933. Yaneshik. My dear Leah, I wrote you this letter a week ago, but could not mail it. There is much trouble here. We are all so frightened, to the very edge of our reason. On Wednesday, market day, all the Jews of the shtetl, and the peasants from the countryside try to earn a few extra *groschen* selling their produce. You remember how it was? The Lithuanian shopkeeper, Gerthe, started a blood libel before the fair began and how quickly it spread among the peasants. Then some agitators came to the store of Zalman Osherowitz shouting about a missing girl hidden there and that the Jews killed her. They broke in to search for her body but they found nothing, of course. They threw stones through the windows and flour onto the floor. Then they set a fire and the fire fighters came with their hoses but they came too late and the building could not be saved. Isaac Mandel was hit over the head, and Abraham, his brother, had his hand broken. Many others were badly hurt. Some died in hospital. Those Lithuanians, a plague on them, *a machaife af zei* defaced the synagogue. We are attacked if we go out in the streets and for the past week all the shops have been closed. We are hungry and everyone is afraid. It is a life-threatening situation we are in, as in Germany. The police, the *knepeldiker*, cannot control it. There is so much hatred against us here, Leah. You and Betty and Rosie and Dina, may G-d continue to bless you, are lucky to be in Johannesburg. Please write soon with your news. Dora and I wish you *Shana Tova* and well over the Fast. Your loving sister Miriam.

How could I know what it was like for them left behind in Yaneshik? How could I know what would happen to them? Those who afflicted my family and my friends, *a cholerye zol zei chappen* – may they all die of plague. I let the letters fall. I cannot read any more.

I wait for Hannahle.

"Daddy, I want to walk with you and Jacob to *Shul*." Hannah importunes Nathan and I anticipate that he'll give in as usual.

"It's too far, Hannah. You must go in the car with Zeida," I say.

I don't go with so soon after the birth. I must preserve my strength though our new little daughter is thriving now.

Hannah spins around in the new summer dress I sewed for her, with a satin sash in red and a flared skirt over a wide, stiff petticoat.

"Mommy, it scratches."

"You'll forget about it once you get there. Off you go now. Zeida's waiting for you."

When the *Torah* is taken out of the Ark, Nathan will go up to the *bima*, make a *brocha*, give a donation to honour Elise and read a portion of the Law. Her name will be announced in Hebrew, Ita Liefsa, in honour of my aunt who died in Lithuania. My mother was very close to her. If we had a son, he too would be named in the Ashkenazi tradition to honour an ancestor, on his *bris* eight days after his birth.

Hannah is radiant when they come back, prancing in with my father and clinging to his arm. She has been the centre of attention at *Shul* as they celebrated our *simcha*.

"Mommy, I had such a good time. I sat next to Daddy and he let me count the fringes on his *tallis*. It's got four corners like four wings. And they shouted *Mazel Tov* to us and then *l'chaim!* And they all shook my hand." She brings me a biscuit, sticky from her hands and clambers onto my bed."

"Here, Hannah, let's put a pillow on your lap and you can hold Elise." Nathan gently lifts the baby from me.

"Careful now, don't give her a fright."

"Alright Mommy. Look how soft her hair is." She caresses the baby's little head as we have shown her, careful not to bump the fontanel. "Oh, Mommy, look! She is so sweet."

Nathan catches my eye and grins.

41

I see Jack.

He is in church in Alexandra township on Sunday. It is hot and there is no grass, no trees to be cool. The roads are dusty and chickens run through the holes in the fences. Goats are tied up and crying. Women carry jars of water or bundles of washing on their head. Children run barefoot with hoops and skip together in the sand. A woman with a baby tied to her back greets me in a friendly manner and I greet her back.

Jack is near the back of the church to one side. If I turn my head I see his face. I look down at my feet, then up at the wooden cross of our Lord Jesus by the altar. Father Timothy says, "Hands together, eyes closed." I do not obey. I can't. I look through my fingers. Jack is the same but smarter looking. He folds his hands and moves his mouth. Is he praying to our heavenly Father to see me again? I pray to know the right thing to do. I try the words for what I must say to him. You have a daughter, Jack. Yes, she is at home so you must come to see her.

A young woman holds his arm. I don't know her.

When the prayers end I go quickly to shake Father Timothy's hand but I am caught waiting for each person in the line. Then it is my chance. I bob and touch his finger with my glove. Outside in the sun the people greet each other, shake hands and kiss mouth to cheeks. I chase Jack and that woman. At last I am near enough to call, but it comes too softly and he can't hear me. I try again, with choking in my throat.

"Jack! Jack! Please." And then he turns round.

"Sina? Is this really you?" He puts his hand on the young woman's arm, pats her and says,

"Wait a minute, Becky, please."

I think, I need the whole day, my whole life.

He comes to me, and stops and gives me his hand. I take it and we shake.

"Hullo, Sina,"

"Hullo, Jack. How are you?"

"Well. And you?" He looks me down and up.

"What are you doing here? It's been very long. How long?" He thinks but I don't say anything. "Sina, I've missed you so much." I think it doesn't seem like that to me.

"Where do you stay? Let me come to see you on my day off. Maybe next Thursday? We can talk."

"Parktown. It is where I am working."

"I stay in Westdene. Near the factory where I work."

"I don't know it."

"We catch a tram and also a bus. Then we walk to come here. And you?"

"On foot, by bus, on foot. Also far."

"Jack, come on, it's getting late." That girl steps from one foot to the other and fixes her hat so it's straight and I can't see her face properly. She picks at her gloves.

"Coming Becky. Sina, I'll try to come to you. Bye for now."

" Go well."

He waves quickly and turns away.

Walking home, I think, at last I know where he is. My Jack. Whom I still love. Even though he dropped me. Then I think how I will be happy when he comes.

If.

Watching Zina embroider the flowers on Hannah's school towel reminds me of the convent; of Sister Boniface who jabbed my fingers with her needle when she saw my ugly herringbone stitches; of how she whipped our calves with her metal ruler when we couldn't get it right. My bruises had faded by the time I went home at the weekend, but there would have been no use complaining in any event.

"Beatrice, remember how the nuns punished us for our crooked daisy chains?" We are sitting on the front veranda, overlooking a vista of Johannesburg in the afternoon sun. "Look." I show her the scar on my right pinkie.

"She was never that cruel to me!"

"She even looked like a gargoyle. We were so sheltered before that, the two of us."

"How old were you, Sue, when you arrived there?"

"All of nine. Hard to believe that my parents sent me away like that. How I begged them to change their minds. I remember my bewilderment on the first day, packing my clothes out into a tiny wooden cupboard, going for roll call in the huge hall, knowing no one. Not as bad as Jane Eyre at Lowood, but bad enough."

"I know. I also cried myself to sleep every night."

"Not that anyone cared. The other girls were too busy crying themselves to notice, after a day of 'Where is your homework book? Where is your white towel? Really, why can't you make sure you have the correct equipment?'" Beatrice smiles at my imitation of Sister Myfanwy.

"I never had the right things at the right time in the right place either. I was always standing in the corner or being sent back to my locker upstairs. I missed half the lesson and came back sweating. As for those black woollen stockings and the starched shirt scratching my neck and my stomach, it's no wonder we were often irritable." She caresses her elegant silk hosiery.

"And woe betide you if you didn't make up the work you

missed. Or if you blotted your page." I rub the lump on my middle finger from writing punishment lines every day and fetch my jar of Pond's hand cream from inside, scoop some out for myself, then pass it to Beatrice. "Once they realised you were vulnerable, they lay in wait, watching until you went wrong. I so badly wanted to go to the government school where Mona and Lily went. They seemed to have so much fun *and* they lived at home. I asked a few times but my parents were adamant, or should I say my father? He took me back on Sunday afternoons, impervious to my tears as I climbed onto the ox wagon and waved goodbye, my suitcase full of freshly washed underwear, shirts, sports clothes, a new tennis racket. My mother gave me five new laid eggs, carefully wrapped in grease-proof paper, one for each breakfast with my own pats of homemade butter."

"Yes. I took apples for breakfast and cheese, and chutney for sandwiches. Most of the other girls had only convent porridge."

"All intended to make up for the loss of family life. Or the culture shock. I ask you! They did me great wrong, Morris and Leah, sending me away. I felt I lost out."

"You must have realised how they wanted us to integrate into the ways of their new country?"

"They could have achieved that without sending me away. My mother never knew anything about my life then. Still doesn't."

To distract me, Beatrice says, "Ugh. Those awful lunches! Cornish pasty."

"And don't forget the bright pink sausage served with glutinous mash. How could our parents, yours *and* mine, overlook the fact that we were eating *treif*?"

"Well, tea with homemade biscuits was a treat."

"After the sweat of a tennis match, don't you think we deserved it?"

"You were always brilliant at tennis, Sue. Didn't you get the award for best player in standard five?"

"I'm amazed you remember. Yes, it helped me get over my

45

loneliness so I soldiered on. The best solution was always action when there was no one to comfort me. How I practised, every afternoon against the wall by the vegetable garden, bounce, smash, bounce, smash. I wanted to be 100% accurate."

"And then we wouldn't play with you socially because you beat us every time!"

"Well, we did play *Running Red Rover, Statues,* or *K-I-N-G spells King* on the weekends. There were always two teams, the cousins who went to Green Park versus Holy Convent: me. I always felt that I was on the losing side. Until you joined me."

"Remember how we skipped with that long washing line, our skirts tucked into our bloomers?"

"All very fine because there were no boys around!" I stare out across the vista as the silhouettes of the houses and trees darken around us.

"Madge and I turned the rope for you to run through and then we changed places. But I know you much preferred to wind the rope round your hands until it was short enough to skip on your own."

"You're right. We did have fun then."

"The best was lying under the pine trees, looking up at the sky, making up stories and anticipating supper of bread and plum jam."

"Or Bensdorp chocolate sprinkle spread. What else was there to look forward to except our next sandwich?"

"Well, the evenings were fun playing *Scrabble* and *Monopoly* round the fire in the common room. And how you used to gloat when you picked up the x or the z or made a seven-letter word."

"I did not!"

"Yes, you did! And then we'd curl up in one of those fat, floral armchairs and read, *Little Women Omnibus* or *What Katy Did.*"

"Those are still my favourites. I want to read them to Hannah someday. If she ever lets me."

"Why ever wouldn't she?"

"Reading together is what she and Nathan do."

"Come, Hannahle, let's make Black Bread." Speaking of it, the rough bitterness of the cheap rye *in der heim* is still on my tongue. As they say, *tsvai mol a yor is shlecht dem orme man* – twice a year the poor are badly off. Summer and winter.

"But I've already eaten, Bobba."

"No, no! This is not to eat! *Du zet*, you see, in my *shtetl* we told each other so many stories. We called them Black Bread." Someone needs to remember the dark Russian nights with snow as high as the window. But. How can Hannahle understand? She tickles the palm of my hand and laughs. *A kind in shtub, ful in alleh vinkelech* – with a child in the house, all the corners are full.

"After the chores were done, when the wagons stopped and the kerosene lamps went out, when Mama and Tati went to bed, Miriam made a sound of a snake. Like this." I put my tongue against my teeth and blow. "It was our signal to sit by the *pripertchile*. We each had a chance. One would begin. Someone else would carry on. We told a different story every time."

"More, Bobba, tell more."

"The fire threw strange shadows on the grey walls. We all snuggled together, whispering. Dora and Betty would tell us love stories that always ended sadly. My brother David spoke of serious matters. About the *Talmud*."

Mama wanted him to be a Rabbi, but he shook his head, no. Well, he was right. Like Morris he ran from the Cossacks, *a cholerye af zei*, may the plague befall them all. But they got him anyway. So much *tsoris*. So much tragedy. This I don't say to Hannah.

"Your great uncle David's stories taught us about life, Hannahle. Listen, this is one about a *kalotel*, a coat." She climbs into my lap and we rock together. As I remember, so I tell. "*Ain mol*, once upon a time, a *shneider*, a tailor, had an attic full of children but only enough warm cloth to make one coat for his oldest son. *Dos dozikke vinter, iz dos geven far em tsu klein.*

47

Tsu hot Elia genummen die mantel…."

"Bobba, I don't understand you." So I must go back to the beginning and speak in English, "At the end of the dark cold winter, the coat was too small for him…." I tell her how the coat was handed down season by season, getting smaller and more torn, until, when the youngest child received it, all that was left was a *kneppel*.

"Just one button, Bobba?"

"Yes, Hannahle, just one button. But they saved even that. *Az zei zoggen*, as they say, if you are poor but happy you can overcome all obstacles – a *lustike dales gait iber alles*.

"Sometimes our Mama came in, shaking her head, with her finger to her lips, 'Shh, shsh, Tati's sleeping.' Then she sat with us and added her filling to the Black Bread. And sometimes when Tati was not too tired he brought his fiddle and we sang *Koem balalaike, shpiel balalaike*." The *niggunim*. The *klezmer*. I sing softly and Hannah's voice joins with my Tati's so far away.

"And you, Bobba, what did you tell?"

"I preferred to stay quiet, *shvaig*, Hannahle. But sometimes I gave in. Read my poems. I used to write them on scraps, of wrapping paper, on the stubs of our shop receipt books where the blue ink ran. Then, one day, there was a brown paper bundle tied up with rough twine. It was *batsolling*, payment for the *Bar Mitzvah* lessons Tati gave Mendelowitz's boy. This was Tati's *parnose*. How he made a living. Mostly people paid with a chicken for *Shabbos* or some eggs or a bottle of homemade wine.

"All of us stood round the kitchen table that time waiting for Tati to open the package. There was a full set of *siddurim* inside, with leather covers and marbled end papers. So beautiful. Precious. And one book with smooth empty pages the colour of tea. Tati turned it over, thinking, then he said, 'Here, Leahle, this one must be for you.' Oh, that night! I copied in my poems and waited for the ink to dry properly before I closed the book, wrapped it back in the brown paper and hid it between the mattress and the iron bed." This

48

reminds me of something else.

"You know Hannahle, when Zeida came here to South Africa, he wrapped his *siddurim* in his *perena* to keep them safe. But he also put the marmalade his mother made in that *perena*. On the ship the jar broke."

I take down one of the tall books from the bookcase to show her the pages that are stuck together and cannot be separated. "So now we can no longer read the words." And I think about how Susan never looks at these books. About how she doesn't know Hebrew. About how she sings Catholic hymns. She thinks I don't know. But. What can I do?

I must write. I must write again. My pen must catch the sounds and the meaning in ink signs on my page. *Tint trikent shnell ois, treren nisht* – ink dries, tears not.

The wireless is playing *Greensleeves* in the breakfast room. I know the tune so I hum *alasmyloveyoudoewrongtocastmeoffdiscourteously* while I sit reading on the carpet. Mommy is darning Daddy's socks and the grey thread goes in and out, in and out.

"Mommy, do you still know *all* the words?"

"Please wait, Hannah."

I finish reading *The Magic Faraway Tree.* I can hear Mommy counting stitches.

"Mommy, please can you take me to the library? I want to get *The Red Fairy Book.*" I have already read the Green, the Mauve, the Yellow and the Blue and I can't wait to get another one.

"Wait Hannah, please. I must finish this row."

I check the hands of my new watch. It is already four. Unless we go now the library will be closed.

"Okay." I fetch *Daddy Long Legs* from my room. I have a collection of other stories too, a fat red book with Louisa May Alcott's stories that Mommy won for playing the piano; also *Girl of the Limberlost* and *Treasure Island.* The boy down the road lent me the whole Hardy Boys and Nancy Drew series that smell of the antiseptic of his father's surgery but I like him so I don't mind. I read them over and over again.

If Mommy doesn't take me soon, I'll have to wait for the travelling library to come past. It's an old bus with shelves of books where the windows should be. I have to write my name and date on a card in the back of the books I choose. The pencil is thick and blunt and the librarian talks over my head to Mommy as if I'm not there. The books are fine though and she showed me the ones about the composers when they were growing up so I know about Mozart playing the piano at four years old and that Beethoven making up music even when he was deaf like Zeida.

I wait for Mommy in the arms of the jacaranda tree outside the front door. I am completely hidden by the purple, popping flowers. I take my cushion with me otherwise the bark scratches my bare legs when I sit. I look up at the ice-blue sky and watch the people in the service lane on the side of the driveway that separates our house from the Millers next door. It is for the milkman and the newspaperman and the coalmen to go from the back road into the main street in front of our house. It is covered with loose stones and sand. Last time I raced home with Laura, I tripped and hit the wall. The gravel dug into the flesh of my knees and hands all the way to the bone. Mommy put on a bandage with aquaflavin emulsion. It's a horrible colour, napkin yellow Daddy calls it. He also says it's a war wound and I first think he says wall. I have a big scar on my knee now.

"Major! Sheriff!" I walk down the driveway onto the Bottom Lawn. I throw my ball and the dogs grab it in their teeth and bring it back to me and I pat their heads. I get very hot and soon we are panting.

Maybe the mulberries are ripe? I check the branches that lean over from next door. Some of the berries are red and others are still green. A few are purple. The little hairs tickle my tongue but the fruit is delicious. Soon my hands are covered in juice. I pick more than I can eat and tip up my skirt to carry them to the house.

Mommy will be pleased. Maybe she knows a recipe for mulberry jam that we can make in her huge jam pot that she keeps in the pantry.

"Hannah, what a mess! Look at you! Zina, come here please."

Zinkie comes but she isn't cross. We go back outside to the garden tap. She brings soap and a towel, and she scrubs and scrubs with lemon juice. My hands are soon spotless but my dress isn't.

"I'll fix it, Hannie. Don'chew worry."

She helps me change my clothes.

I still have nothing new to read. I open *Little Women* and start from the beginning again. Then Elise comes into my room winding up her music box and I can't concentrate.

"Give it to me, please Elly," I say and put out my hand.

She slips away from me and I can't catch her. She starts *Golden Slumbers* again, looking back over her shoulder. Then she's laughing at me.

"I'll tell Mommy," I shout at her. "Give it to me. Now!" I grab and scratch her arm but she won't let go the box.

I wait until Zinkie puts her in her cot for her afternoon sleep and I fetch the box and put it under my pillow. Then I take it out and wind it up. When the music is finished, I turn the box over and open the cover. Inside is a tiny bronze drum with sharp teeth sticking out around it. I wind the key again and watch the teeth click-clack as the tune plays and I hum it, sucking my thumb and curling my fingers across my nose. I also know the words, *golden slumbers kiss your eyes*.

Mommy is standing over me.

"Hannah, give me that box please. It's Elise's. She's crying for it. Can't you hear her?"

I don't move, so Mommy reaches over and takes it away from me. I turn to face the wall. Why can't she leave me alone? Why has Elise got the box of music and why haven't I?

After Elise is asleep, Daddy lights the fire in the breakfast room even though it's not really winter yet.

"Help me here, Hannah. Crumple up those newspapers please." He pushes the paper between the logs of wood and the coal.

"That will make the flames catch more quickly. Watch! Here it goes!"

When the fire is roaring, I lie in front of it in my pyjamas and warm my toes.

"Careful you don't burn your slippers," Mommy says.

Daddy makes the jaffles.

"What filling do you want in yours, Hannah?"

"Eggy, please." He heats the jaffle iron and melts butter into it, cuts off the crust of the sandwich bread, puts one slice in, puts the raw egg in, covers it with a blanket of bread because I don't eat crust, closes the iron and puts it right into the fire. When it's ready, the outside of the jaffle is crisp and the inside is soft and runny. I mop up the egg yolk with some of the soft bread. Daddy makes himself one with melted cheese and gives me a bite of that too. I like my eggy plain but Mommy has tomato with hers.

Then Daddy takes his clean hanky and makes me a *hotinke maizele*, a darling little mouse. He folds the hanky over to make the body and ties knots for the ears and the tail. When it's ready he puts the *maizele* in his armpit and makes it jump out at my nose. It is so cute. We giggle.

Mommy says, "Be careful you don't choke on your food, Hannah. Nathan, you really should wait till after supper." Daddy winks at me.

Then the three of us have a Sunday sing song around the piano. Mommy plays and I sit next to her on the stool. Daddy stands behind us and turns the pages of the music so Mommy doesn't miss the beat. He has a deep voice and knows all the words. Mommy sings some of the songs she learnt at the convent and Daddy does a funny act. He sings *and would you rather be a pig?* And then he points to me! I like *would you like to swing on a star?* much better. We are all sweating because of the fire. It is lucky we don't wake the baby we make such a noise and laugh so much.

I go straight to sleep afterwards with the *maizele* tucked in next to me. Daddy kisses me good night. I don't need him to read to me or hold my hand.

"Maybe you'd like to have piano lessons, Hannah?"

"Yes, Daddy. Please." But maybe I'm too small.

This is my off day. The dogs bark in the driveway like the night I first came here. A man is at the kitchen door with his hat in his hands. He speaks to my Madam and she points to me.

Jack.

I go out of my room. We sit outside my room on my open cardboard box not to mess our clothes on the green grass. He pulls up his trouser legs at his knees and leans back on the warm bricks. We listen to Violet's wireless playing dance music. The penny whistle is high and sharp and hurts my ears.

"Shall I make rooibos?" I say.

"No," and then, "thank you." Jack waits for me to speak, I wait for him and we start at the same time.

"Your mother, how is she? And how are you?"

We talk about Pietersburg. We talk about Egoli. The dogs sit outside the door and I tell him how Major knocked me over the night I arrived.

"Why are you here? You never spoke of it."

"To find you, Jack." His eyes get dark and I am afraid, but I go on, "I need to tell you something."

Violet comes over to us.

"Who is this, Sina? You didn't tell me you have a new boyfriend." Then she looks closely and she greets him, "Jack! Is it really you? Sina has been wanting to see you so much."

She asks if he is in good health and then she leaves us alone. He wipes the sweat from his head with his hand and a drop flies to my cheek. He reaches over to me to brush it away and his touch is as soft as I remember and he looks at me to be sure it is me.

Jack's job is hard. The baas says, "Do this. Do that." No please, or thank you. Jack's job is to pack the furniture into boxes and out of boxes. Boxes of tables, boxes of chairs, roll out the carpets, roll up the carpets. He loads the van with one man only to help. The baas calls, "Boy!" and both must run. Jack sits at the back of the van to make sure the things don't fall off. The wind blows as they drive and sometimes his hat

54

blows off but the baas won't stop. When they get to the place, Jack unloads the boxes and breaks them open. In the house, they put the furniture in the correct place. Sometimes he has to move the sofa from one side of the room to the other. The baas shouts, "Lift it, boy! Don't scratch the floor!" But the money is good.

I tell him about Hannah and Elise and how I am learning English with a small squares exercise book, like at school and how I write the letters that Hannah shows me. She gives me some of her pencils. One she calls indelible because it never can come out. It writes purple and it stains my overall. I make many, many mistakes and I want to rub them away. Jack says,

"Show me," so I bring the book and he goes over my words with his fingers.

"You are learning much here."

"Yes and they are good to me."

Then we sit together and he takes my hand. I do not ask about Becky because I know too much about the men in Egoli. They cannot stay without a woman and they cannot stay with just the one woman. Me, I only want one man. Jack says,

"Next time you go to Pietersburg I will come," but I know I mustn't hope too much. He leans forward and puts his lips to mine.

"Ah, Sina…how I have thought about…." I stop him by putting my finger on his mouth.

"Ssshhh. I have to tell you something quickly."

"What is it? What has happened? Is it your mother?"

"Jack, we have a daughter. I call her Matlina. Ma calls her Maggie. She looks like you."

"Sina, what? When? Why didn't you tell me?" Then he thinks and puts his head down.

Late in the afternoon, after Jack and I have been together in my room holding each other, he kisses me goodbye. He says he will give me money for our Matlina. That one day he will play *morabaraba* and *diketo* with her at my home and watch me make a skipping rope for her. He says he will come back next week.

55

"Zinkie! Zinkie!" Hannah pushes open the door. "Mommy says there's a visitor for you. Who is it?" She turns to Jack. And nods.

"I know you. You are Zinkie's husband. Like my Daddy is my Mommy's." Jack smiles a small smile and gives her his hand.

"Yes, that's right. And who are you?"

"I'm Hannah." She shakes his hand hard. "And you have a little girl like me, Matlina!"

She turns,

"Zinkie, you happy now."

I don't know if she asks me or tells me.

As we drive to Scottburgh, Zina sits at the back with the two little girls, Elise asleep on her lap. The roads are narrow and potholed and we take it slowly, enjoying the bright green veld, the high grass and the cosmos, bright pink and deep red. Hannah stares out of the window, singing softly to herself. I can't hear the melody. Our cream Oldsmobile is brand-new, similar to my father's, American-produced and only readily available since the war.

We relive our honeymoon as we pass the turn-off to the Drakensberg and Cathedral Peak. Nathan reminds me of the potatoes that were served at every meal, even sometimes a croquette and a baked potato together, because of the food shortages.

"Nathan, did I pack the tooth brushes and face cloths?"

He keeps his eyes on the road as I check the bag for Elise's juice bottles, the extra teats and dummies, the steriliser and the pile of nappies, at my feet next to our lunch. I gaze out at the scenery, drifting in thought.

"Do you want to drive, Sue?"

"I'd prefer not. Thanks."

Eventually we break our journey and sleep over in Harrismith. The A-frame chalets are comfortable and we take dinner in the dining room. Already I have the holiday feeling. The next day, we stop to admire the view from van Reenen's pass. Nathan swings Hannah up, showing her the green valley far below. I take Elise from Zina. Nathan has hung a canvas bag of water on the front bumper where it remains cool. We share a long drink and give Zina her own metal mug. Back in the car we play the number plate game.

"TJ is Johannesburg, TP is Pretoria and CT is Cape Town," I tell Hannah. We drive through Mooi River, Escourt and Pietermaritzburg and as we near our destination we see lots of ND cars.

"Durban!" Then Hannah gets very excited at the turn off to Scottburgh and suddenly, there's the Blue Dolphin Hotel.

Ahead of us are two blissful weeks of sea, sand and sun.

No nappies. They must have dropped out of the car when we stopped. But even this doesn't dampen our spirits and we sing as we stroll to the grocers for replacements and for new wooden buckets and spades. Zina unpacks the cases and baths the girls, then goes off to her room at the back of the hotel with the other nannies. She meets Hannah and Elise in the children's dining room at 5.30 to give them their supper.

The weather is glorious, the sea-bathing perfect for the girls in their matching, homemade swimming costumes of bubbly, elasticised cotton. From my deck chair, under the hired umbrella, I watch as Hannah build castles with Zina. Elise, her starched, scalloped bonnet falling over her face, sits on Zina's lap. Zina makes friends with a few of the other nannies on the beach who tuck their aprons up and dabble their feet in the sea water.

Nathan takes Hannah into the waves and I hold Elise. She beams at everyone, sitting on the edge of the surf with the water running between her toes and up her legs. We watch the tiny fish in the rock pools and collect little shells in a bucket to decorate the castle. Zina fills glass bottles with seawater to take home to Violet for medicinal purposes. When Elise demands "Uppie, uppie," I call Nathan and the four of us cuddle together, me on the striped deckchair holding Elise, Hannah standing beside me and Nathan behind. We ask an elderly woman sitting nearby to take a few snapshots with my Brownie. Nathan growls,

"Say 'cheese.'" We burst out laughing as the camera clicks.

We are all sweaty and pleasantly tired at the end of the morning though Elise is irritable with the sand inside her swimming costume. We leave the children to rest after their lunch and go down to have our own meal that is tasty if dull. Nathan and I chat and share a bottle of wine. We are in no hurry to finish and later even manage an afternoon nap of our own until Hannah nags to go out for a drive. We have scones and cream at a tea garden near the beach. On the way back, Hannah takes Elise's hand and pumps it up and down, trying to teach her to sing at the top of her voice *or would you rather be a fish!* As Hannah yells, she pokes Elise in the belly and tickles her, until both are falling over and cackling with laughter.

I go home for Easter to visit Ma and Matlina. Once I am dressed, I pin on my star badge. We celebrate at Zion City, Moria, just like Mount Zion in Jerusalem.

I have plenty sandwiches, and the Madam gives me a thermos of strong rooibos thickened with condensed milk. She drives me to Park Station and puts money for my ticket in my hand. There is a line at the ticket office and everyone is shoving. Everybody wants to be on that train tonight. It will be too full. Hannah wants me to carry my heavy suitcase on my head, "Zinkie, show Mommy how you do it." Inside the case are clothes for Matlina and presents for Ma. My smallest present for her is a tin of snuff.

I can't sleep and stare out of the window at the stars and the moon because the curtain it is broken and won't close. I hum the hymns, *Holy, holy, holy* and *hallelujah*; then the work songs, *Shoshaloza, Shoshaloza… working in the sun, we must work as one.* At dawn, the women are already in the fields cutting grass and making bundles. Men are in the roads digging the tar with their pick axes. Already their shirts are off. In the tunnel at Waterval Boven, the train whistle hurts my ears and it is blacker than coal. When we come out the wheels clack-bang on the line.

At the station, Ma and Matlina are waiting. It's a miracle we find each other. For respect, I hold my mother first, then my daughter. My heart is full. Ma takes my suitcase on her head and we walk from the station. There are wagons and cars waiting to take the worshippers to Moria. We have money enough for a cart but the donkey goes too slowly with so many heavy bodies and baggage. It is late when we arrive and we stand near the back. In the dark are all the pilgrims and the letters Z C C shine in white stones on the hill. We join in the prayers, hands together, eyes closed.

Then the young men dance with bare chests sweating, shaking fur skirts with animal tails that hang in strips. The men have rattles made of seed pods tied round their ankles and they dance their prayers all night and we all sing, Sotho, Pedi,

Shangaan, all tribes swaying together believing, our voices crying to our Great Creator above:

Ke lella moya, I yearn to save the soul.

Ga ke llele marapo. I don't yearn to save the bones.

Ga ke llele nama, I don't yearn to save the flesh.

Ga ke llele taemane, I don't desire diamonds.

Ga ke llele gauta, I don't desire gold.

Ke llela moya wa me. I yearn to save my soul.

So many of us, so many. They say thousands. Around us the land is dark and empty. Where we stand, the land is full.

The men must not eat when they do the dance of the fire, but we are hungry. Lucky for the Madam's sandwiches, I think. The people watch as I bite into my bread, eating with their eyes, but I keep my eyes to the front.

Bishop Lekganyane tells us how we can come to the Kingdom of Heaven. No stealing. No adultery. No killing. As his voice go on, I look at the stars that fly over this good earth, and pray to save my soul.

We drink the blessed tea and the priests lay hands on the sick. Then we sing together *Oh Worship the King, All glorious above*, cold in the night air, sharing our blankets warmed by the spirits and we fall sleep under the heavens. Matlina lies right by me, in the pocket of my arm.

Easter Monday we leave on foot to go to Ma's new house in the location outside Pietersburg. It is a long walk on the sand track that is broken and dry and full of holes. I pray for no snakes. When we get too tired we ride on a donkey cart. The location is smokey. Many families live close together here, sharing fires in tin barrels. The light shines like stars through the holes cut in the sides. All the men stand and warm their hands and the women cook the food.

Ma's house is at the end of a street of sand. G Street. The money I send home and the money Ma's brother gives, helps to build the tin house with windows. Some houses have stones or bricks on the roofs to keep the tin sheets from blowing off. The lavatory is outside.

Inside, the grass mats cover the floor. The curtains hang from a string and I pull them closed. They are made from a yellow material with pink flowers, the same as on my sewing cloth. Daisies.

"Ma," I say, "but these are good! You made the place very nice."

"There is your bed, Sina, next to Maggie. See, I covered it with the cloth you made." She smiles and I smile too, thinking of Violet and the two little girls.

"We should sleep," she says and she blows out the candles.

I wake up with the rain drumming on the roof. Then in the morning the streets are muddy and everything is grey and cold. Ma and I talk and cook together. I tell her about Hannah and Elise and give Matlina the colouring book with crayons from Hannah. When the rain stops, we go out and Ma shows me off to the neighbours.

"This is my Sina, just come from Egoli." She is proud and I take her hand and go for a long walk.

"Let's go home and make curry with beans and mielierys," I say. She looks me and asks,

"What else do you eat?"

"The food that is there, Ma. Sometimes braised meat, sometimes onion with tomato. Always pap."

"Come then, let us fry the onions and tomatoes that I bought at the market." I think how she used to grow her own vegetables, then use them fresh from the ground. This is a better house but the houses breathe together here and I wish for the hills and the trees and our mud hut far from the next one.

At the tap for our street, a crowd of women chat, waiting to fill their buckets and jars. When they see Ma they call her. I see that she is well known and has many friends and when I leave, I don't have to worry. If she needs something, somebody can help her. So I am glad.

Ma says,

"Take shoes off inside, Sina. Don't mess my nice floor."

The days at home are good and too soon it is time for me to walk back to the station. Our celebration is over until next year. I wonder when I will see Matlina again.

I want Hannah to see her too, but how can such a thing ever be?

Laura and Bella and I play in our castle under a hollow bush in the back garden. It's where we hide from Witchie, the Wicked Witch of the West. We peep out but don't manage to catch her. We build a moat with the powder stones from the rockery and decorate it with flowers. Mommy gives us Lecol and biscuits. Inside the castle it is cool and shady and we are very sleepy. There is shouting in the lane next to the driveway. Suddenly the men are here to deliver coal. They carry big sacks on their backs and empty them down the cellar chute with a huge clatter.

I show Bella and Laura my charm collection. Bella wants me to give her my swaps but I say no, she should rather play me for them. Laura says she has a bigger collection than me so I say mine is better. Elise comes into my room and they want to play with her. They say she is sweet and pretty and Bella picks her up and walks around with her. She is heavy now. Mommy says she should be walking properly soon, not taking only one or two steps and then plopping down on her bum. We put her on her rocking horse and she makes funny faces at us.

Bella builds a block tower for her but she knocks it down. When one of the blocks hits her on the head she cries but it is only a pretend cry, I know. Laura has a little brother and she says he breaks all her things. When Laura's Mommy comes to fetch her, she comes into my room. She and Mommy talk about sending us to learn Spanish dancing with castanets and tap shoes. I think it will be too noisy for me and I like ballet best.

Zinkie has gone away for Easter time. She tells me how all her people wear green and white when they come together to pray on the mountain of Moria. They wear silver badges. Zinkie pins hers onto her apron. It says Z C C for Zion Christian Church. Violet comes from the same church and so they are sisters. I can't wear the badge because I am Jewish but Zinkie teaches me some of her prayers. We sing *Hallelujah* and I try to reach the high notes but I miss. Violet joins in. Moria is near Zinkie's home and she will see Matlina. When I ask

Zinkie to bring me a picture of Matlina in their hut she just laughs. I wanted to go onto the station platform to wave but Mommy said no.

Letty comes to help Violet while Zinkie isn't here. She is tall and thin and she stands very straight. Her white overall has a tight belt and her hands shine with Vaseline. She wears a smart red doek tight around her head. Zinkie is much fatter and softer.

"Hannah, please let Letty bath you," says Mommy. Letty doesn't sing to me and doesn't speak until I speak to her. She fetches my pyjamas, the ones with the lace around the buttons, my white dressing gown and my rabbit slippers. She lets the hot and cold water run separately and then checks the heat of the water with the back of her hand. Then I have to put on my shower cap and she makes sure all my hair is under it. I hate wearing it but Mommy says it will stop my hair going like a golliwog. I take off my clothes and I wait and wait for Letty to pour the oil in to make shiny circles on the top of the water so when I put my finger into them, they break into little rainbows. She is too slow. Doesn't she know I want to jump into the warm water and slide myself up and down from the bottom of the bath to the top?

She opens the cupboard to look for the bottle of oil. I jump from one foot to the other.

"There it is! There it is!"

"Sshh. Sshh. I'm coming," Letty says. She looks down at me. I hug her round her legs and yank at her overall. The bottle crashes onto the stone floor. Smash! There are splinters all over the tiles. I jump and step straight into them. Now I'm crying. Letty lifts me up, wraps me in my towel and calls Mommy. There are tiny bits of glass stuck in my feet and Mommy uses a pair of tweezers to pull them out. Letty puts me gently into the warm bath. She sits on the wooden bathmat and I stretch my legs out in the claw-footed bath. The little cuts sting and there are still splinters sticking into my skin. Letty puts soap onto my coloured face cloth and washes my face and hands and then my feet. She rubs carefully, squeezing out the cloth, trying not to hurt me but I can't stop crying. Afterwards Mommy puts on gentian violet and plasters. I shiver even though I am wearing my gown. I go to bed with my hot water bottle and Clementine.

The next day Letty is gone. Crying outside Mommy's room, I beg for her to come back.

"Please, Mommy. Please. Please."

I never see her again.

Our front lawn overlooks a city my parents could never have envisaged, as they starved and froze in Lithuania. It is here that we celebrate Elise's second birthday in grand style with gifts piled at the front door, a new tricycle with a note inked in my father's solid block print. Aunts, uncles and cousins kiss and catch up on family matters. *Kein ainhora* they say when they see the two little girls playing together, both so pretty.

I am delighted with how the summer garden looks, the scalloped flowerbeds filled with hydrangea bushes, day lilies and roses in full bloom. Frans has really done well. Hannah dances across the immaculate lawn to my father.

Zina brings out the spread for tea: fragrant apple tart, scones with jam and cream, chocolate cake. For the children, there are sweet meringues and gingerbread men. The birthday cake is ice cream moulded in a frilly dress around a slim doll.

"Please, Zeida, can we go for a drive?" Hannah pulls him towards his beige Oldsmobile standing on the asphalt driveway.

"Maybe later we can go for a shpin, Hannahle, when our visitors have gone."

"You must say spin Zeida." Then she calls, "Time for candles, Elly. Come, I'll hold you." Hannah hugs Elise closely as the little hands reach around her neck. "There, up you get." They nuzzle cheeks and Hannah blows out Elise's candles for her, then gives her a cone. The baby totters away on unsteady legs, sits with a bump and crawls on her nappy into the middle of the driveway. Playing with the stones, she lets the ice cream dribble down her hands and onto her party dress. She grabs Zina's apron hem with sticky hands, "Uppy. Uppy."

Hannah runs to her.

"You'll hurt yourself, Elly. Come away from here." She picks up the wet ammonia bundle that is Elise and takes her into the house.

"I'll wash your handies and change your nappy and sing you to sleep, you'll like that, won't you?"

67

"Daddy, my tummy's sore." I am bent over in bed, holding myself when I call my father.

"Probably too much party food, Hannah. Let's see what we can do, shall we?"

When he comes back to my room, he is carrying a glass bottle of clear liquid. He sets it down carefully.

"Lift your pyjama top, please." He pours a little of the liquid into his hands to warm it, and them rubs it onto my tummy skin, very gently round and round. The liquid is smooth and it is a very soothing feeling. Soon I am a lot better and I drift off to sleep.

I wake up scratching and scratching. It is already morning and when I lift my top I find bright red lumps all over. Daddy has already gone to work so Mommy comes. I can't stop my nails from scratching. She looks at me and then at the bottle that Daddy has left on my side table.

"Liquid paraffin! Your father!"

My new dress is exquisite, the dark green fabric of the tightly fitted bodice flaring out from the waist to show off my calves. Secluded, I swirl around in front of the long mirror in my bedroom, admiring my handiwork. What a pleasure that I have returned to my old size. The room is cool with the blinds drawn. Elise is having her afternoon nap and Hannah is probably reading in her room, so there is no chance of sticky fingers ruining the silk.

The presentation dinner is next Thursday night, black tie at the Top of the Carlton. I take the cover off the Singer, turn on the wireless to the lunchtime classic concert and place the material under the metal foot. I remove the pins and permanently stitch down the darts, careful not to mark the sheer fabric.

Beatrice helped me choose the material and the pattern so I telephone her for final approval.

"Look at my bargains, Bea, from John Orr's." I show her my new bag with shoes to match. "I'm also going to have a facial. Nathan is to receive an award but he doesn't know about it yet. Zina will stay with the children. She'll sleep in the passage. Then she will be able to get up to Elise at six."

Bea pins the hem and double-checks the placement of the zip down my back. Finished, we have tea with Violet's special cheese scones.

"Mommy, can we go with Zeida?" Hannah bounces in, Elise crawling on her bottom behind her.

"I want to take them for a spin, Susan," my father says from behind them.

"See Mommy, Zeida says yes, so you say yes too."

"Yes, Hannah, very well. Let's call Zina to go with you." I watch them into the car with Elise safe on Zina's lap.

"Make sure you don't drop her," I instruct, "and Hannah, do sit still. Don't make Elise wild. Remember after laughter...."

"...comes tears! Yes, I know, Mommy. I know."

Sitting cross-legged on my bed, I count: sixty-eight sailors, ten clocks, twelve trains and boats and planes, eighty-five Disney miniatures and thirty-seven giants. I have four leaved clovers, rabbits' feet, keys, egg timers, boxing gloves and guns.

Back at school after the holidays, we play *Flick*. We draw a chalk circle and a starting line on the cement of the playground, then stand behind it and each throw down our charms. I never play with my favourites. I crouch, careful that my blue pinafore doesn't drag on the cement. I flick my little horseshoe along. If I get it into the circle first, then I can flick Rachel's charm in too and keep them both. That's how my collection grows.

The tin for my charms has a Spanish dancer with a black mantilla painted on the lid. It is a home for Alice, the White Rabbit, the Mad Hatter and the sleepy Dormouse, for the Cheshire Cat, Tweedledum with his enormous belly, the Turtle swinging his lasso and Peter with a shotgun to get rid of the Big Bad Wolf. The Fairy Godmother flies in a biplane to the ball and Geppetto carves a girl to love Pinocchio. When I have ten or twelve of the same charm, I use them for swaps and I don't keep the black ones.

I hear Elly crying but I take no notice of her and luckily it stops. Mommy must have picked her up. My giant octopus charm has long grey tentacles with rows of tiny suckers underneath. I know it's valuable because I have never seen another one like it. It's like the jellyfish in my fish book that Daddy calls Portuguese Man of War. It is reaching for its prey under the sea. I sing to myself, *the animals went in two by two, there's one more river to cross* as I sort the coloured bears, elephants and kangaroos, the see-throughs, opaques and metallics. Jiminy Cricket sings *give a little whistle, who's afraid of the big bad wolf,* and then *in the jungle, the mighty jungle, the lion sleeps tonight* as I fly away on Dumbo's back.

Elly crawls into the room dragging her blanket. She wants my charms but she can't have them. They are too small for her and she could choke. Mommy says so. She grabs Jiminy

Cricket and I grab it back and she cries. She is such a baby. Mommy comes in and scolds me,

"Hannah, I've told you before you must share your toys. Let's see. Here Elise, do you want to play with Hannah's clockwork frog?" Mommy winds it and puts it down on the carpet. It goes round and round and the key turns round and round too. Elly claps her hands. I sweep all my charms into the tin, close the lid tight and hide it back in the cupboard. Mommy winds the froggie up again. It doesn't sing like Elly's musical box, only croaks.

"Why don't you show her your new ballet book, Hannah?" As I do, Elly yanks it away from me and tears the Swan Princess. Mommy says,

"Oh Hannah, you should have held it for her. Now look."

Now the ballerina will always have a scar across her face. Can I stick the tear together again? Elly pokes my arm and I turn the pages. I wonder about which charm I should give Bella tomorrow for her birthday. I know she wants my Alice in Wonderland but I don't want to give it to her.

"Hannah. More. More. Turn over."

Mommy sits on my bed looking through my books. She picks up *Mr Gimme and Mr Give*. Beatrice gave it to me for my birthday. It has a bright yellow cover with little red men all over it.

"I'm going to have to give this one away, Hannah. I spoke to Miss Levine about appropriate reading matter for you and it's really not suitable." I start to say, but Mommy, I love that book, but she has already taken it with her.

I go outside. How long until I can bring Elly onto the silver roof, I wonder? She can't climb properly and is so slow in her little brown boots. She keeps stopping and calling,

"Hannah. Hannah. Wait for me."

I shout,

"Come on, Elly! Come on!" I want her with me, even though I'm scared. But I can't carry her and she can't do it by herself, so I leave her behind to play in the flowerbeds. Anyway, what can a two-year old know about sitting and thinking and

71

looking at the view. All she wants is her bottle and her blanket and then I have to go and fetch them for her. Zinkie picks her up and puts her on her back.

I dangle my bare feet over the edge of the flat roof over the garages and lean back against the overhanging gutter of Zinkie and Violet's rooms. The metal is boiling hot and I am careful not to touch it. I can feel drips of sweat under my hair and on my forehead. If I come up early in the morning the tin isn't so hot and I can go higher.

Next door, Michelle and Merle are playing in their swimming pool. Once, Mommy took Elly and me there to swim but Mommy isn't here today. And Zinkie can't swim. Maybe Mommy will take us later. I shiver a little thinking about the cool water going over my hair, and ducking and dunking. Why doesn't Merle call me across the fence now? We could play hide-and-seek and run races in our bare feet and have cake and juice and I would have someone to talk to.

Then I turn my head and Zinkie beams up at me from the scullery as she finishes rinsing off the plates. I know her hands are under the water even though I can't see them. She puts the plates in a row, one on top of the other. Then she dries them carefully, one by one. She's got Elly *pepa*. It's what she always does while I play out here after lunch. She waves and then disappears to put everything away how Mommy likes it. When she comes back to check that she can see me, her lips are moving and I know she is singing to Elly.

The dogs roll on the dry grass under the washing line. The sheets are like sailboats on the metal line and Zinkie comes out to finish taking them off. She holds the wooden pegs in her mouth and bundles the washing up to carry it inside.

I pick up a handful of stones and throw them, one after the other, very fast, onto the driveway below. I watch carefully to see how far they go. My arm is getting stronger. I can feel it. Zeida says make a muscle and then he feels my arm to see if it's as hard as his.

Zinkie calls,

"Hannah, you want tea?" I bounce down, trying not to trip

in the holes in the rocks. I fetch Clementine and we sit on the grass. Zinkie has sandwich bread smeared with apricot jam. I gobble my gingerbread, dipping it into her rooibos. It's soft and crumbly. She doesn't mind that pieces of cake fall into her tin mug. She sips loudly like Zeida does. I dance across the lawn and the dogs chase me. I do the runs and leaps and pirouettes that Miss Blount showed me. I spin Clementine round with me and we curtsey, first to Zinkie and then to Major and Sheriff. I sit down with a bump and Zinkie claps. Elly peeks over Zinkie's shoulder.

"Come Zinkie. Let me show you some ballet steps." We stand up together and hold hands. I show her how to take the side of her skirt and hold it out straight and we do point-lift-point-close. My sandals don't point properly and nor do her takkies. Then she shows me other dances. We stamp our feet, first the left, then the right, bending our knees, making bursts of sand. We do a wedding dance and then she gets a cardboard box and bangs the beats to keep in time with the Zulu war dance. When Mommy comes home, she stands and watches us for a little and then goes inside to have her tea.

Zinkie and I pick some of Mommy's white daisies and she shows me how to make a cut in the stems with my thumbnail so we can thread the flowers together to make chains. I put one on my head for a crown and make one for Zinkie too. I give Elly a daisy.

"No, Elly! Not in your mouth. Give it back to me!"

The three of us stomp and dance until its bath time. When Elly finally goes to bed, Mommy comes and switches off my light before I can check through my tin again. My torch battery is flat so I can't do it under the sheets and I still haven't decided about Alice.

Part 2
1956

Hop Scotch

A game that involves hopping into or over squares drawn on the ground. Scotch refers to the scratched line in which they are drawn. Each square may contain a line of the Magpie Rhyme:

> One for sorrow,
> Two for joy,
> Three for a girl,
> Four for a boy,
> Five for silver,
> Six for gold,
> Seven for a secret
> Ne'er to be told.

Hannah and Elly play on the lawn. I feel sick. We run in the sun and I hold them, then I hold my stomach. They don't want me to stop even when Bobba calls them for lunch. Hannah says,

"Zinkie, go, one for her, one for you." I feed Elly, touching the spoon on the back of my hand to make sure is not too hot. We make a game and they finish everything on their plates. Hannah even finishes her pumpkin but pulls a funny face first.

"Good girls," Bobba says and gives them a chocolate to take to their rooms. Hannah climbs onto her bed with her toys and sucks her thumb. Madam wants to put something bitter on it, maybe pepper. Elly keeps two fingers in her mouth. She sucks so hard that she makes big cuts and sores with her teeth. I put her in her cot with her toy bunny and her music box. Now I am afraid of the pain in my back.

"Bye bye Zinkie, see you jus'now."

"Bye, Hannie," and I close the door.

Two o'clock. I want to sit in the warm sun by the wall. I take my rooibos, my thick slices of bread covered with plum jam. I think I must tell Jack about our baby. Again his child.

But what if he thinks it isn't?

I walk slowly to my room, balancing my bread on the jam tin of tea. I try not to think of the pain, so instead I think that one day I will buy a Singer. Madam has an electric one but I will get the one with the handle. Then I can do straight edges for the bedspreads. I can't when I make them by hand, no matter that I pull the stitches out of the sheeting and start over. I want to make many things to sell, first sheets and bed covers and then maybe skirts.

And then the blanket with flowers for my baby that is coming.

I am planning my charm games for tomorrow. I want to win the missing dwarfs from Rebecca who has the biggest collection and who won't share. Perhaps I'll swap with Rachel when we sit under the jacarandas at the end of the playground.

I'm so tired of being inside. I take my flower sandals and tiptoe out onto the back lawn. I wind Zinkie's old rope washing line round my hands to practise my skipping. First I hold my arms to the front, and then fold them across my chest. Up, down, round and round. Up, down, round and round. Sweat runs down my back and I puff my breath in, out, in, out. The water from the garden tap is cool as it drips into my mouth.

When I play with my yoyos, winding them up and down doing string tricks, Zeida watches me. He brings his own piece of string and ties a knot and again tries to teach me to make a cradle. We both look for the cat but can't find it. When he gives me the string, I try to make the patterns too but it always gets entangled.

Zinkie teaches me to play Five Stones. We each have a turn to throw one stone up and pick up another in the same hand until we have cleared all of them away. Sometimes, I make scoobie-doos out of long strips of flat folded plastic. It's like French knitting and I weave them, either tiny or very long, to give away to Rachel and my other friends. Each combination of colours means something important: *yellow and green you don't want to be seen, out with me, you just wanna be free*; or *white and blue, baby I love you.* I have a white and blue one strung onto my bracelet.

But I like my charms best.

"Hannah, you know we are going out tonight. You should be resting if you want to stay up with Zina." My mother pushes my door open and then doesn't close it behind her. I listen as the footsteps go all the way down the passage. Elly is calling and calling. What is wrong with her?

I push my piles of charms to one side of my eiderdown so they don't get mixed up and climb off the bed. I close my door properly but then I think maybe she wants to be held. As I go to her I can hear the sound of Mommy's sewing machine. She is making a smart new dress for herself. She says the material is called satin and it is soft against my cheek. The colour is emerald. She tries it on in front of the mirror and calls me to look. But the pieces are still only tacked together. She goes back to the machine and forgets I'm there. I stand and watch for a while but then I hear Elly is still crying.

In her room, her dummy has fallen. I crawl underneath the cot for it, then dip it into the bottle of gripe water. Sometimes she goes quiet when she sucks the sweet taste off the rubber. It's nice. I know because I tried it once when Mommy was out. Elly's face is bright red and wet with tears and her hair is stuck to her forehead.

"Don't cry, baby girl. Everything's alright." I let down the wooden side and lift her out, then put her on the floor and take off her nappy. I put on a dry one and pin it closed but it is too loose so I hold the ends together and try again. I must be careful not to prick her.

"Lie still, Elly." I lean over and give her a kiss on her cheek and she kisses me back, making a popping noise with her lips. She wets my face and I wipe her tears and the spit off with my hand. She wriggles away from me on her bum to get her dark brown lace-up boots. Her socks are stuck in them and she hands them to me, waiting. It's not easy to push the boots onto her little fat feet but I manage. I tie the laces as tightly as I can. They are very stiff and I can't do double bows so I leave them. Zinkie can do them later. I look at my multi-coloured daisy sandals. The buckles are easy to work. Then I pull my fingers through Elly's hair to neaten it but they catch in the knots. Her hair is much longer than mine, soft and brown. Mine is pitch black and much curlier. I try to fix her ribbon but I can't do that bow properly either. The ends don't come out even and they hang into her face. She pushes my hand away when I try to fix them again.

In the corner of the room is the toy basket. I tip out all her favourite toys plus I wind up her music box. I want to take it

79

with me but she won't give it to me. I leave her playing on her carpet with the door open so she can come to me if she wants to.

I go back to my room and start counting my charms again.

The house is resting. Zeida walks past my door and puts his head in. He comes inside and bends down to kiss me and I turn my cheek to him. Then I stand up and put my arms around his neck before he can stand up again.

"Bye bye, Hannahle. See you later." He blows me a kiss as he walks out of the room and I kiss my hand and blow his kiss back. I hear his steps getting softer and softer.

Next thing, Elly is in my room.

I push her away.

"Wait, Elly. Can't you see I'm busy? Just wait a bit."

She makes a grab for my charms and picks up one between her thumb and first finger. Then she picks up a handful. I don't want her to lose any. And what if she puts them in her mouth? It's dangerous for her, like marbles and jacks.

"No. Elise, no. I said no!" I try to take them away from her but she won't give them to me.

"Go away. Leave my things. Leave me alone." I want to give her a smack. Then I do, but only a small one. She sniffles and I think she's going to cry and then Mommy will be cross with me again. But she stops herself and turns around on her nappy and starts to bump out. As she gets to my chair she stops, grabs the chair leg and pulls herself up. She takes one step and then another and she makes it to the door.

She keeps her knees stiff as she holds onto the doorframe with both hands. She calls me,

"Come, Come, Hannie." She lets go the doorframe and curls her hand at me and I know she wants to go outside and say goodbye to Zeida.

"No Elly," I say. "We can't go. We mustn't." I brush the charms together into a pile as she wobbles towards me. I say, "No! You can't have them," but then she pulls my arm instead.

"Come," she says. "Come Hannie, come say bye bye

80

Zeida."

"Elly, please. We can't. We must stay right here and wait for Mommy. Please come play with your blocks."

But she is pulling me and pulling my arm, so I get up. The charms fall off my skirt onto the carpet. I leave them. They are all mixed up now and I'll have to sort them out into their correct groups when I come back. I think I will make a packet of swaps for Rachel like I promised.

I'm counting Sleeping Beauties in my head. I'm thinking how I like the see-through blue one best as we walk down the passage, me holding Elly's hand. Sometimes she falls down plop and then drags herself along holding onto the passage wall. Then she puts up her hand to me again and I take it and she stands up. The front door is open and I can see Zeida sitting in his car. Elly pulls me. I try to hold her back but she won't wait. I say,

"Elly, you have to crawl down backwards like Daddy showed you or you'll fall." Instead she holds me tightly and we go down the steps together. She sits, then stands, sits, stands. When we get to the bottom she is so happy with herself that I smile right back and kiss her cheek again.

Then we stand on the driveway, me holding her hand as tightly as I can and we wave and wave at Zeida.

"Bye bye Zeida. See you."

Zeida's car engine starts up.

I still have pain front and back. My body is heavy. I hold my stomach. I feel wet between my legs. I come to my door and take my key from my pocket. I lie on the bare cement and my stomach is squeezing hard and then letting go.

Suddenly I hear, "Zinkie, Zinkie!" It's Hannah calling me, "Zinkie, please come! Come, please!"

Why does she need me now? Is it Elly? Maybe they want biscuits? Maybe Bobba is sleeping.

"Ziiiinnnkkkiiee! Ziiinnnkkkiiieeee! Please. Pleeaase."

I try to stand up. My legs fold up under me. Again I try to stand but I can't.

"Zina! Zina! Where *are* you? Come quickly. Please. Come." Now Bobba calls. I wipe my face, my hands and between my legs and keep my hanky there to catch the blood. Straight away, the cloth is red and soaking. I pull myself up, lean against the cold wall and pull the curtain away from the front of the cupboard. From my shelf I take the small piece of sheeting ready to sew a tray cloth. I fold it over and press it between my legs. Slowly I put on a clean overall and button it up. I pick up my doek and straighten it and tie it back round my head. Still I hear Bobba, so far away.

"Zina. Oh help. Help."

I open my door and crawl outside, blinking in the bright light. I have spots in my eyes. I can't go. But I must.

In the driveway, I see Zeida's car stopped in the wrong place. I see Zeida. He kneels. I think the stones hurt him. Hannah is next to him and Bobba behind. They look down and as I come near I hear Hannah's voice. She shakes the old man's shoulder.

"Zeida, what's wrong with Elly? Zeida, Zeida, she isn't talking to me. Why won't she say anything to me? Elly?" Hannah lifts Elly's head but her neck drops. Bobba is crying. She sees me standing there not knowing what to do.

"Oh, thank G-d. Zina, come quickly."

I hold myself straight up. The rag makes a hard wet lump

where the blood pours. I must go to Hannah but what is wrong with my little baby? What is wrong with Elly?

Bobba cries,

"Zina, take Hannah. No, hold Elly. Stay here with them please. I must fetch Susan."

I bend down next to Elly and put my hand under her head, like a cushion against the hard stones.

The stones bite my knees.

There is blood on Elly's face.

Stones in her skin.

Her face lies next to the wheel of Zeida's car at the back.

Zeida is still on his knees. He bends to Elly, holds her head, cries,

"Baby, look to me. Please. "

"Zinkie, what's wrong, why won't she look at us?"

Hannah sucks her thumb and picks her lip. She leans close to me and I cradle her into me, rock her backward and forward. Zeida stares at Elly.

The hearing machine whistles.

"Susan! Susan!"

I drop my sewing down across the machine without folding it properly, run down the passage and grab my mother's arm.

"What? What's happened?" My mother can't get the words out.

"*Koem*, Susan! *Koem*!" She pulls at me and her fingers dig into my flesh. We rush outside and down the steps. My father's car is angled at a standstill in the middle of the driveway and he is behind his car, holding onto the bumper with one hand and supporting his crumpled face with the other, crying, "*Ayayay... ayaya.*"

"Hospital...we must go. I'll drive. You hold her."

I pick Elise up. Her head flops back and she lies in my arms, eyes closed.

"Elise," I shake her, "Elise," but she makes no sound, lies limp.

"What's happened? What's happened? Somebody tell me what's going on." Nobody answers. Behind me, Zina is wringing her hands.

"Susan," I hear my father's voice in the distance, "you must come."

I run to the bathroom with Elly and grab bandages, Dettol, Mercurochrome, cotton wool. Hannah is standing beside me then crumples to the floor.

"Mommy, Mommy.... She...."

"Hannah, get up now and go to Zina. I must wash Elise's arm and bandage it."

I prop the baby on the laundry bin and press her body against my belly. Her arm is gashed and there are bits of gravel imbedded in her flesh. I try to brush them away but they don't come out. I pick the small stones out one by one with my nails and then with a pair of tweezers, trying not to push them in more deeply, dab the antiseptic on her arm with cotton wool. I try to remove the stones stuck to her face. Then I open the gauze and with her leaning against me, cut a few rectangles to cover the wounds on her arm. The gauze won't hold. As I unwind the *crepe* bandage with my teeth, the roll falls to the floor. Not very hygienic. My Red Cross instructions go through my head, but I just keep moving. Holding Elise tightly, I bind the bandage round her arm, gripping the *crepe* between my teeth, then in my fingers, then securing it with a silver safety pin, careful not to prick her skin. I don't know how to cover the round wound on her cheek so I dab Mercurochrome on it and leave it open.

My father is standing next to me, his arms dangling to his sides, sniffing all the time. He does nothing to help. Hannah takes Elise's bib and tries to wipe the saliva off her mouth, picks up her hand and squeezes it tightly, tries to sing but coughs and starts the tune again.

"Susan, we must take her to the hospital!" I know it's my father speaking but the voice doesn't sound like him.

I look at Elise.

"Let's put her in her cot and let her sleep," I say. "She'll be alright in the morning."

Then my mother is there too.

"You must take her in the car, Susan. We must go now!"

Suddenly I am incredibly tired at the thought of the drive and then I think of the hospital. I can't do it.

"No, no. Let's put her in her cot so she can rest. I've taken out the stones and put antiseptic on her arm. Look. I've done a good job, exactly as they taught us. Can't you see?"

One at a time, I pull off Elise's brown boots and drop them on the floor in her room. After I've changed her soaking nappy, I wrap her warmly and put her down. She is resting peacefully as I go out of the room and shut the door.

I thought the girls were sleeping. Why were they outside? What had I seen? My father behind his car. Hannah and Zina holding each other. My mother crying. Did Elise trip on the gravel or over her own feet? She isn't that steady on her little legs, yet is always on the move. Maybe Hannah pushed her? I heard them fighting over that stupid music box. Or maybe Elise was on Hannah's tricycle? I try to think if it had been anywhere nearby.

Where was Zina? I thought she was watching the girls while I put in my zip. Then I take a deep breath and hurry to the telephone.

"Nathan, please," I urge Felicity to put me through. Eventually he picks up the receiver. "Nathan, you must come home now. Immediately."

"What is it, Susan? Susan, I said what is it?"

I try and control my breathing but can't still the beating of my heart in my chest, so that I'm certain he can hear it through the telephone wire. I can't answer him. I don't know what to say.

"It's…there's been an…. Elise…"

"Susan, what's happened?"

"The car…. My father…. The children…but everything is going to be alright, I know it, Nathan. Everything will be alright…but I need you to come home…to decide…."

I can hear him talking into the receiver, still asking me what has happened.

"Susan? Susan, are you there?" I put the telephone back on its rest and sit down in the armchair next to the desk in the entrance hall. Hannah stands staring at me from the end of the passage, holding her blanket and sucking her thumb again. I try to call her to come to me. My mouth won't open. I should pick her up but can't lift my arms. I realize that Nathan walked to work that morning and I wonder if I should drive to fetch him. I go on sitting.

"Ma'am? Ma'amie? Can I get you something, some tea or sugar water?"

"No, no, Zina, just bring some for Hannah. Where is my father?"

"Sitting in bedroom, Ma'amie."

"And my mother?"

"She in the lavatory. She's very sick, Ma'amie. Sorry, Ma'amie. So sorry."

"Oh, what shall I do? What shall I do?"

"Ma'am…?"

"Where were you? I thought you were with the children?"

She is holding her belly and is not standing up straight, moving her balance from one foot to the other. Then my mother is at my side.

"Susan, is Nathan coming home? Do you want me to telephone him?"

"I've already done it."

"Come then. A pot of sweet tea for all of us, Zina please."

"It'll be alright," I say to my mother as she puts her arm through mine and we walk slowly to the breakfast room and Zina goes through to the scullery to fill the kettle. Hannah disappears behind her.

I drift down the passage and open Elise's door. She hasn't moved. I remember the first aid course. I think about concussion and head injuries. I look up the number of emergency services and telephone the ambulance. It rings and rings.

Suddenly galvanised, I call,

"Zina, we're taking the baby to the hospital. Make fish and chips for supper." Zina wrings her hands and then wipes her face with her apron. I think, I must teach her not to do that, it's so unhygienic.

In Elise's room, I pick her up out of her cot, wrapped up in her favourite blanket. She doesn't make a sound. She was always such a good baby. I snuggle her to me.

Now I am in complete control. I call my father. He follows me out to the car and goes to the driver's seat. I sit at the back and Hannah gets in next to me. She should stay at home but I don't have the energy to tell her.

"Look how Elly is sleeping and that's good. Sleep is healing," I say as I rock her to me. "Everything will be alright, you'll see."

"Which way?" My father's voice is so soft I can barely hear him. I direct him down Twist Street and feel Hannah pushing her hip against me. My father shakes his head all the while and I wish he would stop it.

Every robot and stop street is a delay. The journey takes forever and he mumbles over and over,

"*Ayayay, ayayay. Vey is mir.*"

87

The poles in the street whiz by. I think Zeida is going too fast but I don't say anything. When he slams on brakes at a red robot, I crash off the seat. I try to think about the charms I'll swap with Rachel tomorrow, but I can't remember which ones she's got that I want. I say,

"Mommy, what's going to …?" but we have stopped at the gate. I read the big letters on the signboard: General Hospital, Hillbrow. Whites Only.

"It's an emergency," Zeida says and the guard points to where we must park. We drive into the place for ambulances and he stops. He yanks the brake up and the car jerks and turns off. Suddenly people are all around us. Zeida jumps out and opens Mommy's door. Mommy holds Elise very tightly. I try to hold Mommy's arm but she is running. The nurses take no notice of me. Inside I'm behind Mommy and Zeida, watching the stretchers go past. Mommy says hurry up and I walk behind her, watching my sandals and listening to them squeak at each step. I think everyone can hear Zeida's hearing aid whistling and see him fiddling with the little black knobs.

The nurse at the desk looks up.

"An accident. A terrible accident," Zeida says. "Please. Get somebody," he takes a deep breath, "Quickly!" His face is white and his lip hangs over his false teeth and he cries and the nurse says,

"You need to fill these forms in first." But then she looks at Mommy with Elly and says, "This way, please." Suddenly Mommy is gone, they are all gone and I'm alone in the middle of the passage. I walk on a little but I don't find them so I sit on a bench to wait. The lights are a yellow-greenish colour and the walls are the same. Doctors and nurses are rushing by. They wear white and there is a lot of noise and shouting but no one talks to me. Some men pass, carrying a man who is dripping blood on the floor. I swing my legs and watch the flowers on my sandals going up and down.

"Hannah, I have to stay here with Elise. Zeida will take

you home."

Zeida doesn't speak to me at all as he drives but keeps saying *ayayaya*, *ayayaya*, like the doves in the morning except that he never stops.

Back in my room, I close my door, put on my shortie pyjamas and climb into bed. I pile my charms in front of me and start sorting them from the beginning. Again. I think about climbing onto Pegasus's back and flying over the storm clouds to the clear sky.

I tie my bracelet of string with the horseshoe, rabbit's foot and four-leaved clover onto my wrist. Around my neck is my gold *Magen David*. It is like Zinkie's silver star. I hold my hands over it until I fall asleep.

Elise is hooked up to tubes and drips, alone in the ward. Her eyes are circled with blue, the lashes stark against her ashen cheeks.

Nathan strides in, panting. He bends over the cot.

"My father has taken Hannah home."

"Susan, what's happened?"

I look away, thinking of our two little girls playing that morning, their heads bent over a tower of blocks, knocking it down and rebuilding it. At this moment they should be running down the passage to Nathan as he arrives home from work, Hannah standing back, Elise calling, "Uppie, Daddy, uppie." Then they'd play the swinging game, Nathan giving them turns to put their legs around his waist and whirl, screeching with laughter. Hannah would say, "Daddy's our merry-go-round. Daddy's our clown! Go Daddy, Go!" Then she would step onto his feet and they'd march down the passage with Elise bumping after them.

I know Nathan is thinking the same. He steps out into the corridor and lights up a Mills Special. He coughs as the nicotine catches the back of his throat. I touch my hand to my cheeks. They're wet. Suddenly he is back beside me, reaching for me. As he puts his arm around me, I flinch.

There is no one at home except Zinkie and me and I wonder when Mommy and Daddy will bring Elly home. From the top of the rockery, I watch the clouds changing shape. The rockery is covered with aloes and cactuses and I scratched my legs scrambling up. I climb higher, onto the silver roof, then onto the steep red tin. My feet burn as I grip the metal ridges tightly with my toes. I hold onto the chimney so I don't fall and the bricks are cool against my face. Down below there are rooftops to the horizon. I hug my knees, push my curls off my face and close my eyes.

Zinkie calls me to wash my hair. She tries not to hurt me as she smoothes the hair away from my forehead. There is a plastic ring around my head to keep the soap and water out of my eyes. She pulls up a stool to the basin in the bathroom and I kneel over. She dips her fingers into the running water and pulls them away. I hear her say, *chissa*, too hot. Then the basin is full of lovely warm water. Perfect.

I bend over and she pushes my hair under the tap and pours on the see-through yellow shampoo. She soaps up my hair, then rubs and scrubs. She rinses it out and then does it again, then checks to make sure it squeaks. If it does, it means it's clean. Then she squeezes out the water and wraps my head in a huge towel. The Johnson's only washes out the dirt, not the knots and I cry as she combs them out. Rubbing the water out with the towel only makes it worse and she has to comb it through again.

Then she sits in the sun with me, waiting for my hair to dry and I keep running my fingers through to check. I've brought *Up the Faraway Tree* with me, but I don't read. Instead we play cards. I teach Zinkie *Old Maid* and *Snap!* and *Cassino*. I show her how to count the cards as we play them out, like Bobba showed me. We don't keep our cards secret, but put them on the grass so we can see what we've got and we play out the hands together.

When my hair is dry, Zinkie takes a bow and ties it around

my head to keep the hair off my face. She makes the bow exactly the same on both sides and it stands on top of my head like wings. My ribbons are always smart because she mixes starch in a bowl and then soaks them. When they're dry, she irons them so they are crisp.

"Zinkie! Zinkie!" I call her to pick me up and we sit in her room on her cardboard carpet that says Surf-Surf while she finishes her pap. She wants to give me some but I can't eat. My tummy's sore. Zinkie is rocking and making a noise in her throat. I catch a tear on her cheek with my finger. When I lick it off it's like the sea when we were all in Scottburgh, when it was still Daddy and Mommy, Elly and me.

We go back outside for Zinkie to take down the dry clothes but she doesn't sing anymore. She gives me the wooden pegs, one at a time, then rolls up the sheets and clothes into the big bath, ready for ironing. She says if I drop the pegs they'll get full of grass and spoil her clean washing and if Sheriff gets hold of them he could choke on splinters. That's why we don't give him chicken bones to eat. Zinkie puts the washing under the kitchen table and makes my supper, soft eggy and toast how I like it. I try to eat because she wants me to.

Daddy will come home soon and I'll be dressed for *Shabbos* in my new dress with blue stripes, my white socks and my shiny white shoes. He'll say,

"How's my big girl, then?" and run his hands through my hair. He doesn't say anything else. Does he think Elise is prettier?

Home from the mortuary, Nathan says,

"Neethling was on duty. I've dealt with him for clients on a few occasions before but when I went up to the desk, I couldn't get the words out, Sue. He said, '*Ek is so jammer, Mnr Kramer*, so sorry.' He put out his huge hand and gripped mine and I had to look away. I couldn't bear the pity in his eyes. He waited patiently and then said, '*Kom saam met my, asseblief.* Come, please.' He took me through to the icy storage room and uncovered her. I bowed my head. I felt him squeezing my shoulder, then he left me alone with her. I had to sign the death documents."

Nathan went alone even though his brother Harry offered to go with him. Now he is out of control, crying, choked and breathless. I only half-listen, pulling the blankets round me, hearing the sounds of life from the kitchen, from the passage outside. He starts up again,

"He telephoned the *Chevrah Kadisha* straight away and said I mustn't worry. That I could leave ...."

Nathan's sister Fay works for the burial society so I am fully aware of the ritual required for the washing and preparation before they put her body in the pine box.

"...but I waited. When they came we arranged the funeral time. Then Neethling released her body to them." I stare at the curtains, tightly closed.

"We need to keep a *yortseit* light burning for the whole of *shiva*. One night of prayers is enough, don't you think?" I point to the mantelpiece where I've already placed the glasses of candles. "You and I have to sit on the low bench in our slippers."

"What about my parents?"

Tonelessly he repeats what the Rabbi told him.

"Morris and Leah have no official obligation. If my parents were still alive, Morris would be obligated to say *Kaddish* in my place. Luckily my parents are not alive. Unbelievable. First she was at home, then in the hospital cot. Now nothing." He seems to forget himself, then goes on,

"We aren't allowed to do any day-to-day chores and I'm not allowed to shave. After *shiva*, things can go back to normal." This is the most we have spoken to each other since it happened.

"I'm going to call Felicity and get her to put a notification in *The Star*. What shall I tell her to say?"

"Beloved daughter of…."

He stares at me.

"I can't forgive myself that she died alone in a hospital. One of us should have been there, holding her." He brushes his eyelids with his fingers then takes his handkerchief from his pocket. "Where's Hannah?"

"With Beatrice."

"I want her here. With us."

"This is no place for a child."

Nathan picks up the candles and goes out, clicking the bedroom door closed behind him. My parents are in their room. His brothers and sisters arrive and I hear them all go into the lounge. After awhile, they come and sit with me and wait for me to speak. Fay brings me tea and a sandwich. I can't swallow. I watch Nathan. He doesn't eat either.

Maybe if he'd taken the car to work that day, if he'd come home sooner, if he'd taken Elise to hospital immediately…?

When Beatrice brings Hannah back, she leaps into Nathan's arms. He lifts her up and buries his face in her neck. She is silent; then I send her to her room.

Harry signs for countless telegrams of condolence. Beatrice opens them and reads aloud to us, the formulaic words, so well meant, so empty. The telephone rings incessantly. Beatrice takes messages and makes a list so I can write thank-you notes to everyone.

At the cemetery, the Rabbi rips my blouse over my heart. Also Nathan's shirt. When Hannah's twin died at birth, Nathan buried her on his own. That grave is marked with a number, SB292. There is no head stone.

Now there are only a few of us at the gravesite. I didn't

want anybody at all to be there but Nathan's siblings insist, come with their spouses, stand at a tactful distance. Fay holds Nathan's elbow and I stand stiffly on the other side of him. Zina and Violet wanted to come but I didn't think it necessary and Nathan didn't argue with me. My parents, heavily sedated, stayed at home.

The funeral service is brief. Watching the little coffin being lowered into the earth, I stare ahead. Nathan reads the *Kaddish, Yitgadal vi'yitkaddash*…. His well-practised Hebrew allows him to get through it with no mistakes, mechanically. The Rabbi says a few words about the beauty and fragility of life and how we must comfort each other. His voice quivers, *may Hashem comfort you with the other mourners of Zion and Jerusalem.* I don't look at Nathan.

To bury a child is a parent's worst nightmare but I don't cry. I have no idea who shakes my hand or wishes me 'long life' at the cemetery, nor of who comes to the house afterwards to share our *bagels* and hard-boiled eggs. Fay reminds me of their ritualistic meaning, how they represent the continuation of the cycle of life. She instructs me to force a few bites down my throat. Otherwise there is silence. It is a strain while other people are here, but even more so when they leave us and Nathan and I are alone.

He maintains a polite veneer, but still I feel his accusing eyes.

I am wearing the little pink playsuit that Mommy made for me and the sun is on my bare legs as I swing. I look for Selwyn, my friend at the park, but he isn't there today.

When we came here before, Zinkie had Elly on her back, tied in a blanket. Elly also wanted to swing, but Zinkie said,

"Wait. Wait. Hannie first." I remember Elly was nagging and nagging.

Then Zinkie said,

"Look, Hannie, let's give Elly a chance."

She pushed Elly for so long that I stood up and pushed myself, swinging my legs up and down, up and down and Zinkie said,

"Hannie, you are such a strong girl now."

That day when Mommy came to fetch us it wasn't cold and she came into the park and watched us. I wanted to go on the Witch's Hat but she said it was time to go home and picked Elly up under her arm. I walked with Zinkie, holding her hand.

Today, the swing chains squeak as I hold onto them very tight, then bend and straighten my knees, bend forward, bend back and the wooden seat creaks. My hands are sweaty and the chains slip so I hold tighter. I call Zinkie to come and push me,

"Higher, higher," and I stand up and balance my feet next to each other, exactly in the middle, the sandal buckles shining. From here I can see the flower clock on the other side of the park. The numbers are made of white flowers but I can't see what the time is. I had lunch before Mommy dropped us and she said she'd be back soon and then it'll be time for tea.

I can see Zinkie in her starched white overall and her doek far below. I'm swinging up and up trying to look over the tops of the buildings, even though I'm scared that the chains will swing right over the top of the swing frame and I'll go flying off.

The shadows are dark and my skin is cold. Zinkie and I are

the only ones in the park and I'm the only one on the swings.

From high, high up I can't see anything properly. The tar ground is very far away and I can't hear Zinkie singing anymore. I breathe in and my hands let go. I put my arms out in front of my face and crash-land on the stones. They cut me everywhere, my hands, my knees, my forehead, in my mouth, up my nose. Zinkie lifts me and carries me to the tap, talking softly to me. She wets her hanky and wipes the blood from my lip and tries to brush the stones off my skin.

I look for Mommy, turning my head as far as I can, this way and that, looking for the beige car.

"Where's Mommy? I want my Mommy."

"Shshsh. Mommy's coming now-now, Hannie."

Nobody else is here. The sun is gone. Zinkie helps me to put on my jersey but there are no long trousers and no socks. She carries me to the green park bench and curls me into her arms against the scratchy starch of her overall. There's blood all over her apron. The wooden bench is icy against my legs and I crawl onto her lap.

"Shshshsh." She sings to me and strokes my hair. My bow falls onto my face and the corner of the ribbon catches my eye. I think I see Selwyn, my friend from the park, coming to me but when I look again it's the man who cleans up. He is behind the trees on the other side of the path.

"There's Mommy!" She sticks her arm out of the driver's window to show that she is stopping and Zinkie and I climb into the back seat.

"MommyMommyMommy, where were you?"

Bobba is sitting next to her and she turns around and gives me her hand to hold. She is not wearing her glasses and her eyes are red. She dabs them with her hanky. We pass the hospital where we took Elly and Bobba squeezes my hand harder.

At home, Zinkie runs my bathwater. I sit on the toilet, bent over so I can hold my tummy. I forget to get off until Zinkie touches me. Then I step into the bath with lion paws. The water is lovely and warm, but then it burns my wounds and I scream. The scrapes have dried on my face and I keep touching them. When I lick the cut on my lip, I feel the hard blood. It tastes like tin. There is a big lump of blood on my forehead. I put on my flannel pyjamas but I am still shivering, so Mommy sticks the thermometer under my tongue.

"Don't bite the glass, Hannah. If you get the mercury in your mouth, it'll poison you." She tucks me into bed and pats my head and I lie in the dark and think about Elly. Then I hear Mommy and Daddy talking in the passage.

"We were wrong to be away from her for so long. And I still think we should have taken her with us to the funeral."

"And how would we have coped, do you think?"

"I would have held her tight and we could have cried together. Don't you think she wonders what happened, where Elise is? What if she thinks we're also going to disappear?"

"There's no going back on it."

"Yes, well you made the decision as usual."

"I can't have this discussion now."

"We need to spend more time with her. Perhaps we can take her with to the unveiling?"

"It's much too soon to think about that."

"We should have it sooner rather than later."

Tomorrow I'll ask Daddy what unveiling is, if it like my bride doll's veil. I'll also ask when Elise is coming back. I know he'll know. I listen for her crying so I can go and give her dummy and her blanket. Bobba and Zeida don't come out of their room for supper and Zinkie takes them their food on a tray. But then she has to fetch it and she says, "All the food in this house is going to waste."

Daddy is talking again.

"Do you know that no one telephoned the bridge club? Goldie only found out what happened when she got her newspaper this morning.

"I thought that Beatrice called her."

"She said they would have come to the funeral. I reassured her that only the immediate family came."

Mommy's skirt rustles as she turns to walk to their room.

"Anyway she says she'll come tomorrow and visit us."

I think I'll get down my charms and check them, but I don't. I turn to the wall and put my thumb in my mouth, then take it out. Tomorrow I must check the thumbprint. Daddy says if I don't stop sucking, I'll suck it away. Mommy says she is going to put something bitter on it.

My door opens and I snap my eyes shut. Daddy comes and stands by my bed and watches me in the dark. I don't say anything but lie as still as I can and he thinks I'm sleeping. He goes out softly not to wake me.

Suddenly I sit up straight. I left Clementine on the park bench. It will be freezing cold now. And so dark.

"Mommy…."

"Hannah, how could you? What a nuisance!"

We fetch Clementine the next day. The park man kept her in his office for me. I check her from top to toe but she's fine, not a scratch. I hug her and kiss her forehead.

"You're lucky this time, Hannah."

In the car, I put Clementine into Elise's car seat and my thumb back in my mouth. Mommy keeps shaking her head.

At home, Clementine and I crawl into bed.

Nathan and I must wear the same clothes every day of *shiva*, those we wore for the funeral and spend each day in the lounge. Zina has taken the big cushions off the sofas in order that we sit low down. The mirrors and paintings are covered with sheets – we may not look at ourselves or at anything beautiful that might give us a feeling of joy. When parents pass away, children are obligated to mourn for eleven months. The obligatory mourning period for a child is thirty days because parents need no external directive to keep them mourning forever.

Nathan and his siblings reminisce about their pranks and achievements when they were growing up, about the time when their own parents passed away. Then, Nathan said *Kaddish* in unison with his brothers Harry and Ben. Their shared history and memories brought them close to each other despite their sadness.

Now, mealtimes pass and visitors come and go, shaking hands or kissing us. My eyes are scratchy. Sometimes I catch Nathan looking at me but I don't look back. I am lost in thoughts of school days and holidays that will never happen and each minute drags by.

Sometimes Hannah sits on Nathan's lap, always neatly dressed with her hair brushed back and tied in a ribbon. She says nothing and I wonder just how much she understands.

Eventually I tell Nathan how I found them all that day, where my father stopped his car, about Zina and Hannah. I think: there were no eyewitnesses at the moment of impact but I know what happened. I know what I did and I don't need a coroner to tell me or a judge to decide. We all know who is guilty even though it is my father who is standing trial.

Nathan tries to explain the legal ramifications to us.

"At the inquest the coroner tries to ascertain what happened, to whom, when and how. This is essential to the process. There is no placing of blame at this juncture. That will only occur if and when the case goes to trial. Any witnesses would be called to clarify what happened but the aim is to avoid all emotion."

From the stone steps at the front of the house, Nathan stares at the driveway. Hannah rests her head against his knee and he pulls her close so I leave the two of them sitting outside and go into Elise's room.

Zina and Violet haven't tidied up because I forbade it. I put the linen in the wash basket, wondering what happened to the clothes Elise wore that day. Her alphabet blocks and teddy bear are still lying on the carpet, the last things she touched. The bear still has her baby smell trapped in its fur. Inadvertently, I knock the winder of the music box that my parents gave her on her first birthday, that she played over and over, winding it up with the key underneath. The last notes of *Golden Slumbers* chime softly as I lean back in the armchair in which I used to feed her.

Then Hannah is there.

"Mommy, where's Elly?" She climbs onto my lap, lifts the box out of my hands, its marquetry decorations chipped in places, and turns the key. I take it away from her and set her down on the carpet, watching as she tips Elise's blocks out again and starts to build a tower. Then without warning, she bashes it down and one of the blocks gashes her eyebrow.

"Come, Hannah, let's have something to eat." In the kitchen I make a sandwich of peanut butter on soft white bread and leave her with Zina. Later, I hear her putting herself to bed, leaving the light on. Nathan checks on her to make sure she is covered and switches it off but then I hear it click back on.

The events of that day replay themselves on a tape that winds and rewinds itself against my will. I swallow my sedative and wait for dreamless sleep.

101

I bring some pap to my room. Hannah watches me but I don't eat. I push the plate of gravy next to her and she sticks her finger into the tomato and licks it. I look away. I don't want her to see my eyes.

The blood still comes. I must go to hospital but I have no strength to walk. I think how the blood started. How I tried to breathe slowly, the pain deep like a knife cutting me, waves coming and coming.

If Jack knows that I carry his child, maybe he'll come back.

"Hannie," I say, "you want tea?" But she doesn't answer, she just stays sitting on the floor.

Soon more visitors will come so we must go back inside. There is cake for them and I must boil water and put out clean cups for my Madam. She lies on her bed all day and looks out the window.

Violet comes in.

"Sina, you must go to hospital, you know." She puts her arms around me and we rock together. "You need to get well." I hold her body away from me and look in her face.

"Madam needs me now. I must be here for her. And maybe I'll lose the job if I go."

"But you're sick, Sina."

Hannah listens to each word.

"Zinkie, what's the matter? Are you sore, Zinkie?" I can't answer with words so we hold hands with our hearts full. Suddenly Violet says,

"Sina, I must tell the Madam. She will help you."

What can I do? When Jack comes I will be gone.

The little girl in white sails through the window, waving her arms and calling me to go with her. She flies over my bed. Her hands flutter and her legs go up and down. She is not smiling. She keeps away, doesn't touch me at all. I reach out for her to make her stay. There is bright light around her in the black night. I want to hold her but she disappears and my room is empty once more.

I wake up crying, the dream still in my body. The light from the passage makes a boogeyman on the wall. Mommy and Daddy's door is shut so I wait on the carpet outside their room. Sometime soon they'll come out, I know.

Daddy finds me there asleep on my arm with pins and needles. He lifts me up.

"Come, Hannah."

I don't see Mommy that night and not the next day or the next. I don't go to school because Mommy can't take me. There are lots of other people in our house. Some of them I know, like my cousins and my aunts and uncles. Everyone brings food. They whisper to each other. When Daddy comes out, the people go up to him, shake his hand and ask about Mommy. No one speaks to me.

Daddy still takes me to bed.

In the middle of the night, I call, "Daddy, Daddy" and he always comes.

I want Elly," I say. He cradles me and he is crying too.

"Daddy, Daddy, what's the matter?" But he doesn't answer me only holds me tighter. He brings me a glass of water and then switches off my light.

"No, no, on please."

"You can't sleep with so much light."

"Please, please." He leaves it on. He leaves.

I put my thumb in my mouth, then take it out. I hum, *Go to sleep my baby, Go to sleep…Rozinkes mit mandlen, dos vet zain dain baroef.*

I call again,

103

"Daddy....Daddy." Why can't he just stay here with me? Mommy is sleeping. I know because when I tiptoe into their room, Mommy is turned to face the wall.

I'm still bleeding. So today I'll go to the General Hospital, to outpatients. Hannah is at school. When she left she waved at me from the back window of the Master's car. Still Madam lies in bed.

I finish making the beds and hanging the washing, smear Vaseline on my legs and pull up my stockings. They stick to the Vaseline. I tie my money into my handkerchief and put it in my brassiere. Then I button my overall to the top of my neck.

The walk to Hospital Hill is the same as to Park Station. The hills are difficult and sometimes I trip on the broken pavement stones. I think about Matlina. Will she ever have a brother or sister? At the hospital the room is full, people wait on chairs and also on the floor. I give my name and they give a piece of paper with a number. After a long wait the doctor gives me pills to stop the bleeding and aspirin for the pain and tells me to come back next week. He says that I must have an operation to fix where my body is torn. I don't know what this means only that it is time away from Hannah and from my job.

Slowly, I go home. The bus goes past me and I wave. It doesn't stop.

Nathan and I first became acquainted at the tennis club. He must have seen the way I looked at him but never acknowledged it. He didn't have time for a social life, immersed as he was in his studies and then building up his law practice. He once told me that the nearest he came to a date was to take his sister Fay's friend, Alice, to the Yom Kippur social because she needed a lift. She was fun to be with, he said, but not his type. His sisters liked me and I took his nieces and nephews to the circus and the zoo and bought them ice cream.

My father too thought him the right kind of man for me, intelligent and attractive. He respected Nathan's profession and his family's standing in the Jewish community although they were poor. Nathan admired my father in return. Where he is formally educated, my father's wisdom is innate. He is a self-made man whose advice is careful and whose demeanour is modest. He weighs up issues from every side and often sees aspects that have not occurred to Nathan. My father tries to leave nothing to chance. So it was that he approached Nathan's mother, may she rest in peace, arranged our marriage and planned our future. Presumably Nathan was satisfied with my looks, my thick curly hair and green eyes, my small nose and freckles and thought I would make a good mother and wife. I was pleased to consent.

The wedding was all I could have dreamed. I wore a dress of guipure lace that fitted me snugly and emphasised my slim waist and round hips. My train and headdress were fit for a princess, nestling on my dark curly hair. The arum lilies in my bouquet were freshly cut and interlaced with baby's breath. Nathan wore a black dress suit and stood upright and slim next to me, his reassuring hand firmly on my arm as we posed for the guests and the camera.

"Nathan, I'm not ready for a child!" I was overwhelmed by my immediate pregnancy. "Where will we put a crib, let alone a cot? This flat's too small." It was our first quarrel. While he agreed that the baby shouldn't have to sleep in the dressing table drawer, he wanted to wait until he was more established before we bought our own home. My father agreed with me that we should move immediately and insisted on paying as we signed the title deed to the house on the hill. I recognise now that the cost of its upkeep remains a strain for Nathan.

Today, Nathan will ensure that my father receives the most accurate legal advice and the best hearing. He reassures my father,

"The court will take into account the actions of a reasonable man. I'm sure you will be found not guilty. We will call character witnesses to testify to your unblemished record."

I think about how we will have to endure the due process of the law, how it will drag on interminably, how none of us is in a fit emotional state to take it. I brace myself for what is to come. Later Nathan asks me,

"Susan, how the hell did it happen? Why didn't he look? Didn't he hear the children?" I can almost hear him saying, Where were you? What were you doing? How is it that Hannah was in charge? Do you ever think that she could have run behind the car too? You lock up your jewels but leave our children in someone else's care? My father says he called Zina. Then where was she? Nathan should confront her but I know he won't. I say nothing.

"Daddy, where's Elly?" Nathan folds his newspaper so he can do the crossword in his head and eat at the same time. Hannah rests her head on his shoulder.

"Susan, perhaps Hannah could have arrangements again. A friend to visit would be good if she doesn't want to go out."

I don't answer.

"Susan, she needs you," Nathan says, but the darning thread whispers as I pull it through his sock. I keep my head down. "She needs a haircut." So I take her to the barber's for a quick bob. "Oh, Susan," he says when he sees her that night, "where are her beautiful curls?"

"Zina couldn't manage them. They were like coir. Nathan, can you please see to the gutters? You promised to do them weeks ago. The water is pouring over and ruining the woodwork. I think this is the perfect time."

He rocks Hannah and holds her, then pours his tea into the saucer, blows it cool, gives her a sip. She pulls a face, not sweet enough. I flick my head towards her.

"Don't you think you're pampering her too much? She's going to have to get over it sometime, the sooner the better."

I stalk out of the room. Behind me there is a bruised silence.

Even though he knows I disapprove, he is teaching Hannah to read difficult books. He insists that it gives her something to take her mind off what happened, that because she absorbs everything so quickly it is a pity to hold her back. I know it will cause problems when she goes to school.

Nathan plays endless rounds of golf, works late. He wants to make love. He clings to me until he must know he's hurting me. We lie close but we are miles apart. Eventually I turn to the window and stare into the darkness, waiting for the solace of sleep. When I wake, he has already gone.

I am afraid. I am afraid of my own feelings and thoughts. And I think about what has been said and of how tomorrow will be, and the next day, and then all the days after that.

I cannot have any of Elise's belongings around anymore, reminding me of what was and what might have been. Each item is a trigger: the little dress with the rows of deep crimson smocking on the pale pink muslin bodice she wore to Hannah's birthday party; bootees knitted by Auntie Betty, wrapped in tissue paper; sheets embroidered by my mother with tiny flowers and butterflies; cotton bonnets with starched brims, floral and plain; knitted bonnets with earflaps; a box of hair ribbons, each perfectly ironed and ready to be worn again; all the reminders of a previous time, an ordinary life with special days, the seemingly endless days of being a family. I force myself into action and when Beatrice arrives she finds me in Elise's room.

"Sue, don't you want to wait before you do this? It's too soon."

"Nothing about the situation can change. Give it all to a

good cause. Someone else can benefit." I hand Beatrice Elise's ABC wooden blocks, "Here, put these in that box, please." Then I pass her the rag doll with its auburn plaits, Elise's colouring books, the fat grease crayons, broken and worn down, the music box. I take a little velvet jewellery box that I've brought from my dressing table and remove my cameo brooch of the Three Graces. In its place, I put Elise's gold heart locket, opening it one last time to look at the photos of Nathan and me facing each other. Then I put it on top of everything else in the Surf washing powder box and Sellotape it shut.

Hannah dawdles in and settles down on the rug. I wish Zina wouldn't let her wander around like this. I call down the passage. Zina comes out of the kitchen, wiping her hands on her overall.

"Zina, please take Hannah. I'm busy here with Miss Beatrice. And we can have tea in the lounge. Is there still some gingerbread?"

"Yes Ma'am. Come Hannie, let's go and put out the tea things. You must choose the cloth for the tray." When Hannah shows no sign of moving, Zina lifts her up, as she were not too big to be carried, and takes her into the kitchen. I hear her saying,

"We should use the pretty tray cloth with the yellows flowers that you like. Come now."

"Don't you think…?" Beatrice starts, but I look at her and she stops. She sees I don't want her lecture.

"Please cancel our booking for the dinner, Bea."

"Don't worry, I've done it already. The tennis girls want to visit you tomorrow afternoon. Will that be alright?"

"I suppose so. It's very difficult though. People I don't have anything to say to come and there's nothing I can do to cut their visits short."

"They mean well, you know that. What do want me to do with these?" She points to a forgotten pile of cloth nappies lying in the corner, some new, some torn from Elise's bum-crawl.

"Can you find another cardboard box, please? Ask Zina."

When we've finished packing up, we have tea. Beatrice steers the conversation towards safe topics, the sewing class she wants me to take with her and the new recipe that Hilda gave her that flopped.

"This gingerbread is delicious, Sue, as usual."

To me, it's like eating the Surf box.

I want to find her but I can't get out of here. It's all black. Very slowly, I feel along the wall for the window. There isn't one. There are rows of high, huge cupboards. The shelves are packed. The darkness smells bad. Like poison. I move along the walls. I need to find the doorway quickly.

I know I mustn't make a sound.

I feel for a door handle.

There is a pinprick of light at the end of the long passage.

Suddenly she's there, the little girl in white. I hold my breath in tight and the air is a cushion over my face.

Then I'm calling, Mommy, Daddy.

I wake up to find my father tapping my shoulder. He speaks gently, then goes out, leaving the light on. I look around. My room is empty.

We are in the kitchen, Zinkie and Mommy and me. Mommy says,

"You were supposed to be looking after the children. Where were you?" Zinkie is looking at me. She holds her hands together in front of her but doesn't say anything.

"Mommy, please...."

"Hannah," And I hear her voice and she's frightening me. "Hannah, this has nothing to do with you. Go back to your room now."

"Please Mommy...."

I wait on my bed until my mother goes out, then I take Clementine to Zinkie's room. I also take my breakfast but I don't eat. I sit on the Surf-Surf carpet by the door. On Zinkie's bed is a big brown box. It says Swift Washing Powder for the Cleanest Wash. Her bed has bricks underneath the bottom feet like Violet's so *tokoloshe* can't get her. *Tokoloshe* is a bad thing that comes when people aren't careful enough. Zinkie told me.

Zinkie folds all her clothes and packs them. Then she takes her pillows out of their covers with the red and blue flowers. She folds the covers too and puts them on top in the box but leaves the pillows on the bed. She says they are Mommy's. From inside the cupboard she takes the white sheet she is sewing for a present for Ma. That's Zinkie's mother. It has satin stitch all the way around the edge.

I stand up and put the pillows in the box too. She doesn't argue. She just goes on packing.

"Zinkie, you alright?" Hannie looks at me with her sad face.

"Come," I say, "let's help Violet bring in the washing." Hannie walks behind me and I give her the pegs. This at least is still the same.

Tomorrow I must leave this place. I don't know where to go. Perhaps I can find Gertrude. I still have her address. But it is so long since we spoke together on the train and maybe she found her brother and went home. I think about Jack, but only for a minute and then I shake my head. He came here when I was in hospital but he has not come back. I don't know where he lives. What does he think about me now?

The wireless plays penny whistle music. I switch it off. Hannah stays with me. Quietly. No dancing. No singing. Not like before. The light is out in her eyes. Like my eyes when I look in the mirror. She puts her hand in mine. Violet comes into my room.

"Sina, can I help you? You can leave some of your things here with me if you can't manage." How will my life be in Johannesburg without her? She's kind to me all the time. Everything I know about my job, I know from her. She is a good woman, truly. I stop packing and we sit quietly together. Hannah crawls onto my lap and I hold her tight.

Violet gives me a piece of paper.

"Here. This is where you can find Josephine, my sister. She will let you stay there until you find a job. Her place is not far from here."

I take the paper with the letters written in pencil and Violet explains how to get there.

"If Jack comes…."

"I know, I know," she says softly.

There is nothing more.

Part 3
1957

Blind Man's Bluff

One player, designated as 'It,' is blindfolded and must grope around to find the other, concealed players.

Today would have been Elise's third birthday so Nathan will go to *Shul*. His voice drones on,

"I'll say a special *Kaddish*, Susan. Then everyone will shake my hand at the *brocha*. I'll look away because I can't bear the pity in their eyes. I'll make pleasant conversation, as if I am the same Nathan." Nathan, the man who never confided his feelings before now just talks, talks, talks. But I can't.

"You know, when I walk to *Shul* with Jacob…it's not the same. Before, we'd chat all the way. He could match me joke for joke. He'd cross-examine me, seeking answers to the ways of the world. He wants to be a lawyer – like me – but he's afraid of me now." I don't look up from my book. "I envy him and the other *bochrim* playing outside without a care. I can't even get annoyed when they sneak two chocolates from the *Rov* instead of one. I cannot wait to get away and we walk home in silence, though he sometimes puts his hand on my arm, but then he lets it drop. When he leaves me to go to his own home, he waves jauntily, trying to smile. But it's all an act." His voice becomes reflective. "I remember my father's words as he spoke from the pulpit. How I wish I had his wisdom. I lose my place in the *siddur* and have to force myself to follow the service." He doesn't notice that I make no comment.

"Don't forget to wish the Mirvises Mazeltov on the birth of their new baby," I say.

When he comes home, I'm still in our bedroom and still in my dressing gown. I turn my cheek to him for a kiss, then go on sorting out my drawers. "There are sandwiches for lunch if you want, leftovers from dinner last night," I tell him.

On Sunday, he invites me to walk with him as he plays a round of golf. He says it's good exercise, that I'd enjoy it. He says it's good for the heart. I refuse. His game has improved, his handicap down from twelve to five. It's the best it's ever been, perhaps because it doesn't matter to him anymore. He puts one foot in front of the other, assessing which club to use and checking the lie of the ball the way I check my stitching, without thinking and when he comes home, he does the crossword puzzle. Hannah eats her fried egg, dipping the *kitke* into the yolk. She watches me all the time with huge black eyes that make me feel guilty. I have nothing to give her. The only time my pain disappears is when I eat, but it rises again immediately after I swallow. Nathan hounds me,

"Susan, you don't need that slice of bread, do you?" Why does he think he has the right to tell me what to do? He eats frugally, of course, watches his cholesterol intake, showers in cold water every morning, and strides to work.

I go to my meetings held at the home of a different committee member each week. At Goldie's, we are cramped but she is welcoming, her manner warm and relaxed. She shares her recipes and the table is laden with tasty treats. When we are at Millicent's, the butler serves us our tea and cucumber sandwiches. However, our agenda is always the same, to raise money for the less fortunate.

On the tennis court, I stand in one place. I haven't either the energy or inclination to run around. The girls are considerate and hit the ball within my reach and my serve is as accurate and lethal as ever. So my partner and I still win. I look at the stretched skin on my arms, the flesh bangles around my wrists. My watchstrap cuts. My skirts are tight and I think I shouldn't wear them short anymore. I think my blood pressure is raised and I should go for a check up, but the doctor will nag me about a new pregnancy.

Otherwise I go to John Orr's or Anstey's or Stuttafords, check each dress rack for my size, riffle through piles of collared shirts. One day, I buy twelve boxes of flat sheets, all white. The saleslady parcels them up in brown paper and string and the porter fetches a trolley and helps me to the car. Then I go back inside and buy a pillar-box red coat for Hannah that has been reduced to quarter price, too big for her now, but she will grow into it. I keep the till slips folded together in my handbag in case I want to return anything. When I buy a bargain, a new dress or pair of slippers, I feel better for a while but only until I drive back up the driveway. Today I was sweating coldly when I switched off the engine. I put my head down on the wheel and wept.

Nathan brings mounds of paperwork home, covering his desk with printed and handwritten notes and spending the night behind a barrier of lawsuits. His only distractions are coming to the supper table, and putting Hannah to bed. This absolves me. What a relief it is when I hear, "In the high and far-off times, the elephant, oh best Beloved, had no trunk. He had only a blackish, bulgy nose as big as a boot...." and I know that I will have a half hour of peace.

"More, Daddy, more please." She is so demanding of him. I'd go mad but he is incredibly self-disciplined, my Nathan, attending to her every whim. When he asks me to come and sit with them, I see the same appeal in his eyes as in hers. I don't go.

He comes to bed later and later. In the bathroom cupboard is my tiny bottle of sleeping tablets, hidden at the back and I take two for immediate oblivion between tight sheets.

"Have another child," everyone says. Nathan has pinned his hopes on a new baby. I know he wants to kiss me, bury his head on my breast until we are both overcome but *Rov* Goldring told him he must be patient.

For me it is inconceivable and my arms lie immobile at my sides, my legs heavy. Nine months of pregnancy and the subsequent delivery would be a life sentence. My labour with the twins was forty-eight hours long and by then it was too late for a Caesarean section. Passing out between the doses of pethadine, I discovered that only one baby had survived: Hannah. The death of the other little girl still weighs me down and is another blank space on the family tree. When Elise was born I missed out too. Exhausted after another long labour, sleeping in my room, I left Violet and Zina to run the house and look after the little girls. Another baby would be right, logically. But the child would be deprived of its birthright, its mother's love. And how could I even look at another little girl and not imagine Elise, or have the energy for a little boy, for its squalling demands, for the decisions. If only I'd had a hysterectomy after Elise as I'd wanted to.

So I don't need my diaphragm. I can't let Nathan near me in that way anymore, touching me, stroking my skin, my face, my body. How I flinch thinking about it although he was always both gentle and manly, caressed me as if paradise were within our grasp, so that when I felt his hand arousing the warmth and the wetness I knew a love for him that I could never have imagined and that at the precise moment we conceived the twins, there was a wave of heat from our conjoining bodies. It seems ludicrous now that this act of intimacy could ever have brought us pleasure.

I can barely prevent myself from walking away every time I look at my father, every time I look at Hannah. I bite through my lip and dig through the skin of my palms with my nails. I stay away from home to avoid Hannah's eyes. To amuse her we go to the library four times a week. For myself, I can't concentrate on any book.

The house is silent. Hannah hides out with Zina in the back yard or alone in the rockeries. She drags her cushion, her book and her doll, sucking her thumb as she disappears after lunch. I retreat to my room and rest in the cool darkness, the Venetian blinds shadowing the walls, and listen for a baby's cries.

I am dried up where once I was soft, a woman with no future, old before my time, without hope or joy. Last night Nathan was reminiscing about the holiday we had in Scottburgh on the beach with the two little girls. He wanted to look at the snaps we had taken. I told him I'd given all the photograph albums away with Elise's things and I didn't want to talk about it again.

It's as if I'm watching someone else.

I have lost the child of my heart.

The gates of tears are never shut – *di toiren fun treren zynen kain mol nit farshlossen*.

Morris must go to see the advocate, Frank Gordon. So I go too. As we drive, Nathan tells us what will happen in the court, about the judge with two assessors. They have to make sure of Morris's innocence, he says. I wonder if assessors will be better than a jury.

We pass by the Old Fort. Johannesburg's prison. Grey cement with one opening. It is the same as the *turme* in Yaneshik, the prison block. Where the Cossacks, may the cholera befall them, *a cholerye af zei*, beat and broke the Jews. Those that survived were conscripted for twenty-five years into the Russian army. Siberia. Conversion. Lost to their people as they served the Czar, may he burn in hell's fire, *zol er brennen afn fyer*. Morris's brother Mendel smashed his left thumb deliberately to avoid such a call up. Their brother Ben escaped to Palestine, a Zionist like Jabotinsky who began the Betar movement. If the Russians had caught him, he would have been shot straight away. Like my David.

Mr Gordon, a very bright young man, goes through all the possibilities.

"They have to take the foreseeable, not the unforeseen circumstance into account. You could be found guilty of culpable homicide, Mr Gerson, but even murder in the third degree is a possibility." He speaks like a gentleman, softly so I cannot hear him too well. I try to listen carefully. The language of the law is difficult for me to understand. My questions in my Litvak accent would sound like *tsebrogene tseine*, like breaking my teeth. So I keep quiet. Stay *shtoem*. Morris's life is at stake. Also mine. But. The facts are the facts.

Nathan speaks.

"What happened was totally without warning."

"Yes, and for that reason alone it's unlikely that Mr Gerson will be found guilty." Mr Gordon looks kindly at Morris. "Such episodes are not taken in isolation and the judge will use the

121

behaviour of the average man as a benchmark. There are many different ways of looking at any one case. Where a pedestrian has stepped into a street without warning and been knocked over, the judgments have gone equally to 'guilty' and 'not guilty.'"

And I think, every stick has two ends – *ale shtecken hobben tsvei zyten*. Will anyone ever know what really happened? Did Morris look properly? Could he have stopped what happened? Did Hannah call him? Did Elise? Will the court find him negligent? So whose fault, whose fault? So who is to judge? Tears falls from my eyes. *Dos iz nit fain*. This is not good – in front of everyone. I take my muslin kerchief from my sleeve and dab my cheeks and my nose. *Dos gantze leben iz a milchome* – the whole of life is a struggle.

Mr Gordon warns that the State will make it difficult. He tells Morris the questions they will ask. This is called cross-examination. I start to worry about anger and the Jesus cross and what that is to us.

"Above all, Mr Gerson, you must remain composed, calm. The verdict may very well be that it was an accident but you may lose your driving licence nevertheless, or receive a heavy fine."

For the first time, Morris speaks,

"In the early days, we could buy a driver's licence for 2/6 or 5/-. Many of my friends did, but not me. After the war, I learnt properly and earned my licence first try. At the same time, I changed my name by deed poll from Moshe to Morris to be part of my new country and to have new hope.

"Then I learned to drive the new Oldsmobile. In thirty-six years I never had even the smallest incident. I was always so careful," he says kerreful and I know he is wrong, "especially because of this." He points to his ear on the right side.

"The judge will certainly take your previous driving record into account, Mr Gerson."

But Morris was the only adult there. He should have taken more care. Nobody else to blame. Only him, *im alein*.

"Nathan has told me that the baby hadn't been walking for

122

long and her ankles were weak. They will ask you whether she tripped, Mr Gerson."

"Yes, yes. She wanted to go with me for a drive. A shpin we call it. She had special boots to keep her legs steady. But they didn't...." I want to tell him to say spin.

This is not the *shtetl* where a child slipped on the muddy street under a donkey cart or was trampled by the hooves of a Cossack horse, G-d forbid, *nisht do gedacht*. There, Ben pinched Morris's arm when they were feeding chickens or milking the cows to tell him, lunchtime, suppertime. And to tell the truth, *der emes tsu zoggen*, I didn't even know until the first time we walked by the lake.

"You mean you don't hear a word I say?" I made a joke of it.

His sister grabbed him from his *viggele*, his cradle and dropped him in the *blotte*, the mud, when she ran from the Cossacks, may the cholera be upon them, *a cholerye af zei*. Afterwards, they had to wait for the *feldsher*, the doctor. He gave Morris a draft for sleeping. But. They did not dare take him to the hospital in the city because maybe there would be another pogrom. Later, his parents, *zol zei lieggen in ru*, may their souls rest in peace, spoke to his left side only. As I do still. Now all I can think is what if the verdict is guilty?

Mens tracht un Got lacht – Man dreams and hopes but G-d laughs.

The gift is delicately wrapped and tied with a bow.

"Perfect, Nathan," I say, "thank you."

Inside, on his personal notepaper, Nathan has written an anniversary card in his minute script. I jump up and collect the little cardboard boxes from my top drawer. Hannah tips my rings and necklaces out of their cotton wool beds and rearranges them on the velvet lining of the new leather jewellery box. Sitting on the edge of the bed, we bend our heads together and as Hannah prattles, I describe:

"Look, this is the cameo brooch of the Three Graces that *my* Bobba gave me. And Daddy bought me this necklace when you were born. Let's put it round your neck, shall we?" I undo the gold clasp, lift the chain over Hannah's head and centre the pendant. The blue enamel wings of the butterfly match the colour of her dress.

As I lift the wrapping paper to throw it away, a whisper of perfume lingers in the air and suddenly, I see it all in my mind's eye, Felicity finishing taking dictation, appropriately dressed in a smart, fitted skirt, a plain blouse tucked in at the waist. She has on low-heeled black court shoes and stockings. Softly spoken and unobtrusive, she reads Nathan back his words without error. As she turns to leave, he calls her back.

"I must buy Susan an anniversary present. Could you look for something for me, please?" Stepping into the realm of women's finery is beyond Nathan's capabilities, I should know.

"What do you have in mind, Mr. Kramer?"

"A jewellery case. Would you go to Anstey's? Or perhaps John Orr's? That's where my wife would look." He reaches for his wallet. "Here, this should be enough." She puts the money between the pages of her notepad and her face lights up.

"I'll go at lunch time, shall I?"

"Why don't you go right now? You can take your lunch thereafter. It is office business, after all," and he beams at her.

Hannah fingers the butterfly and admires herself in the full-length mirror. She does a few turns and her skirt flares out.

"Look, Daddy!" She points to the necklace and he bends to kiss her forehead, then swings her up onto his shoulder and puts her down so that she is facing him. Her feet rest on his as they waltz down the passage.

Pine trees black against the horizon.
No voices, no song. Only crows.

I write the words down, alone in my dark bedroom. Later we sit down for supper. Hannah is next to me. If not for her I would stay in my room all the time. Under the tablecloth her hand is in mine on my lap. So her mother can't see it. Susan calls and rings the bell at the same time,

"You can bring the food, please, Violet." Violet carries in roast beef, potatoes, peas, and *burikes* salad, beetroot with raw onion, *tsibele*, like we ate at home. Nathan carves the meat. Susan serves the vegetables. We are all silent.

Morris is in his usual seat next to Hannah. His face is red, swollen and wet. Then I stand up, shaking, and my insides tumble round and round. The words burst from my mouth,

"*Du bist a moerder*!" My finger points at him. "Murderer. That's what you are! Murderer!" I take a deep breath. "Why did you …? You had no right …." I grip the table. My knuckles are white. There are no tears. Only boiling rage as I get more and more worked up – *Ich bin azei oevgerecht*. I could be a killer myself at this moment. I put my hands to my cheeks. *Azei hais*, so hot. I can't hear what I'm shouting because of the *tumel* in my head, the noise, the *gevalt*.

Der tsoren iz in hartzen a doren – the anger in my heart is like a thorn. "You have destroyed us. All of us. Why? Oh why?" I am trembling, holding the table and my words die. I am empty. Like I vomited. Now nothing is left and everyone stares. They are staring at me. Then they all look away. *Zei zoggen kain vort nit* – no one says a word. Morris holds his head and bows his body over the table, crying. I look into the child's bright eyes.

"Bobba? Are you alright, Bobba?"

I sit down and take her little head in my hands. I look into her face. Then we are all sobbing.

After a time, Nathan takes my arm, helps me up to leave the table. Hannah runs to her mother and puts her head in her lap. Susan's arms hang by her sides. The child's head is in her lap

126

and Susan's arms hang by her sides.

In my room, I lie down, then sit up and unlace my shoes. I turn the bedspread over my feet and turn my face to the wall. A long time passes. The doctor comes and gives me an injection. My mouth is mud and my tongue sticks. I put my hand on his sleeve to say, "Talk to Susan. See to Hannah. Please. Tell them the warmest bed is the mother's – *di varmste bet iz di mames.*" But I can say nothing.

When I wake up it is dark, silent. *Zei zoggen az der shlof iz der beste dokter* – sleep is the best doctor, they say. But. I feel the same as before. Susan and Nathan's door is shut. What goes on behind it? I only know what goes on behind our door, mine with Morris.

Not guilty the court may say.

But.

I look for it all afternoon, Elise's tiny gold heart locket on a golden chain like my *Magen David* and like Mommy's butterfly.

When I find it, I'll ask Mommy to put a photo of me in one side so I can see my wild hair and black eyes. Elly will be in the other with her soft brown kiss curls. I want one where she is smiling at the camera so that when it's in the locket she's smiling at me. When Daddy holds the box camera, he checks where the sun is. Then he looks through the hole and says: "Say cheese." He always smiles with a closed mouth because his teeth are crooked, but he wants me to laugh. Once the camera clicks we stay that way forever, so the photos must fit perfectly.

I'm worried Mommy'll be home soon but still I go through all her drawers. I lift her underwear and my hand bumps against the knives wrapped in her satin scarf. I know exactly what they are because Zeida told me they are his tools for raw meat on the slab. They are very sharp, one for chopping, one for slicing between the chop bones and one for carving. I touch the heavy wooden handles and the cold blades. Daddy calls them dangerous weapons so that's why Mommy hides them.

Mommy's silk bloomers are with her brassieres that have hooks and eyes at the back and a metal ring on each strap. They are beige, white or black and made of stiff elastic and she tells me that they are tight and uncomfortable. There is a pile of corsets with suspenders attached for her stockings. I lift a pair of stockings and hold it to my cheek and feel the electricity as I pull it away from my face and my hair rises up. I put the stockings back, careful not to ladder them on my hangnails.

No locket.

In the bottom drawer next to Mommy' petticoats are boxes of black and white snaps, pins, curtain rings and buttons. I find Mommy's red plastic View Master. Mommy keeps promising me that she will give it to me when I'm big enough to look after it. I put one of the cardboard circles in and there is Sleeping Beauty in 3D. I mustn't tear it, I know. Quickly I pack the card back in its box. Mommy'll be home any minute.

In her top drawer, everything is in compartments, all her little knickknacks that we sort together. I open the jewellery box from Daddy, clicking the lock and lifting the lid. The locket must be here in one of the three layers of maroon velvet. At the bottom is Mommy's pearl necklace, her heavy gold chains, a black disc with a gold coin set into it and a ruby pendant. There are also bracelets and bangles in silver and gold.

The top layer has rings and brooches: a pearl bar brooch with a pink flower that Mommy told me was amethyst, two ballerinas joined to each other with a tiny silver chain, and the shell-pink cameo of The Three Graces, her favourite.

I close the jewellery box and put it back in the drawer.

There is still the wardrobe. Do I have time? I fetch the dressing table stool and climb up. I open the right hand cupboard door and feel my way along each shelf with jerseys, careful not to crumple them. Then the top drawer. There are gloves and scarves and hankies and a muslin *pot-pourri*. I move the stool, close the wardrobe door and go to the other side. Under her dresses are piles of boxes reaching up to the hems of her dresses. Mommy sometimes can't find what she is looking for. Some of the boxes have shoes inside. Some big ones have John Orr's printed in a green bouquet and are full of sheets or towels. Other boxes have smaller empty boxes inside: chocolate boxes, card boxes, scarf boxes, empty button boxes, empty cotton thread boxes whose labels say filosheen or silk on their lids. They are all shapes, sizes, colours, striped and plain, floral and spotted, black and white, pale and navy blue, silver and gold. Some lids lift off and some are hinged. Here's her favourite scarf carefully packed away in a chocolate box, her hankies are in a Bicycle card box, her manicure set is in a button box. I open every one.

Her car is coming up the driveway. Quickly I stack everything back, trying to be neat but I can't remember properly what goes where.

Violet comes in to put the washing away.

"Hannie. Whatchew doin'?" I run and put my arms around her. She nearly drops the towels she is carrying on her head and the dresses draped over her arms. I start crying as she puts everything down on the bed and then I hold my breath in to stop hiccupping.

There's still the material cupboard with the rolls of coloured cotton, cambric, silk, viyella, cordella, ticking, floral, striped, plain. There is a safety pin on each with a handwritten label showing how long it is and the price, 2/6 for half a yard of calico; two pounds for 3 1/2 yards of maroon velvet; 3 guineas for a strip of shiny beads. On the bottom shelf of that cupboard are boxes of paper patterns that Mommy uses for her clothes and mine and Elise's. There are also some that are brand new, waiting for Mommy to cut them out.

Tomorrow is Mommy's tennis day. I won't go with to play with Mark. I'll stay at home and look some more, also for Elise's music box so I can wind it up with the silver key and listen to *Golden slumbers kiss your eyes, Smiles will await you when you rise, Sleep little baby do not cry, And I will sing a lullaby.*

In my room, I sit on my bed and write a letter.

Dear Isabelle,

Please bring me a little gold locket.

With love from Hannah.

Ich bin azei farmatert. I am so tired. Every night my husband lies and cries but to tell the truth, *der emmes tsu zoggen*, I can't look at him. And so my mind is made up: I must leave here. *Ven men lacht zen ale ven men vaint, zet kainer nisht* – when you laugh everyone sees. When you cry, no one cares.

"Violet. Violet." She comes from the kitchen. "Please, you must take out my clothes for me." I rock in my chair and I can hear little noises from my throat. Violet holds up my dresses for me to choose, careful not to crease the cloth. The lace collars are hand crocheted and pinned, to easily remove them for washing.

"Yes, give me that housecoat, the floral, and my new morning gown, please, the pink one. And another summer nightdress." Morris must take me as soon as I'm ready.

"Also, bring down my hat box. I want the straw sunhat with the black ribbon and my white panama with the silver hatpin." Susan bought it on the sale at John Orr's. I don't want to go out in public but I know Betty will want to. She is so much stronger than me. She will also want to talk but I make up my mind that I won't say anything.

Violet packs my toilet bottles into the leather vanity case and tucks my hairnets into a brown paper packet with my tortoiseshell combs. They say *der shverster ol iz a laidike keshine* – the heaviest burden is an empty pocket. But this is not correct.

"I want my body lotion and bath oil. Also the Johnson's baby powder." She busies herself silently and then stands with her hands underneath her apron, waiting.

"Violet, where is Zina?" I ask. "What has happened to her? Where did she go?"

Morris barges in.

"Not guilty. Leah, Mr Gordon is certain they will find me not guilty." He stops when he sees I am waiting, suitcase beside me, hat in hand. My checked parasol leans against the bench.

"I want to go away, Morris. Now, please." My voice is soft.

He looks at me with deep grey eyes but doesn't ask me anything. Maybe he's expecting this. He takes my case with one hand, my arm with the other. I support myself on the parasol. All the way to Betty's house, I look straight to the front. Morris keeps to the extreme left as we drive. He waits behind the white line at stop streets. At orange traffic lights. He is so careful. But. The stable door is locked after the horse is gone – *zei zoggen az men ganvert avek dem ferd, farshlist men di stal*. I *shvaig*, say nothing. I don't know what it's like to be the driver. At Betty's, he takes me in. She settles me in the spare room.

"I hope you will be comfortable here, Leahle," she says.

Morris leaves, putting one soft kiss on my forehead, and then I cry, far away from Susan and Nathan and Morris and Hannah. Later Betty brings soft-boiled egg and toast. She cracks the shell for me because my hands shake all the time. While I eat she stays, watching and waiting. I force myself to swallow. Sometimes I choke. I haven't eaten properly since that day. *Nisht ale tsores kumen fun himel* – not all troubles come from heaven.

Betty switches out the light. I sleep. I bathe early the next morning and scrub and scrub until my skin is red and sore. I try to write, in my looping English that someone will have to translate for them, another letter,

"Dearest sisters Dora and Miriam…." Then I write my *Mame-loshen*, "*Ich veis nit vi ich ken far dir dertseilen….* I don't know how to tell you this…." But. My mind sticks. Instead I say,

"We are all fine. Nathan works too hard. Susan still does charity work. You well remember Shira, our *landsfroi?* We went to her daughter's wedding. The *kale* looked lovely. Her dress was handmade with beads sewn in patterns across the bodice. She carried white gladioli, nothing like the summer flowers of Litte. The bridesmaids did not carry lighted candles as was our custom. It is very hot here now. The children play on the lawn when we water the garden. *Ich bagrist dir.* I greet you. Your loving sister, Leah."

132

I blot the paper, fold it carefully and put in the drawer. I need to address it but I will ask Betty. I take up another sheet.

"Morris, I want to be there but something worse may happen. I will let you know my plan. Leah."

I take up my knitting, the pink jersey still on my needles. Quickly I pull it all out. The wool falls in baby crinkles like little girls' hair and I wind it up into a ball. My arms are heavy when I finish. I put back the needles and the wool in my tapestry bag. Then, though it is bright daylight, I put back my nightdress and climb back into bed. Here there is no Violet or Zina to care for me and so I don't expect supper. But soon Betty is there with my tray and when I finish, she takes it away. I move my legs and she comes to sit next to me on the bed.

"Leah, what is all this? Why are you here? Not that I don't want you, but surely your place is with your husband, your daughter?"

"I can't stay there. He's a murderer. I told him in front of them all and you know the tongue is the pen of the heart – *di tsung iz di feder fun hartsen*."

"How could you say such a bitter thing? It was an accident. He needs you, now more than ever."

"*You* don't know what happened." I want to turn my back on her. I breathe in deeply. "Dora and Miriam. I want to tell them."

"But Leahle," and I see she looks strangely at me, "but Leahle, you know...*du veist*,... Dora, Miriam,... they...they are not alive anymore. You remember? *Du gedeinkst...?*" Gently she puts her hand on my shoulder. Then we are weeping together, our bodies shaking and shaking. For all those who we left behind, all those who did not survive. At last we dry our eyes. She says,

"Shall I read to you? We can start the Isaac Bashevis Singer book if you like."

"*A greisen dank*, Betty. Thank you."

I close my eyes. Afterwards she kisses me. Like Mama did at bedtime, Mama who never missed a night even when she

133

was worn out. I pull my *perena* over my head to keep the light from my eyes.

"*A guten morgen.* Good morning." Betty shakes me. "Morris is here to see you."

"*Ich ken nit.* I can't."

"Leahle, you must. I've given him tea. Come, I'll help you to get dressed." I want to run away. But I cannot escape the ghosts – *Ich ken nit antloifen funem shaidim.* Betty chooses my clothes. She pulls my dress over my head and bends down to button my shoes. She leads me to the bathroom and I splash cold water on my face. It wakes me up but does not chase away the darkness.

"Morris." My voice is shaking. He stretches his hand out and takes mine in it so I feel his strength and his weakness. He leads me to the sitting room.

"Leah, I am so glad to see you. *Koem, lomer trinken a glezele tei.*" We drink together, draw the lemon tea through the sugar in our familiar way. I put a sugar lump in my cheek. The sucking is soothing, the tea sweet and sour at once. It makes the sound of pain. I speak. I stop. *Ven di hartz iz biter, helft nit kain tsuker* – when the heart is bitter, no sweetness helps.

Morris clears his throat and his hearing aid whistles. He fiddles with the buttons and begins,

"I need you with me, Leah. Please. Come home?" His words come out in little splatters, like coughing. I keep my eyes on my glass and sip. Slowly.

"*Vos vet dos helfen?* What will it help?"

"It's where you belong, by my side. We promised each other.... Remember?"

"We have lost Elise and this was never home. You took me away from that long ago. The language is not ours, the people not our people and I cannot be with those who are here. What happened, happened. *Azei iz azei.*"

"I know. I'm...."

He takes both of my hands in both of his and caresses them like he did that very first day, on the banks of the river when he kissed me for the first time and set our flame alight. Now, even now, I see my eyes in his eyes. I say,

"It can never be the same. I make it worse for you."

"But what's the point of us each being alone? There is no way back, but maybe, maybe it will be less hard if we hold hands?"

"I don't know…." I am heavy like the zinc bath full of water when Zina washes the curtains. Morris walks me to my room and leaves. I crawl back under the *perena* and spend the whole day there. Sleep. Wake. Sleep.

I think perhaps I will dress again but I don't. Nathan telephones. I don't speak to him. My daughter telephones also but she doesn't come to see me and I don't want to see her. I long only for Hannah.

That afternoon.

My two little girls. My Hannahle. My Elly. Resting after lunch. Me knitting in my room. The wireless on. Iron. Steel. Engineering. Then screaming. Crying.

I dropped my needles and wool and ran.

Hannah.

"What? Tell me?" I shook her. Hard.

"Elly, Bobba. It's Elly."

"Hannah? Where is she?"

"Oh Bobba, it's all my fault. I took her out of her cot, Bobba! Come! Quick! Please!" She was gabbling, grabbing my hand. Then I left her behind.

Morris.

Moaning.

Crouched over on the driveway.

Elise.

The wheel of the car.

By her head.

"Zina, I must find Susan. Take Hannah. Quick."

Last night the Hellmans came round to visit us. Madge was dressed to the nines and spoke in her most affected tones. Her single topic of conversation is children, even now. She and Alec are terribly kind but their sympathy gets on my nerves: Madge put her arm around me at one stage during the meal, but when I recoiled slightly, she withdrew. Alec discussed my father's case with Nathan in undertones and I caught the words "reasonable precautions" and "reasonable man." I am grateful that I can leave the legal matters to Nathan and know he will be meticulous working on the case. Hopefully, if my father is found guilty, he will only face a manslaughter rather than a culpable homicide charge.

Madge didn't kiss me goodbye when we parted and I was relieved. Why do people have a constant need to embrace me, people who would not have done so before? She telephoned me this morning to go with her and a few friends to see *Private Lives* at the Library Theatre, a matinee with Moira Lister. Without thinking it through, I agreed.

Now I'm sorry. I have no interest in Coward's brittle lovers. I'll have to wear make-up and my tightest smile. Those women mean well but have no idea about my life now, of Hannah's clinging or the tears that stain my skirt. Before, she was satisfied with the chocolate that I brought her after my outings. Preoccupied with the baby she hardly noticed I wasn't there. Now it's such a relief for me to drive down the driveway and out of the front gate and leave her with Violet.

I chew up the whole roll of toffees that I've hidden in the cubbyhole by the time I reach the greengrocer, so I buy more. Chocolate is a better pick-me-up, but the last time I ate it in the car, I had to drive with sticky fingers. Wiping off the steering wheel afterwards with a tissue dampened with saliva, I was disgusted with myself.

Hannah is on the lawn eating Violet's bread and jam and my mother is back from Betty's. She rests in a deckchair, her parasol shading her face. My father isn't here and I'm relieved:

I'm afraid these days of what I might do or say. Nathan joins us.

"Come Hannah. Let's show Bobba and Mommy how you ride the two-wheeler." My parents gave it to her as a surprise and she and Nathan practise on the lawn next to the driveway in the twilight. He holds the bicycle steady and Hannah mounts, then he runs with her as she turns the pedals. She keeps falling off but persists, calling,

"More, Daddy, more." Nathan picks up the bicycle and steadies it again. Eventually she manages a few rounds alone own.

"Look everyone. It's like the circus. Look at me!" We clap and smile until she skids and falls again and I go inside, exhausted.

Nathan has this notion that there is a Guiding Hand and a Greater Good. I can't go along with it though he cajoles me to change my mind. He finds comfort in the Rabbi's words and blessings where I do not, so I cannot discuss my feelings with him: his map of understanding is poles apart from mine and we inhabit totally different worlds. How can he be right?

In my wardrobe, in the pocket of my silk dressing gown, are my rosary beads. Tentatively I start, Hail Mary full of grace… and the beads are solid and cool in my fingers.

In the breakfast room, I find my father is lying on his stomach on the rough brown carpet. I have no idea how long he has been there, banging his legs up and down.

"*Vei iz mir, ayaya, oy, vei iz mir.*"

"Dad, stop that at once. Pull yourself together."

He gulps a few times, his face buried in the carpet until the crying becomes softer, then less, then stops altogether. He sits up, wipes his nose and cheeks on his handkerchief, takes off his spectacles and cleans the glass. His earpiece dangles. The machine screeches.

"*Ay, vie dos fyft.*" Breathing heavily, he turns the tiny black button back and forth until the piercing noise stops. Then he leans on the arm of the wooden chair, stands up and leaves, not saying a word.

Did he switch the aid off that day? This is a question I can never ask.

Azei zogt men, as they say: *Gan-Aiden un gehenem ken men baide hoben oif der velt* – in this world there is heaven. But also hell.

Nathan finds Morris by the Dam in Emmarentia. Looking for stones. He brings Morris home. Holds his arm as they come into the dining room. Morris's hair is sticking up. His shirt is creased. The candles burn and he blinks at the reflection in the mirror.

The place of the highchair is empty. Nathan makes *Kiddush*. We have wine and break the *kitke*. Violet brings the soup. Hannah says,

"Where were you, Zeida? Didn't you know we were waiting for you?" Morris only stares at his watch, puzzled. Hannah reaches into his pocket. There is no Nestlé but he takes her hand in his.

No one eats and the soup gets cold. We sit in silence as Violet comes to take away the plates. She brings the roast chicken and vegetables. We leave it untouched. Even the potatoes.

In Litte – nothing. Here – nothing.

"Zeida," Hannah says, "Today I heard my *Piet-my-Vrou*. That's its name in Afrikaans, you know. In English it's called Red-Chested Cuckoo. Daddy told me." What would it be in Yiddish, I wonder? But in Yaneshik we didn't ever hear it. Morris used to try to copy how she said it – before – and she would laugh. Before we would all have laughed. Who were those people who could laugh?

We *bensh* but without song. Morris and I go to our room. He takes off his shoes and socks. They are soaking wet.

"I am to blame…whatever the court will say…I drove around all afternoon…in the rain … through the jacarandas… everywhere is green…full of life…then I parked at the Dam…." He is talking to himself, not to me, "…my hands were in my empty pockets… I held them there not to pick up the stones…, but the water was over me already…."

I don't want to listen. He taps the top of a cigarette on the Mills Special tin, puts the tip in his mouth, wets it and lights up. One cigarette. Then another. He stubs them out just before they burn his fingers.

"I flicked the stompies into the water...they floated... disappeared...so peaceful. I thought about Hannah...I thought about Susan... I want to be there... with Elise...."

I look out onto the dark green lawn, to its trimmed edges. The purple agapanthus plants sway between the bright blue garlic plants. *Az zei zoggen, az men ligt oif der erd, ken men nit falen* – they say, if you lie on the earth, you cannot fall.

Elise lost. My family lost. But they must be given honour, *koved*, must all be remembered. Mama, Tati, David, Ita Liefse, Miriam, Dora.

On the round table in the corner of the room, I move all the ornaments. I rest my inkwell on a plate not to knock it over onto Susan's pretty floral cloth. Thoughts, memories, keep on coming.

Everything is still so clear. Like yesterday yet so long ago. I write in English letters. But my words inside remain Yiddish.

Night of the Cossacks.
Pine trees black against the horizon.
No voices, no song. Only crows.
Fists pounding on the door.
Hurrying footsteps.
Father's voice. Mother's cry.

The words don't stop when the book shuts. Sometimes if I close too quickly, the ink smudges.

Horses breathe smoke. Steel blades whistle.
Hurry up! Arois! Arois! Out! Out!

Morris and I were lucky – *a glik hot unz getrofen*. We escaped from it. Then. All the black memories are back now. Open scabs. So I must write everything down. *Ich muz dertseilen* – I must tell. So everyone will know. Not forget. I want to tell Hannah. But she is too small to understand what happened to my family then. What is happening to us now.

I close my eyes. Life is sweet and too short when we are happy. But, *oisbrukirt mit tsores iz der veg tsum bais-hakvores* – when a wrong cannot be made right, it such a long and terrible road to the cemetery.

Why don't Daddy and Mommy ask *me*? Daddy keeps saying,

"Susan, what happened? Tell me what happened? Please."

But Mommy doesn't know. Mommy wasn't there. Mommy was far away inside the house and didn't hear me calling. And Zinkie wasn't there. Zinkie doesn't know. Zinkie was in her room. Only Zeida and I know and Zeida doesn't talk. Mommy closes the bedroom door. Daddy is on the phone. I need to tell them. Tell Mommy and Daddy. Why don't they pick me up and say,

"Hannah, what's the matter?" Then I'd tell them she wouldn't listen. I held her hand as tight as I could. I told her to stop. I said, "Stop, Elly! Stop!" But she wanted Zeida. She wanted to run. She wanted to go for a spin and she pulled her hand away from me.

But no one says anything and they don't see me. It's like I'm not here. Just like Elly isn't here. Like we both disappeared when she ran behind the car even though I didn't run after her. I took her out of the cot and then I let go her hand. Mommy doesn't look at me or speak to me because she knows it's my fault.

Zeida lies on the breakfast room floor, kicking his legs up and down and Mommy tells him,

"Pull yourself together." What does that mean? He used to sing to me. I go to him and get onto his lap and touch his shirt and put my hand in his pocket for a little Nestlé but there isn't one.

The maitre d' of The Three Ships brings us the menu. We are celebrating my birthday. We choose smoked salmon on rye for hors d'oeuvres. I decide on a grilled sole while Nathan has the kabeljoe with baby potatoes and courgettes. I know I have dark smudged lines beneath my eyes and my mouth is tightly set. I wait for him to speak first. He tells a quick joke that I don't find funny.

"Susan…?"

"I…." Crying in public isn't my style, so I focus on cutting the fish flesh from the bones. He tries again to distract me.

"What are we going to do about Hannah's schooling next year? I know the timing is poor but the decision has to be made."

"You know that the school you're suggesting isn't the best one, Nathan?"

"Perhaps, but at least there she'll have her cousins with her for support."

I think of how lonely I was at the convent when I started, how my Latin and English studies sustained me, learning the roots of words and the conjugations off by heart and how Sister Theresa encouraged me to explore the wonderful library as an antidote. She often brought out her own stories, written in pencil in small square exercise books. They always finished, 'And darling Eddy loved darling Nora and he took her in his arms and kissed her.' We raised our eyebrows at these soppy bits and wondered if she had come to the convent because she had lost her own true love in the Great War.

"Hannah will make new friends soon enough but it will be easier for her if she is with Bella and Laura in the beginning. You know what little girls can be like and I don't want her suffering needlessly."

"Yes, it did make a difference to me when Beatrice was old enough to join me. Perhaps you're right."

Luckily the Jewish girls gravitated towards each other as we all sang the Lord's Prayer and then a hymn every morning.

141

Eventually I made friends with Maisie and Sheila and though we competed for first place, it didn't ruin our friendships. Surprisingly.

"You know I played the *Moonlight Sonata* in the annual concert, not to mention that I accompanied the choir for their Carols by Candlelight? How badly I wanted my parents to be proud of me. But carols…!"

"I'm sure they were proud just seeing you on stage, in the limelight, considering where they had come from…."

Nathan knows nothing about my rosary beads or recitation of the catechism, of course; how, at *Shul*, the *brochas* mingle with the Hail Marys I learnt instead of Hebrew.

"I guess that they were, in their own way. When I went home for the weekend, they made me play for the family and for the shop staff. Then my cousins were jealous of me and Mona and Lily giggled as I sat down and adjusted the piano stool. They all clapped at the end, but I could see that they thought I had gotten above myself."

"The fact that the convent offered you piano and violin lessons was a good thing too. We must enquire what the school can offer Hannah."

I have never told him of the control of the metronome when Sister Bernadette rapped me over the knuckles because I was out of time, or of Sister Boniface's sewing lessons. But there were peaceful times too, practising alone in the music room, high up in the tower, fulfilling times when I won Royal College of Music prizes.

"We need to play and sing on Sundays as we used to do, Sue, so Hannah can benefit from what you know. And the music could be a solace. Maybe we could even get a teacher to come to the house for her."

"My father believed he had done the right thing to send me to a private school, an opportunity he never had. Did it give me airs and graces, do you think?"

"I know Madge and Alec's children learn piano. Don't you want to ask her about a teacher?"

"I think Hannah will have enough to cope with going to

142

a new school, with the homework and school extra murals without overloading her with other activities as well."

"The way she walks around sucking her thumb and carrying Clementine wrapped in Elise's blanket. It breaks my…. She needs…."

"Yes, she needs to get rid of that blanket. I don't know how I overlooked it. I thought I'd put it in the boxes that Beatrice took to the Benevolent Shop. Now she just won't give it to me. I've even tried to bribe her. It's ridiculous."

He puts his hand on my arm and looks round in alarm in case anyone has heard me. Quietly he says,

"She'll give it up in time, I'm sure."

"Yes, well, you know yesterday at the grocers, they were all watching her sucking her thumb. She is much too big to still be doing it. And she never says a word to them even though they are always so friendly towards her."

"I think we should go away for a few days, perhaps to the coast. We could do with a change of scenery and the sea would be invigorating. What do you think?"

I think about not having to pretend in front of our friends for a few days, of the sea air blowing away the past.

"Getting away and spending time together sounds wonderful!"

"And it would be so good for Hannah too. I know she'd really like it."

"Do you do that on purpose?"

"What? What do you mean?"

"Have you heard anything I've said? Why is everything about her? Why does she always have to be part of everything? Of everything you and I should be doing together?"

"Susan! We can't leave her alone, especially now."

"Don't you think you and I could do with some time alone for once? Especially now? You're obsessed with her."

"Perhaps we should order dessert. Let me get the waiter. What are you having?"

We order Pavlova and eat in silence. Nathan downs another Scotch in one gulp. I wonder if he realises what is happening to us or just doesn't want to see.

Once home, he unzips my dress at the back, taking care with the hooks at the top of my spine and bending to kiss my neck.

"You look lovely, Sue. The dress turned out really beautifully." Perhaps the evening would have gone better if he'd complimented me immediately on the garment made so painstakingly for the unattended awards dinner.

I step out of it and hang it away. Putting on a dressing gown over my underwear, I go into the bathroom and close the door. When I come out, Nathan is in his railroad pyjamas, reading the Britannica, but he takes off his glasses and looks up.

"Don't you want to tell me why you are so angry with me?"

"It's you who are angry with me," I snap back.

"I was only trying to talk to you. Why won't you answer me?"

"You are such a liar, Nathan. You know you blame me for what happened. You blamed me when Hannah's twin died and you blame me now. I know you think the whole thing was my fault."

"Susan, how you can say that. How can you even think it?"

"Because everyone knows it's true. I was here all the time so why did it happen? Don't you ever ask yourself that?"

"It's not me who blames you…."

I feel my tears rising and my breath coming painfully and I cover my face with my hands. Nathan moves towards me.

"Leave me alone. Keep to your books and your darling little Hannah. Please." I go back into the bathroom and bang the door.

I picture him returning to his encyclopaedia, focusing on the battle of wits between Monty and Rommel, the support of the Allies by the Americans, the impact of the Sherman tanks, the use of the Hawker Hurricanes and the difference that these anti-tank planes made to the outcome of El Alamein, facts he will want me to share when I get into bed as if nothing untoward has happened or been said.

He couldn't go to war because of his damaged eyesight, but Joe, his partner, was in the 8th battalion. On his way home from North Africa, Joe spent *Shabbos* in Nairobi with the Rabbi. He met the daughter of a newly arrived Czech family and they fell madly in love. Within six weeks they were married and living in Johannesburg and are still content, which is why Nathan is certain that a Greater Power directs everything.

As I come out, I know Nathan can smell the Pepsodent on my breath and the Pears soap on my skin. I don't look at him but switch off my light and watch him through half-closed lids. Eventually I fall asleep, but later I am aware that the place beside me is cold. Nathan is wandering around the house somewhere and it is still dark outside. By sparrow-chirp, he has dressed and eaten and left.

"Daddy. There is someone outside the window." I wait a while and call again, "Daddy,… There's something behind the door."

And there's someone under the bed. I know it. And behind the curtain is a big, black something. And also inside the cupboard.

"Daddyyyy. I want you." The light from the passage shines in through the fanlight above my door.

My father comes into my room, barefoot. He switches on the light and shakes the curtains. He opens the cupboard. Nothing. He lifts me up so I can see through the window into the garden.

"Nothing there, Hannah. Look."

"Please can I have some water?" He fetches a glass from the bathroom and I sip. Then he switches off the light and goes back to bed.

"Daddy. Daddy. I need a wee-wee." I know my potty is under my bed but I can't get up by myself. My father follows me down the dark passage to the toilet and waits while I finish.

"Daddy, I'm thirsty."

"Daddy, I want water."

"Daddy, there's someone outside the window." I can see their shadows beating on the ceiling so I point.

"Daddy, there's someone under my bed."

Each time I call him, he shows me that there is nothing there.

"Daddy, there's someone in the cupboard."

"Daddy, I'm thirsty."

"Daddy, I want…"

"If you call me once more, Hannah, I'll give you a hiding."

For a long time I swallow my breath. I lie in the dark and suck down hard on my thumb with my teeth, my heart banging so loudly I can hear it.

Then there it is again, outside the window.

146

"Daddyyyyee."

A man of his word, my father. He clicks on the light.

"No, Daddy. No. Please, no." I put my arms out straight to stop him. Then I cover my face.

He turns me over like a limp fish, spanks me twice on each cheek and turns off the light. My tummy shudders and breaks and I mess myself. And the bed.

"Mo-mmy. Mo-mmmmy."

This time, it's my mother who turns on the light. The smell is horrible.

"Why didn't you go to the toilet? Now look."

She lifts me up and holds me away from herself. She carries me, sobbing, to the bathroom, fills the basin with warm water, finds my washcloth, grips my arm and wipes my bum and legs roughly. It's the only way to get it all off. Then she changes me into clean, soft pyjamas. My body is still heaving.

"Bring your cushion and come to my bed."

Soon she's breathing deeply. Behind her, staring and sleepless beneath the squares of the pressed ceiling, I watch the black night change to grey light through the Venetian blinds. As soon as I hear kitchen noises, I slip out of the tight, hot sheets and go to Violet and she presses me to her warm body.

When Daddy comes into the kitchen, already dressed for work, I am sitting on the wooden stepladder. Violet is giving me Milo and rusks. He takes his newspaper and says he is ready for his Jungle Oats please. When he goes into the breakfast room, I follow. He mixes peanut butter into his porridge and sits me in the chair next to him. He does one for you, one for me until the plate is empty.

Then Mommy comes in.

"I can't believe you are feeding her. Hannah, wipe your mouth and let's get you to school."

In the car, I sit on the armrest in the middle of the back seat. I am wearing my striped skirt and my button down top and I hug my brown suitcase. I have my towel and my milk but Mommy says Clementine can't go with because Miss Levine won't allow it anymore.

At school, Mommy leans round and opens the car door. She is still in her dressing gown and slippers and she doesn't come in with me. Laura is there with her Mommy and I walk in with them. When I put my suitcase in my locker, Laura says,

"Do you want to come and play at my house today? I've got a new kitten. She is called Sooty. She has a white star on her face. You'll like her."

"My Mommy doesn't like me to go out after school."

"We can make Marie biscuit faces with pink icing for tea."

"Alright. I'll ask."

We walk into the classroom holding hands but I know that I won't go to Laura's house.

I need to be home for when Elly comes back.

It is only mid afternoon but Nathan has walked home.

"The Cane case is worrying me, Sue. I'm too exhausted to think. I need to be more alert. Even with my notes in front of me, I can't find the discrepancy in his evidence. It's probably obvious and I'll kick myself when I eventually do see it."

"Mmmm."

"I have some niggling doubts about his innocence. For example, why didn't he go straight to the police after the shooting? Where was he really in those crucial two hours? I must discuss it with Joe before it comes to court. Perhaps with his experience he'll be able to give me a lead." I go on with my sewing.

"I called Cane to set up an urgent meeting. Susan, are you listening to me?"

"I thought you walk to work early to clear your head for just such problems?" I picture him surrounded by law reports and his collection of leather-bound editions of the writings of Lincoln, Jefferson, Churchill. The room is a cocoon of silence where he plans strategies and makes decisions, a place where no one presumes to disturb him.

"It's getting too much for me. I've been looking at all the invitations. There are so many functions coming up, and another conference where they want me to give the plenary address." I know he is both a popular raconteur of funny stories and an insightful speaker on the minutiae of the law. "I must get Felicity to sort through and make some impact on my in-basket. These things need to be kept under control. At least there I can try to make some sense of things."

I look up. His face is wet.

"A piece of grit flew into my eye. As I walked over the bridge a train puffed underneath. They run according to a strict timetable, like clockwork, but they send up a rush of dust each time they pass. I tried to use the corner of my hanky to get it out. Please can you try?"

The carpet is covered with all my things. I took out all the toys to sort them but now I'm under my blankets. Mommy brings two big suitcases into my room and puts them on the floor. The last time we used them was when we were going to Scottburgh with Elly. Elly and I shared one case between us, her clothes on top of mine with our sunbonnets next to each other.

"Hannah, you need to get rid of some of these toys. We can't take them all with to the new place. Come and help me or I'll have to do it myself."

Mommy opens my cupboard and takes my dresses out. She folds them one by one into the cases, then my swimming costumes, then my button shirts. She holds up the pink one, then the red, then the white.

"I think these are a bit small. Or perhaps I should just give everything away? Hannah!"

I suck my thumb and don't care about bitter aloes.

"What do you think, Hannah?" What I think is I wish Mommy would go away and leave me alone. "Will you wear them again?" I know I should tell her that I won't but the words don't come. I stare at the wall until I hear her turn around on her heels and go out.

I hold Clementine. Then I fetch all my dolls and put them under the blankets with me. I take my tin of charms from their hiding place in my cupboard and put it under my blanket too. The dinky cars and my jacks are in the cupboard. Also my marbles, my glassies and puries and cats' eyes in their Snowflake bag Mommy gave me when the flour finished. I like the blue and red letters but I don't care if I leave it behind.

When I wake up, it is completely dark and still. I tiptoe down the passage without my slippers. The light is on in Mommy and Daddy's room. I hear them talking and I wait.

"I still think this is a mistake, Susan."

"Why would you want to stay here even one more day?"

"This is the place we know. Hannah is settled. She has been through enough already, Zina leaving, then your parents will be going away too. And then a new school...."

"There are too many memories here. It'll be better once we're in the new house. We'll be able to get on with our lives. You'll see I'm right."

"Do you really think that any move could erase the memories or the pain? We'll carry those wherever we are."

"Well, I think it will be better once Hannah is settled somewhere else. Maybe then she will stop expecting Elise to come back. She is like a shadow walking around, looking in every room, over and over. When I say that she should sit with me in the breakfast room and read her books, she looks straight through me. I don't know what to do with her and quite frankly, I can't take it anymore."

"It is early days yet, Sue. I was speaking to Beatrice yesterday. She gave me the name of a book that gives advice on how to handle these kinds of situations, how to help children who have suffered a bereavement. We need to try and help her."

"Why are you speaking to Beatrice behind my back? You know, she said I should keep Elise's things! How would that help anything and how can she possibly know what I am going through?" Mommy's voice gets louder and louder, like when she shouted at me when I left Clementine at the park.

"But I do. I've lost my little baby too, you know." It sounds like Daddy is crying again, but I can't be sure. Maybe it's Mommy. I push open their door and step into the light.

"Mommy, can I please sleep in your bed?"

"You see," Mommy says, "this is exactly what I mean. Now she'll get into my bed and I won't be able to sleep." She looks at me. "Go and get your cushions." She doesn't kiss Daddy but turns onto her side with her back to me and switches off her bedside light.

I walk slowly back to my room and get back into bed, but then I fetch the little torch that Zeida gave me for my birthday. I hug Clementine and sing to her. Then I kiss each of my dolls one by one. I yawn and yawn but I don't put out the torchlight. I don't want to sleep in case the little girl in white comes again.

151

It's Wednesday afternoon and Nathan is playing golf with clients. Supposedly. He tells me how golf is the only thing that calms him. Now he's trying to get Beatrice's brother off a fraud charge and is under pressure with the Cane case.

But he's having an affair, I'm sure of it.

Our old friends don't know what to say, are on guard not to hurt our feelings. Yesterday in my sewing room, he sat on the couch arm and continued his on-going soliloquy.

"I am no longer Nathan. Instead, I am the father who lost his daughter in a terrible tragedy. No one can get past that. They talk about me when I'm not there rather than to me when I am, and stop speaking as I come into the room, cross the road when they see me coming towards them."

He is probably with her this very minute, sharing a meal and a glass of wine. Felicity.

I can just hear Madge,

"It's no wonder, you know. The poor man needs some comfort and warmth." And Alec would agree with alacrity, in support of his own sex. I wouldn't be surprised if Nathan's taken her to that new Italian bistro that everyone is recommending.

"Would you like to share a salad?"

"That would be lovely, Mr Kramer, thank you so very much. Perhaps we could have the one with olives and feta? Then I'd like a margarita pizza with mushrooms, please."

"Please, call me Nathan. And yes, that sounds good to me too."

He orders his pizza with anchovies and pineapple. She bats her long lashes at him and asks obsequious questions about his career, about how he put himself through night school while clerking during the day. No doubt he believes that, unlike me, she is actually interested in his answers. When he asks her about herself, she confides in him about her difficult growing up years, her family, her relationship with her mother who is in the throes of Alzheimer's. He is caring and she is enthralled.

"They say Parkinson's disease is worse for the patient,

but that senile dementia is worse for the family," he says, sympathetic and enrapt.

"I can't bear to be with her anymore. It's heart-breaking how she doesn't know who I am and calls me Grace, her late sister's name."

They keep to safe subjects and he is too much of a gentleman to ever mention me. But still he confides,

"I am hoping to go to a sculpture class. One of my clients teaches and I like both his manner and his work. I need an outlet. Something besides golf!" They share a conspiratorial laugh. When they finish eating they look intently at each other. He is aware of the softness in her face, in such contrast to my own drawn features. When did I last smile? Smile at him? I can't remember, so I'm sure he doesn't either.

Felicity flicks her wrist to check her watch.

"I must go now, Nathan. It's been wonderful. Thank you very much."

He is disappointed. He assumed they would spend the afternoon together. He settles the bill and gallantly helps her into her jacket. When she leaves, he is at a loss.

It is seven o'clock when he comes home. He describes his walk around the golf course, the ducks and the clouds, the 19th hole and the few Scotches with his friends, discussing their rounds in minute detail.

I picture it all as he spends another night poring over the Britannica.

I am peripheral.

Clementine wears her white dress and white booties and the cape that Bobba knitted for her. I wear my green and red striped sundress. The straps are made of ribbon that matches the bow in my hair. The air-hostess takes my hand and cares for me on the aeroplane after I kiss Mommy goodbye at the airport. We are soon high up in the sky and I watch the clouds float past. I think about climbing up the rockery at home and sitting on the silver roof. That's the highest I've been before this. I think about when I tried to take Elly up because we wanted to touch clouds. She pointed at the birds and laughed but she couldn't get past the first set of rocks and I left her. I look out into the clouds but I still can't see her. When I ask Daddy where she is, he goes quiet so I don't say anything about Elly anymore.

Zeida and Bobba and Beatrice fetch me from Durban airport to have a holiday with them.

"We are so happy you came!" They are sunburnt and they all talk to me at once while Zeida drives us to the Greenfields Hotel. I have a bed in their room behind a curtain. I fall asleep with the sound of the waves crashing outside. When I wake up I watch the sun rise over the sea.

Zeida loves swimming. He gets up at dawn to go to the beach and then comes back to wake me up. He jumps from one leg to the other and up and down to shake the salt water out of his ears and then rubs himself dry, making a funny wet sound with his lips. Brrrr. We go in to breakfast. A smart waiter in white serves us paw-paw slices, then Maltabella porridge, then fried eggs and toast. They bring me bacon and Zeida sends it back. The fried eggs aren't crisp and golden around the edges the way Zinkie used to make it.

Later we go to the beach together. I have my swimming costume underneath my shorts. Bobba wears her thick stockings and a dress with long sleeves even though it's hot. She opens her gingham sunshade.

"I don't like the sand or the sun," is what she tells me, but she comes with us anyway. We sit in deck chairs and then I like to lie on the sand and bake. Bobba inspects my sand castles and tells me stories about the place called *in der heim* and all her sisters. I count them on my fingers, Miriam, Dora, Rosie, Dina and Betty plus her brother David and her sister Ita Liefse before she died. She tells me how they played by the river and washed their clothes when they were my age. They made *mensele* out of mud. We try to roll the wet sea sand into heads and bodies but they crumble.

Later, Beatrice meets us on the beach with Isaac, her husband who is the handsomest man in the world. She buys me an ice cream and a cold drink. When I swim, Beatrice or Zeida hold my hand and we jump over the waves. Sometimes I get dumped if the waves are very strong and then water goes up my nose. My hair is tangled and sticky and full of sand so I shower off at the beach in freezing water.

Every day Bobba and Zeida sleep after lunch and I practise my dancing. I wear my long dressing-up skirt and spin my pink parasol in my secret bedroom behind the curtain. It's like backstage. I bend and stretch, and point my toes and wind one of Bobba's scarves round my head and another one round my waist for an extra swirling skirt. When Bobba and Zeida wake up I do a concert for them. I sing, *Ce sera sera, whatever will be, will be*, and *All day, all night, Mary-Anne* and dance at the same time.

One afternoon, Zeida takes me to the Snake Park for a special treat. The South American and Australian snakes are the prettiest but they are also the most poisonous. Some are small with diamond patterns, bluish and greenish. Some are large and plain. Their forked tongues stab in and out of their slit mouths and some of them spit. That's why there are glass panes to separate them from us.

I show Zeida my favourites, reading the labels on the cages, vibrating the words through my lips and teeth like Daddy does: viviparous, oviparous, venomous, herbivorous, omnivorous, carnivorous. Then I roll the sounds round on my tongue, reptile, arboreal, diurnal, nocturnal. I don't know what they all mean. Nor does Zeida. He likes my words but he doesn't like

155

the snakes as much as I do. He says that in Russia snakes kept the mice away but they were afraid that they'd bite the babies in their cradles.

In Johannesburg, I have my own snake. Daddy killed it in the bright moonlight when Violet and Zinkie and Frans were screaming and shouting and he went out to see what was happening. Daddy broke a branch off the loquat tree and hit the snake's neck. When it was dead, he wound it into a glass bottle and preserved it in pink methylated spirits. He labelled it HOUSE SNAKE with the date, 10 January 1956. For a while, the bottle stood on the breakfast room mantelshelf and I couldn't stop staring at it. Then Mommy put it away in the bathroom cupboard next to the gentian violet and the bath oil. A common house snake is nothing to be afraid of, Daddy says.

At the snake park, there is a demonstration at 3 o'clock. They bring out the snakes and put them in a huge pit, mambas, cobras and vipers on one side, non-venomous snakes and constrictors on the other. The man with the microphone tells us about their habits. Then we're allowed to touch or hold the non-poisonous snakes if we want to. We stand in a line waiting for our turn. Samson the attendant has a two fanged fork and he picks the python up for Zeida. Zeida pulls a face and holds it far away from his body with both hands round its middle. He won't hang it round his neck, but I'm not scared of it.

"You must take it like this, Zeida, see." I hold its tail in my left hand and its neck in my right and dangle it round my neck like long, thick rope. I don't squeeze but stroke it and I don't touch its face. Its skin is smooth and dry and decorated with bronze diamonds and isn't slimy at all. It feeds on dead mice, rats and rabbits and is related to boa constrictors and also to the Bi-coloured Python Rock Snake in *The Elephant's Child*. Pythons and boa constrictors crush their prey and swallow it whole, but I'm sure it won't hurt me. Zeida gives Samson our Brownie camera to take a snap of us with the python. My hair is pulled flat because it is sticky with salt water and I'm wearing my ugly grey jeans because they are warm but it doesn't matter. I squint into the sun.

Back home in Johannesburg, I draw the geometric patterns of the snakes' skin, the diamonds, squares and circles. In the bathroom, I stare at the black scars on the skin of my snake curled up forever in its graveyard bottle and look up its picture in my new snake book that Zeida bought me.

It's not a house snake.

It's a mamba.

"Hannah, come, we'd like to measure you," Nathan calls. She comes to her new bedroom and stands tall and straight in her socks against the newly painted white doorpost. He places a book on her head, rules a neat pencil line under it and writes the date.

"Three foot, two! What a big girl! We'll do this each month and watch how you grow in our new home, shall we?"

He mends the doorknobs and erects bookshelves on bricks. Hannah follows him as he replaces the leaking tap washers, watching intently as he puts the parts together, asking which piece goes where. She carries the spanner and screwdriver in one hand and the small pair of pliers in the other, pointing the implements downwards carefully and passing them as he needs them. Because she can't criticise, she is the perfect helper.

At the bottom of the garden, one of the taps has snapped.

"That's a job for a plumber!"

We hear the *Piet-my-Vrou* again and Nathan imitates the call, two short followed by one long whistle.

"Is it the same one that we had in the Stone House, Daddy?"

"I don't know about that, Hannah. But I do know after it lays its egg, it doesn't look after its baby."

"I want to see one, Daddy."

"Well, they are very difficult to spot. We'll go to the zoo and look at other varieties. I think you'd like that."

He takes her with him to pick plums. Although there are only a few fruit trees at this house, their basket is full.

"The fruit is ready for cooking. You and Mommy should make jam." We bite into the delicious flesh and the juice drips down our chins. In front of us, the whole of the western side of the city glows in the afternoon sunlight. I point out the vermilion roofs to Hannah.

"It's the same orange as those." She points at the strelitzia that are in full bloom.

"They are called Birds of Paradise," Nathan tells her.

158

"More birds, Daddy!"

"Shall we cut a bunch for Mommy? Let's get the pair of secateurs."

She waits for him singing to herself, a song she learnt from Zina long ago, in another life, *kwenene kwenene; kwenene kwenene….*

Inside, Nathan pours himself a Scotch and soda and coaxes Hannah to have a taste. She makes a face but doesn't spit it out. He pinches her nose and she giggles, then he mixes her a drink of granadilla squash and soda water. I bring out a platter of snacks and we watch the sun set.

"What steps did you learn at ballet this week?" Nathan asks, and Hannah demonstrates points, pliés and pirouettes. Then she fetches the paintings she has done at school. One is a full-length portrait of herself with a single area of colour, her bright blue tutu. He suggests that we should get the picture framed.

"We can hang it up in Hannah's room." I agree to take it in. "Will you make me another one for my office, please, Hannah?"

"We have to go, Nathan. Bridge starts at half past seven."

"Oh, blast!" He's obviously forgotten and seeing Hannah's crestfallen expression is sorry to leave her. He promises her a sweet for under her pillow when she protests about staying at home with Violet.

During the break at bridge, Beatrice provides smoked salmon on rye bread and egg mayonnaise bagels and cheesecake. As usual there is far too much food. We stand around, chatting and catching up on the week's events. I dislike standing and eating, balancing my tea and my food plate. I look around for an empty chair.

"Susan, how's Hannah doing since I last saw you?" Madge asks

"Fine, thank you."

"It can't be easy…."

"I said she's fine." I turn away, my shoulders rigid, and take another sandwich. Silence has descended around us but Madge continues undeterred.

"I've heard of a good counsellor who specialises in children's trauma. She lets them paint while she speaks to them. Perhaps she would be suitable for Hannah?"

Now everyone is listening.

"I said, Hannah is fine. Thank you." My voice is a door snapping shut. Beatrice claps her hands.

"Come on, time for one more rubber, I should think." She shoos everyone back to the game. Somehow I must get through the evening.

"One spade."

"Four spades."

"Double."

"Redouble."

I have to play out the hand but my mind is not on my cards and I go down. As we leave, Nathan slips two chocolates into his pocket for Hannah.

"The way that woman violates one's privacy...," I say in the car.

"Her idea is not such a bad one, though. I don't see Hannah as being alright at all. Why don't you...?"

I turn and face the window. The court case will follow protocol and Nathan will coach my father and anticipate the cross-examination and pre-empt the trick questions, setting down aspects that he wants the advocate to include; however, he has no idea about how to talk to his wife.

I lie awake. I know Nathan does too, but he makes no move.

Bella and Laura come to my new house and we practise our ballet together in the lounge, pointing our toes out, doing our leaps. We put on our flared skirts and black leather shoes and watch each other from the ledge in the bay window and do duets, holding hands as we run on tippy-toes across the floral carpet. It's called Persian. Once Bella trips on the fringes and bumps her head on the mantelpiece and then I run too fast and hit my leg on the sofa leg. I have a bruise there, mauve and blue and yellow.

We want to get good parts in the concert so we go over our steps again and again and then we correct each other. We make believe that we are on stage when I switch on Daddy's gramophone and play his record of the *Nutcracker Suite* and the *Waltz of the Flowers*. I am careful not to scratch the vinyl because then I won't be allowed to do it again.

When they leave I write a letter.

Dear Fairy Queen Isabelle,
I want to be the Blue Rose.
Please can you fix it?
With love from Hannah.

I fold the piece of paper and put it in the box at the end of my bed. In the morning, the letter is gone.

Nathan and Madge may be right, that Hannah needs an outlet, and, as I do dislike the mess when she paints at home, I take her to an art class. At least then Nathan will stop hounding me about helping her.

We drive to Clarendon Circle. I park outside Crown Heights where other children are carrying in their art equipment and go in with her. A still life is set up in the centre of the room, spring flowers in a striped vase with pinecones, apples and oranges arranged next to it on a black cloth. Around it are wooden easels with large sheets of paper clipped to them. There are children kneeling on the floor over their drawing boards while others lean at a long trestle table. Hannah clings to me, as she does in the morning at school.

She has brought her own tin of watercolours, but Pamela suggests that she use the big pots of already mixed powder paint.

"Plenty of bright colours for you here, Hannah dear. Have you done anything like this before?" Hannah hesitates as Pamela sets her up in front of an easel next to some children whom Hannah knows, including Madge's boy.

"Please stay, Mommy." I assure her that I'll fetch her in a little while and leave without looking back.

An hour and a half of freedom. I pop into the small dress shop nearby. I decide on two new blouses, a blue silk with a mandarin collar and one in cream that is off the shoulders. Both will go well with my new black linen skirt. Time flies. As I leave I imagine the accessories I will wear. Perhaps I will treat myself to a pair of new earrings.

Hannah hands me a very wet picture of the beach with a dark green sea. We place it flat in the boot. She holds onto her still life that is already dry.

"How lovely Hannah," I say, as the other mothers do when they hug their darlings. Silent at the back, staring out of the window, she volunteers nothing about the lesson. At home, she takes both paintings and goes straight to her room. The door bangs.

At supper Nathan asks how her day was. She takes him to her room to show him her pieces. When he comes back he is alone.

"Thanks, Sue. It will be good for her, I think. I wouldn't mind doing a still life with her one of these days. Perhaps I could also join a class?"

He picks up the newspaper to do the crossword puzzle, but gazes at the jacarandas for a long while as I finish stitching the last flower on my tapestry cushion.

I'm kneeling and drawing behind Mommy in the breakfast room. Daddy brought me a pile of paper from his office. I like the way the pencil makes dark thick strokes if I press very hard, but it can also go very light if I just press softly. When I say, "Look Mommy," she says, "Please wait a minute."

Pamela is nice, but there is too much noise there and too many people. Last week a boy spilt water on my painting on the floor. I tried hard not to cry when I had to start again and I didn't like the new picture as much. Then one of the girls tried to talk to me and I said, "Leave me alone." She went to tell on me.

"Mommy I don't want to go back to art lessons."

"Oh," Mommy goes on sewing but then she says, "you like drawing so much and you know Daddy will be very disappointed." I don't answer. I don't like having to copy things like Pamela's still life. It's the same at school when my teacher makes me cut out shapes and stick them down and then colour them in. Here in my pencil drawing, I can see things that nobody else can see. They are my secrets. While I make my patterns I hear songs in my head, but Mommy doesn't know. That's another secret.

I am so tired. I didn't sleep last night because the little girl came again. It was dark, but she was lit up brightly in her nightie. I think maybe I should say Mommy, who is she? but I don't. Instead I hum Elise's song for going to sleep, the one I should have sung to her when she was crying that day instead of taking her out of her cot.

I finish shading the paper. Mommy doesn't notice when I leave the room to put it on Daddy's pillow. Maybe he'll take it to his office. When I go back to the breakfast room, Mommy is finished sewing and she makes tea for us. She pours mine into my saucer to cool it. I blow it and then drink like a kitty. I don't spill a drop and Mommy says, "Good girl" but then I make a little burp with my mouth open and she frowns.

When Daddy comes home, he kisses me first then Mommy,

then hangs up his jacket and goes into the pantry to make himself a sandwich. He calls it a *nush* and that means a snack. He gives me a bite of the meat with pickles and mustard and it burns my mouth, but I like it. He says we mustn't have too much because we don't want to spoil our appetites for supper.

"How was your day, big girl?" He ruffles my hair and puts his hand under my chin.

"I made you a drawing, Daddy."

"Bring it and let me see."

"I put it on your pillow."

"Lovely, Hannah. I'll show my partners and have it framed, shall I? Thank you."

He gets down the encyclopaedia with pictures of a famous artist called Van Gogh. He signed them with his first name, Vincent, in paint. Daddy shows me how to sign Hannah in the bottom corner, very small, so it doesn't spoil my picture.

He also tells me how Vincent cut off his ear. There must have been a lot of blood.

It is inappropriate, according to Nathan, that the wife of a professional man should work for a living. Instead I assist at the Women's Zionist Organisation and sort the books for the charity sale.

"How was your meeting today?" Nathan asks as he pecks me on the cheek.

"Busy. We have lots of plans because we haven't hit our target yet."

"Come and have a drink with me."

"Can't. We've got the sale tomorrow and the banquet next week, remember?" He pours himself a whisky and returns to where I am sitting. Hannah brings him a new drawing.

"Sue, the classes are really making a difference. Have you seen these intricate patterns? It's a real development from her previous pictures, don't you think?"

"She's stopped going."

"Why? When?"

"She said she didn't like it. About a month ago, I guess."

"I thought that it was so good for her. I can't believe this! Why didn't you tell me?"

"Listen to you. This is exactly why. You make everything my fault. I can't force her. In any case, she's doing perfectly well on her own as you can see – which is what I told you and that busybody Madge in the first place." Why can't he take my word for it? Not being there during the day, he has no idea how Hannah is or isn't functioning.

"Sorry, Sue. I don't know why you won't share any of this with me. I guess you're right, if she's reluctant. I just don't think she should spend so much time on her own, is all."

"She doesn't want to go to her friends and the mothers don't seem keen for the children to come here at present."

"I'm sorry to hear that. I only hope it eases up. She's lonely, poor kid."

"Nathan, it's my grief too, you know. You seem to think that it's worse for her. Or you." I stop. I must not let my guard down. If he knows I'm vulnerable, he'll think it gives him the right to tell me how to handle the situation.

I know he weeps when he thinks I'm sleeping and I feel as if I am about to snap. I go back to packing books. Nathan does the crossword, checks the definitions and finishes it before supper.

"Hannah, why don't you invite Bella to come and play tomorrow? Mommy can telephone her now, if you like."

Her head is down and she plays with her food. Nathan leans forward to coax her, almost challenging me to say something. But I don't. I peel a banana, slice it and offer her my plate. She checks my expression and takes two small slices, popping them into her mouth. She helps herself a few times when I am not looking and soon the plate is empty. Then she says, "Excuse me please," and leaves the table.

Down the passage, we hear the door of her room closing. Nathan goes and stands outside. He beckons me. She is talking to Clementine and we can only guess at the content, but her voice is tremulous. Nathan taps his signature beat on the door, "Shave and a haircut! Bay rum!"

"Who's there?"

"Daddy."

"Oh, Daddy, silly, you can come in anytime."

"Thank you." I watch as he sits cross-legged on the carpet opposite her.

"Do you want to have tea with us? Clementine has just made some delicious scones with jam." The room is spotless, everything in its right place, the clothes hung away, the dressing table neat. There is no sign of her paints or even her charms and the books have been shelved.

When their little party is over Nathan comes back.

"I was thinking about the drawing she gave me, Susan. Have you noticed she has abandoned her wonderful colours?" He fetches the picture to show me. The detailed picture is densely shaded, as are all her more recent ones: cross-hatchings in pure pencil. Solid grey.

Beatrice spends the afternoon with me while Mommy has her book sale. She sits in the striped green deck chair on the front lawn and I'm up in the branches of the jacaranda.

"Hannah, it's Rag on Saturday. Would you like to watch the Parade?"

"Oh! Yes, please! Where?"

Last year we sat on the gateposts at the Stone House and the floats went past in the street below. We took a break to walk up the driveway and have a cool drink from the garden tap. I remember the *Piet-my-Vrou* was calling loudly because Daddy came home and told me its name. He said I may never see one because it's very shy. It hides in the tall oak trees behind the house. This afternoon I hear it again so I know it must be Rag time.

"I thought we'd watch the float procession in the centre of town for a change."

"Maybe we can go by bus?"

I watch the red and cream buses travelling past every day and Daddy sometimes takes one to work. When he comes home, he tells us how it stops suddenly because the trolleys come off the overhead wires and the conductor has to get out and use a long pole to hook them back. Everyone waits to go, tapping their feet and reading their newspapers. All the cars behind hoot until the bus moves. It makes Daddy late for work.

"I think it'll be easier if we take the car. We'll ask your Dad if we can park at his office building, shall we?"

We go in very early because Beatrice wants to avoid the traffic. I am wearing my favourite red spinning skirt with its tight waistband and straps that go over my shoulders. It has smooth gold buttons at the back. Mommy made it to fit me exactly. Under it I wear a bright-white short-sleeve blouse with puffy sleeves and my snugly button-down jersey. I have short white socks on and my best patent leather black shoes.

We park in the basement where it's very dark. Later it will

get very hot but now the streets are grey because there are no sunbeams between the tall buildings. I shiver as we walk, saying the street names aloud: Kerk, Pritchard, President, Commissioner. Beatrice tells me what they mean and the famous men they are named after. It's all to do with long ago when Johannesburg was built in the gold rush. I hop on the paving stones and she holds our packet with peanut butter and plum jam sandwiches. We also have apples and water bottles.

There are hundreds and hundreds of spectators. The pavements are packed and people shove but we manage to find a place near the front. At the bottom of my driveway there was nobody else and it was our own private viewing spot.

Mommy has given us lots of copper pennies to throw at the floats and Bea keeps them in little money packets. We wait and wait. We chew apples. Some children are perched on their fathers' shoulders and there are people on the balconies and on flat roofs leaning over and looking down. What if someone falls? I hold Bea's hand tightly, sometimes kissing it and staring at her sparkly ring, sometimes looking into her smiling face. Everyone waves at everyone else and suddenly there is shouting.

"They're coming! They're coming!"

First come the walkers, the fairies, dwarfs, clowns, witches and magicians. They are made up with white or coloured face paint and have red cheeks and shake their metal boxes at us for our coins. A giant on stilts with long red striped trousers leans down and takes a penny from my hand. He laughs and waves his white glove at me and makes a popping sound with his huge fish lips. At last the floats are here decorated with garlands of tissue paper flowers, yellow and white and pink. I pick a fallen flower off the street and put it in my pocket. I see all the fairy tale characters that are also in my charm tin, Beauty and the Beast, Cinderella, Snow White and Sleeping Beauty and we keep throwing money.

The Rag Queen sails by in her white shiny satin dress, wearing a diamante crown and carrying her mace like the Queen of the Fairies. She has long black hair and long white gloves and she waves her hands and smiles and blows kisses. We all cheer and she catches my eye and blows me a kiss and I blow one back to her.

"Here, throw her a shilling," Bea says. I pull my arm back and throw as hard as I can. It lands near the Queen and one of her fairies picks it up and laughs thank you. I throw a penny and then another one and then I throw a whole handful at once, using my strong arm like Daddy showed me. They fall onto the float and into the street and roll under people's feet. Some roll into the gutter. I let go of Beatrice's hand. I must put them into the moneyboxes for the poor. I crouch down to try to pick one up in the street. Suddenly the wheels of a huge float rush past my face.

I freeze stiff. I hear voices far away. Then Beatrice is there next to me. She lifts me up and carries me away from the street. I can't hold her because my arms are too heavy. The people crowd around us.

"What's wrong? What's wrong?" Their bodies close in. I keep my hands over my eyes and I can't breathe.

"No, no! Please...No...."

I lie in Beatrice's arms all the way back to her car. I hear her,

"Excuse me, excuse me. Please let us pass." Her chest going up and down hard but she soothes me all the time,

"Shh. Hushhsh, Hannah. It's alright. It's alright."

We have to drive home slowly through the people in the road. Once we have to stop so I can open the car door and vomit. Beatrice gives me a tissue to wipe my mouth and looks in her bag for a peppermint. I suck hard to take away the sour taste.

"Nearly home, Hannah. Alright?" She talks softly to me. The cars behind us hoot and hoot and Beatrice keeps saying, "Sssshhh, everything will be fine."

At home in the kitchen she gives me to Mommy and mixes a glass of sugar water.

"Drink this Hannah. That's it, slowly now," she says. "Okay, let's clean you up." She gently wipes away my snot and tears.

"What happened?" Mommy asks but Beatrice shakes her head and doesn't answer. Instead, she takes me to bed and tucks me in with Clementine. Mommy is standing by my door holding her head in her hands. I am still whispering,

"No, no. No, no."

I lie awake, *in der finster*, in the dark. So many months of waiting for the case to come to court. Is this Morris's last night in his own bed? Will he be sent to jail? Will it be straight away? When do they decide? Nathan must explain when Hannah and Susan are not here.

The wire of Morris's hearing aid is caught in his tie.

"Come," Nathan says, "let me help you." It is the morning of the trial. Nathan helps Morris put on his jacket. I am grateful to Nathan. Not once has he looked with anger. Or spoken in bitterness. He holds the car doors open for us. Morris sits in front, me at the back. Susan does not come.

"Nathan, I want to give you the money for the funeral. Also make a donation to the *Chevrah*," Morris says. I watch Nathan's face. His hands are steady on the wheel. He takes his left hand off the gear lever, puts it on Morris's knee,

"You must not worry about that now."

"And I must pay Mr Gordon. You must let me see his accounts, please." How can he be talking about money now? Children are more precious than gold, *kinder zynen tyerer vi gelt*. "Mr Gordon also told me that my automobile insurance will pay damages."

"We'll see." Nathan talks solemnly about how the day will proceed and reminds Morris to stand straight up, look at the one who is asking the questions. Nathan catches my eye in the front mirror as if to say, how am I?

In der heim, there was no justice for Jews. Cossacks came, may the cholera kill them all, *a cholerye af zei*, with shotguns and sabres, *mit biks, mit shverd*. They locked Jews up. Tortured them. Shot them before they could escape. I remember how those Russians, *a magaife af zei*, a plague on them, took Kaplan's boy Reuven for questioning after a scuffle with some local Lithuanians. They needed a Jewish scapegoat! When I passed the *toerme*, the prison, to collect our *Shabbos* chicken from the *shachat*, I heard screaming. I blocked my ears. I ran. I was the last to know Reuven alive.

Outside the court we park and go up the stairs. Morris and I wait on a wooden bench. Many people walk past, some holding hands, some with bowed heads. Nathan goes to find Mr Gordon. Next to me, an old woman sits with her daughter. She winds her handkerchief round and round her fingers. The daughter pats her mother on the back and says,

"Mummy, it'll be fine. You'll see. You mustn't worry." I think this is like my own empty promises to myself – *allezding vet zyn fain*. As if that can ever be. Nathan comes back.

"They're running late, as usual."

We wait and wait. Morris remains quiet. Even the hearing machine is quiet. At last we are called to the courtroom. Number eighteen, *chai*, the number that means Life. There is a special place marked for Non-Whites/*Nie-Blankes*. In Litte it was Jews who were separate. Without a voice. There is no one that we know in the public gallery for *Blankes*/ Whites. Strangers lean over the rail. Stare at us. *Peruvniks* with no politeness and no manners. They look on our lives as a *Chanukah shpiel*, a play for their entertainment. But for us there can be no *neis* like there was for Judah the Maccabee – there can be no miracle here. The law must take its course.

The lime-green walls are stained. Many men smoke cigarettes and pipes. Morris, at Nathan's suggestion, has left his Mills Special at home. He sits separately in the dock, far away from me. Fiddles with his braces. Everyone stands when the judge enters. The *knepeldiker*, the man in uniform, gives the name of the case: "The Crown vs. Mr Morris Gerson Esquire." He speaks like *a ware Afrikaner*, a true Afrikaans South African. "Your Honours, Mr Gerson is accused of causing the death of Elise Kramer by the negligent use of a motor vehicle on Thursday the eleventh November, in the year of our Lord, nineteen hundred and fifty five at eleven minutes past eleven o'clock, before noon. The charge is culpable homicide." He turns to Morris and puffs up his chest,

"How do you plead?"

"Not guilty."

Again I wonder how this is possible but remember what

Mr Gordon told us. About the two ends of the stick. About the different sides to a case. How young children behave erratically. The court must decide if a reasonable man in sound mind could have predicted or stopped what happened.

"Call the first witness. *Roep die eerste getuie.*" They call the coroner. He is the one at the mortuary who looked at Elly. "Describe your findings for the court please." How can he choose to be with dead bodies all day, bodies of victims, bodies of babies? Choose to talk about bruises, breaks, blood, about the injuries that cause death? In a voice that does not shake? He states that the injuries coincide with those that would be inflicted by a motor vehicle. The state's lawyer questions him.

"Were the cuts on her face what you would expect in an accident of this nature?" I have no idea how long it goes on for. I check the brown station clock behind me. I can hear the big hands as they drag round, one long minute, then another.

"*Ja*, Your Honour. They were."

"And the abrasions on her arms?"

"*Ja*, the skin was broken and there were stones in her flesh."

Morris looks at the assessors. But they don't look at him. Have they already found him guilty? He looks straight at me. I put my head down. I try and follow the state's evidence, how the lawyer presents the case. There are many words I have never heard before. But I understand what he means. It's all clear to me. Black and white.

The *knepeldiker* puts down the Bible. Morris puts his hand on it.

"Do you swear to tell the truth, the whole truth, so help you …?"

"I do." His voice is soft but still I hear how it breaks.

"Mr Gerson," the state attorney speaks again, "please describe for the court what happened on that afternoon, the afternoon of the eleventh of November 1955."

Morris's hearing aid gives a small blast. He looks at me, then at Nathan. Always the same problems.

174

"It was at my daughter's place...Susan's and Nathan's. It was time for me to leave." He keeps his eyes down.

"Speak up, Sir, we can't hear you. *Ons kan jou nie hoer nie.*"

"I kissed Hannah and then Elise. My grand-daughters...."

"Hannah is the older, is that correct?"

"Yes, Your Honour. I kissed...then I went down the passage, out of the house. I left the little girls to sleep... in their bedroom. They always had an afternoon nap, at least Elise did.... I went to the car...."

But my thoughts slide away. Past his voice. Past the grinding noise of the fan. Out of the boiling courtroom.

Morris is kissing me. It's not the first time a boy touches my face with kisses. Innocent kisses on Sunday afternoon in full view of our parents. Child's play. Now Morris's lips touch mine, his brown to my red. His tongue is in my mouth. Our saliva mingles. I feel him pressing hard against me and our bodies incite each other. I don't know how I will be able to stop. It is all heat and breathlessness.

He takes his hand from my back, places it on my breast, then where the white cotton blouse and my skirt meet. My breath comes in gasps like pain. I run my hands up and down his sides to feel his flesh. My body wants more but I know it's crazy, *meshuge* – before marriage there can be no touching, no kissing, no desecrating the body with carnality. Our codes are simple, strict. We are out of bounds and both of us know it. He draws away and I make no further move.

In the gallery of the court there is a loud scraping of a chair. Someone whispers,

"Sssshhh!"

"Is it your own vehicle?"

"Yes, Sir."

"Was it in working order?"

"Yes, Your Honour."

"The accelerator. The brake?"

"Yes, Sir."

"What happened then?"

"I started up. The engine didn't catch at first, so I revved it

175

hard. Once it started, I had to reverse. You see…."

"Yes, yes, we got that. Go on." Morris wipes his eyes.

"…the car was parked outside the front door…."

He may be going to jail but still I don't want to hear any of
this. I try to concentrate on the trial, but I cannot and so I turn
away.

At last, Morris drags his mouth from mine. Breathing deeply,
he takes his hanky from his dungarees' pocket, mops his face.
He offers me the cloth, turning the damp section away from
my hand. My cheeks are flushed as if I've run all the way from
Yaneshik. I know nothing about what is supposed to happen
next. Betty always said I'd find out when the time was right.

We walk back to my house, deep in thought, hand in hand.
We have been so close to each other. But we are strangers. And
I am a stranger to myself.

"Alright?"

I nod. Morris smiles. I go inside.

That night, I nudge Betty, lying back to back in the bed
we share.

"Are you sleeping? I need to talk."

"Why now? *Ich bin farmatert*. I'm tired."

"*Dos iz vichtik*, it's important. Please." I need to know –
about the need for intimate connection and procreation; about
how to balance this conflict with spirituality; about how to
control urges powerful enough to keep the whole human race
alive; about the meaning of the Universe.

"What's on your mind?" To me it sounds like "hurry up."

"After kissing…*vos noch?* What next?" She laughs. I wish
I'd never asked but I plough on, "Don't try and get out of it
this time. Please." Realising I'm serious, she stops laughing.

"What's happened with Morris? How much do you know?"

"Nothing and nothing."

"Do you want to…? Sorry. Stupid question." She leans over
me, intense and determined now to tell it right.

"The thing is, the boy has to show the way. He should
sweep you off your feet. Details? Yes, very well."

By the time she finishes we are giggling. The facts seem

176

ridiculous. Horses, chickens, cattle, yes. But people…? What black comedy has *Hashem* devised for us? What does this act have to do with the emotions and passions of love? As much as Betty makes it sound like the natural outlet, I feel uncomfortable about it. How is it that He made my body yet forbids me to soothe it? She explains the physical process, but she is no deep thinker. I want to know how she manages her own needs. My elder by two years, she can be no stranger to them, but we have never spoken before. Well, the time wasn't right for me before.

"Lucky you, Leah. He's so nice!" She turns over and is asleep straight away. I lie awake for a long time reflecting on morality, on need, thinking about Morris. I ache with guilt. Then I wonder if Morris worries too. Maybe he has already been with a girl – a sin. And if it's one of the village girls, a Gentile, another sin – G-d forbid, *nisht do gedacht*. But then I think, impossible.

From the witness box, Morris's voice breaks,

"Then I reversed…."

There is a long silence. Could he have known that she would run? He should have been prepared because she was testing her legs. He knew she wanted to drive with him, that she wanted to go for a spin. He says shpin. Hannah would have corrected him.

Eventually the state's lawyer says,

"Yes, yes, and what then?"

"The car…I felt…."

"Please Mr Gerson, we must have the facts. What speed were you doing?"

"Maybe… ten…maybe ten miles an hour. I had only just started the car. I felt a bump. I turned the key, switched off the engine. Got out…."

I see it all in front of me again. As I know he must.

"I reversed. I felt a bump. I pushed the brakes down hard. I opened the car door. I got out. I saw…. I opened the door. I saw…." Morris is talking too fast and now he is repeating himself. The lawyer holds up his hand,

"Yes, yes, you've said all this before." And, I think, no one can understand him because his accent is still thick Litvak. Like mine.

"And what did you see when you stepped out of the vehicle? Explain to the court, please."

"She was lying, Elly was lying...behind the car, by the wheel...."

"Was she still alive?"

"Yes."

"What did you do then?"

"Nothing...."

"Was the ambulance called?"

"No, no, my daughter...."

The courtroom is *a zei heis*, so hot. My lace collar scratches. I try to listen, try to keep my eyes on Morris. His face is downcast and his fingers are between his shirt buttons. They grip the hearing machine and the cord is looped around to his ear. The hangman's noose. Soon the court will decide but to me he will always be guilty. My mind wanders

My husband is in the dock. He may go to prison, G-d forbid, *nisht do gedacht*. But I can't think about it now. Maybe not even tomorrow. I want to be somewhere else. Away from here.

My mother is baking bread with Mrs Kuperowitz. They roll out the dough and plait three strands together for the *Yom Tov challahs*, large breads enough for all the guests but there will be no bread for us during the week because there will be no more flour. She eyes me. My hair is neat with a straight middle path and my skirt is spotless.

"You look pale, Leahle. Sleep well? *Host gut geshlofen?*" I kiss her good morning. "Is something worrying you?"

"I'm fine, Mama."

I take porridge in my bowl, add milk. I eat with my face towards the plate. Finished, I wash up and scuttle outside. I don't want Tati to arrive and start with his questions too. There is a knock on the kitchen door. Morris comes in.

"Eggs from the stall over the way! My Mama wants to know how we can help you with tonight's meal. She can do some

178

baking for you if you like."

"That would be a big help," Mama says, "Thank you, Moshe. Perhaps your father could help us with the fire. My Zev has gone to fetch the wood." She pauses, "There's so much to do for these *Yom Teivim*. Leahle, do you want to peel the potatoes for the *burikes* soup in the meantime? Then Mrs Gerson can help me with the *gehakte* herring."

I stand fixed to the spot. Mama looks at me seriously.

"You two should go for a walk first, before we start," she says. So I know she has caught on. And approves of my choice. Now they won't force me into an arranged marriage, a *shiduch*. They know that Moshie is my *bashert* and I found him myself, with *Hashem*'s help. My heart sings.

The judge bangs down his gavel. I jump, forced back to the hot courtroom as the talking in the gallery stops.

"Mr Gerson, I see you wear a hearing aid."

"Yes, Your Worship. I am deaf in my right ear."

"On the side of the car on which the two little girls were calling goodbye to you?"

"Yes, sir. But I didn't know they were there. I thought...."

"Just answer the questions please. Was the hearing aid in working order on the day in question?"

"Yes."

"According to your daughter, Mrs Kramer, the machine gives you a lot of trouble and so you sometimes turn it off. I put it to you that on the day of the accident, you switched the machine off as you left your daughter's home and this was why you did not hear your grand-daughters."

"No, no. That is not right!"

"Nevertheless, you did not hear them, Mr Gerson. That is all for now." He turns to Frank Gordon. "Your witness."

"The court will adjourn for lunch."

Once more the hammer crashes down on the desk. The judge and his assessors leave the courtroom as Morris is led away. My son-in-law walks behind him through the exit marked Whites only.

We are at a loss in the break, waiting, waiting. I have no

179

appetite. I want to just sit on the bench but Nathan takes my arm.

"Come, Mom," he says, "let's walk a little, shall we?"

I have not brought my parasol so we stay in the shade. The leaves are bright, dancing in the soft breeze. Round the back of the courthouse there are lines and lines of black people, some quiet, some chatting. Some women have blankets tied around their waists with babies inside. They all wait their turn.

"Why are they all here, Nathan?"

"They need to fix their papers to allow them to work here in Johannesburg. They must have the right stamp in their passbook."

"Where do they come from?"

"The countryside where there is no work and no food." So many of them. So long standing and waiting. A young boy plays a penny whistle, a tune Zina used to sing to Hannah, something like *fannegalo, fannegalo, a Zulu boy will understand*....

"Back home, it was Jews who were like this. Allowed to live only inside the Pale of Settlement. You know?" I grip Nathan's arm more tightly.

"Yes. I know." He says nothing more and we are both lost in our own thoughts.

Back inside, I stare at the painting of the Prime Minister behind the judge's desk until I see right past it and the courtroom voices disappear.

"Look Leah. Muscovys!" Morris says as a pair of ducks glides past. "It is said they stay together for life."

"I heard that too."

"Do you think they have feelings for each other? Like humans?" My heart bumps and jumps and I worry he'll hear.

"How can ducks fall in love? What keeps human beings together is shared history and heritage." I can't help laughing. Morris laughs too. "Look at their colours in the water."

Our reflections float together like the ducks in the dark lake. His black hair is brushed across his forehead. He took great trouble with his appearance, I think. My own hair blows across my face so he can't see my eyes. I tremble a little. He leans his head to one side, listening.

Our heads bend forward. He should make the first move, according to Betty the *maven* because if I do and he doesn't want to, I will embarrass myself. But I can't stop. At the same moment, we turn towards each other.

"You want to kiss again?"

Quickly we rise and he draws me into his embrace, lifting my golden curls back. Little breaths escape from my mouth. We put our lips together once more, cool as summer's blackberries, warm as the syrup from Mama's *teiglach*. He clasps his hands around my neck and touches my skin, gently at first, then more intently. I link my arms around his waist, touch him, feel where his waist dips in. Over, down, back. Faster and faster, we breathe together. How long we stay like this, I don't know.

But nothing is perfect – *mit ale meilis iz nito*. The ducks squawk and we break apart. I quickly smooth the back of my skirt down and brush off the dry grass. On the other side of the river, the local Cossacks *a cholerye af zei*, may the cholera be upon them, are out for their Sunday fun. The soldiers see us together. Bayonets glint and horses stamp their feet. My body heat drains away and I shudder.

Nit ale tsores kumen fun himel – not all trouble comes from heaven. I try to stay calm. I don't dare to look at Morris. The Colonel turns to his troop. Barks in Russian. Spits the word, "*Zhid.*" They bellow with laughter. He points his gun. Two shots and duck feathers scatter. He orders his men to collect the bloody bodies and they leave without another look at us.

I curl into Morris's arms, my bravado gone. Sobbing, I turn my face for his kisses. How I need him to hold me now. His hands grip me hard. I cannot pretend that I am not aroused.

We are going too fast. But I can't stop it, can't stop myself as I feel his hands move over the front of my blouse, seeking the opening and finding bare flesh swelling into his palm. I can feel he wants to kiss me there, feel my nipple in his mouth, as we yearn towards each other.

But we are totally exposed without the ducks to give warning. I am frightened now and not only of the soldiers and what they might do to two young Jews. We move into the grove of trees where it is cool and offers a little protection. Morris sits, leans back against the trunk of a fir tree and parts his legs. I rest between them, my back to him, my breasts under his hands, my hands pressing his, showing him how hard he can touch me without hurting me, though it seems to me that pain is a natural part of this too. I half-twist and latch my mouth onto his, then turn completely so I am facing him again.

I wonder if this is how we are going to have to live out our lives, Morris and I, where Cossacks, *a cholerye af zei*, mock Jews for their sport, rape our women, decapitate babies in mid-air.

I toss around all that night, lying in bed with Betty. When Morris comes the next morning, he says,

"Leah, I am resolved. I have already told Mama."

"Told her what?"

"About what happened yesterday. I said, 'I'm afraid, Mama, afraid for us all. We must leave this place. At once.' She was pouring fresh milk from the dairy pail into a jug for the table. As my words tumbled out, I saw her sadness.

"I said, I heard that in Africa, *der goldene land*, there are opportunities for a good life that Jews in the *shtetl* in the Pale, can never hope for, more to eat than herring brine and *bulves*, more to look forward to than subservience, conscription and pogroms. Here I wear Ben's cast off clothes and hand-me-down shoes and there is only one chicken for the *Shabbos* meal"

"How did she answer you?"

"She said, 'At least we have chicken.' But then she saw I was serious." He fingers the fluffy hair on his face. "Then she wanted to know how we'd manage boat fares for seven of us? How I could know we'd be safe? How Tati could earn a living when the only languages we know are Yiddish and Litvish? She says she's too old and too tired but that I am right to make plans.

"I have never seen her vulnerable or needy before. She is always our pillar, does everything without fuss, as if everything were as simple as *beis* following *alef*. Tati relies on her strength so he can teach and learn without worrying about us. A meal is

182

on the table no matter when he comes home after helping at the *Bikkur Cholem*, visiting the sick and the poor.

"At that moment, my father walked in and wiped the smudge of flour off her nose. Then he started with me too, '*Nu* Boy, what's this? So serious? You should be making your Mama laugh on this festival day. *Koem shein*. Come.' He grabbed me round the waist and we went to chop the wood, light the fire and set the huge pot filled it with water from the vat on the stove so Mama could boil the potatoes and roast the chicken. We also put on the samovar to heat for lemon tea and honey after our *Yom Tov* meal.

"'Golda, is it herring or beetroot with the potatoes?' he said. 'Both tonight, of course.' It was as if I'd said nothing. 'Morris, can you please call Bluma? I think she's with Leah and the other girls outside.'

"My cheeks were burning and I couldn't help smiling, even though my heart and mind were weighted down with my decision. I watched all the girls but I couldn't take my eyes off you, Leah."

I am flooded with memories. But how I pity him now. How I pity us. His eyes are shadows as we wait for the court's decision.

Later Nathan shows us an article about the case in *The Star*. He says it is better he shows us or someone else will. Better he warns us that Morris may get no sympathy. In big black letters I read, Oupa runs over granddaughter. Murder?

The moon is a snake egg hanging in the dark sky. Pine trees stand like Cossacks behind the house on the edge of a cliff. Around us is a chain of lights like tears.

I feel alone and afraid. The truth, *der emes*, is that everything ends in weeping – *altsding lozt zich ois mit a gevein. Az men zogt*, as they say, *yeder mentsh hot zyn pekel* – every man has his burden.

Sitting on the armrest in the centre of the back seat of
Mommy's car is like sitting on a horse. I bend my knees and
hold on tightly. Mommy's arms are curved around the steering
wheel and I stare at the wall of her back. I can see her eyes in
the mirror. They don't smile. She moves her head from side to
side like talking to herself.

"Mommy, what's wrong?"

"Nothing," and her head moves, left, right, left again.

"Where's Elise, Mommy?" I know she won't answer and
she doesn't. She parks the car, heaving against the weight of
the steering wheel and mops her forehead and cheeks with a
hankie.

I step onto the pavement and bang the car door shut,
carefully going around a black bicycle chained to a lamppost.
My mother marches on with her handbag hanging from her
elbow. My mother turns to check where I am. I feel see-
through like Alice as I hop along the paving stones, careful to
miss the cracks... *one, sorrow, two, joy, three, girl, four....*

"Hannah. Come on."

At Pandora Greengrocer, the bakery, fruit and veggie shop,
the owners who are huge and friendly always say hello. Their
wives behind the counter are dressed all in black. First we go
to the fruit section. My mother tests the paw-paws and melons
with a light thumb, but doesn't speak to me. I tag behind,
enclosed in the warmth and the noise. The smell of newly
baked bread and pastries makes my mouth prickle with spit.
The bakery-woman gives me a biscuit and the hundreds and
thousands melt sweetly on my tongue.

Then we go to the general store. Mommy inspects and
I copy what she does, picking up, putting down, picking up
and putting down. I sniff the soaps, the Lifebuoy, the Lux,
the Pears and we both cough at the sharp soap smells. The
shampoos are in coloured glass bottles pine green or deep red.
Mommy looks at the prices and puts the one she likes into
her shopping basket. I want the baby shampoo but Mommy

184

doesn't offer and I don't say anything.

Wandering down the aisles, I find the toothpastes. They often have gifts like a flowery container or a small sample of perfume stuck onto the boxes, or even maybe a surprise inside. Today, Pepsodent toothpaste has a tiny plastic charm as a bonus in each box. It's a lucky dip even though it isn't Christmas time. I open the cardboard boxes one by one and sniff at the peppermint and spearmint flavours of the toothpastes. I peek inside, careful not to let anything fall out. I slide the usual sailors, aeroplanes and trains out into my hand, inspect them and slide them straight back into the boxes, closing the lids without bending them.

Then, into my hand falls a tiny blue doll with a perfect face, its eyes open wide its red mouth smiling up at me. It lies safely in my palm, so light, almost not there.

My hands shake. I cannot see my mother. There is no one else in the aisle but I check once more, stretching my neck as far as I can to be quite sure.

I press the lid of the toothpaste box neatly in place and put it back on the shelf, one box among hundreds. I stroll to the end of the aisle where my mother stands at the till. She is paying as I drift towards her. We push through the turnstile, she in front and me behind.

A giant steps in front of us.

"Tell her to open her hand."

My mother glares down at me.

"Do it."

I uncurl my fingers and a huge fist lifts the charm away.

My mother strides away, her back stiff.

"Please, Mommy. Please don't tell Daddy."

She opens the car door for me. I climb in and she slams the door and starts up the engine. Her mouth is shut tight all the way home.

I don't know if she tells my father or not.

In my collection, there is no little girl.

185

I stare at the stained walls. People stare at Morris. I think they point at me. The voices of lawyers go on and on. Then I no longer listen.

Morris and I walk across the market place with our families to the *shtiebele*. I wear my long pinafore, neatly mended. My blouse cuts into my wrists. My cracked leather shoes are worn down at the heels. Stuffed in the front, old rags press on my toes. I never did grow to fit them after Betty passed them on to me. It is as they say, *mit shnei ken men nit machen gomolkes* – from snow you cannot make cheesecake.

Tati and Mama walk ahead together, not touching each other. How will I dare talk about leaving here? Where will the money come from? If they take a loan from Mr Miller, my father will have to pay interest. Then they will say seventeen is too young to leave home. Adulthood has caught me. I am no longer that girl without care, the girl I was.

And oh, never to see them again? Or my brothers and sisters? Their hearts will break. *Einems mazel iz an anderes shlimazel* – the truth is, my luck will be their bad luck.

Outside *Shul*. The men and women say, "*Gut Yom Tov.*" We go through separate entrances, the women to their hidden place behind the *mechitse*, the curtain, not to distract the men from their prayers. But I'm sure Morris can feel my presence. And I feel temptation even though I can't see him.

Does Betty have such a conflict? Has she ever been interested in any particular boy? Perhaps she is afraid. So how can I, the younger, be so sure? We *daven* together, Mama and my sisters and I, sometimes by heart, sometimes reading from the *siddur*, always softly, never to draw attention to ourselves. We bow. We stand. We feel each other's rhythms, each alone with our G-d. I pray, "Let me make the right choice at the right time. Please let Your hand guide me to find my right path."

I am afraid, yes. But also so excited. Through the veil, my eyes seek Morris.

Going home he catches up with my family and walks next

to my father. They discuss the *parsha* to be read from the Torah next morning, how the Israelites lived in the desert for forty years. What flimsy dwelling place will we have, he and I, away from the support of our dear families?

The aroma of the delicious *cholent* reaches us from home as hoof beats crash towards us. There is the loud neighing of horses and Russian voices:

"Hey, you there!" Colonel Alexandrovitch shouts.

I slide next to Morris without thinking. Brush against him. Touch his hand. Mama and my sisters quickly move near to Tati.

"Don't just stand there. Move *Zhids*. In the road." Run and they'll slice our throats. Or shoot. Stay and they'll mock us first, then slice our throats. Morris straightens, salutes and clicks his heels.

"Good evening, Colonel. Did your wife make a fine casserole with those beautiful Muscovys you shot yesterday?" Alexandrovitch stares, puzzled. Around us, the evening holds its breath, our two families forming a huddled black shape in the darkness. In place of the *cholent*, I can smell our fear. Morris stands stiffly waiting. Recognition crosses the colonel's face. Then,

"Where's your girlfriend?"

I step forward where he can see me. Morris slips his hand around mine. Are we crazy, drawing attention to ourselves? But, I think, we are damned anyway – we have already touched, so it makes no difference now if my father forces him to marry me. My hand is small and sweaty in Morris's and our fingers grip tightly. We could still run, perhaps? Suddenly Alexandrovitch bursts out,

"You know, Jewboy, I think you brought me luck. Me and my missus, we slit those ducks from mouth to gizzard. Tonight we're roasting them for supper, with vodka to wash it down. The smell of Jew blood will spoil my appetite." He turns to his brigade, "What do you think?" No one answers. If he lets us go straight away, *Kiddush* will still be on time in our *succah*. Hands wait on bayonets as the moon rises in the sky. He turns.

"Come my fine fellows. These are meagre pickings. Let's go home and enjoy a grand meal and drink to the Czar of all the Russias." The soldiers' arms fall to their sides and they are gone as quickly as they came. So we know we are not yet inscribed in the Book that decrees who shall pass away before next *Yom Kippur*'s judgement.

Subdued, we make our way home. My father begins to sing. We all join in and gain courage. Each word is a prayer of thanksgiving, a psalm. "*Az ich gei durg di tol fun di shoten fun toit, bin ich nit dershroken*…. Yea, though I walk through the valley of the shadow of Death, will I fear no evil…."

My father gives thanks when he says *lesheiv basuccah*, and dips the *challah* in honey for a good sweet year. I help Mama dish up and we hand round carp and potatoes, *kreplach* soup and *cholent*. We even have pears in wine for dessert, a treat for our guests. And for us. The *succah* is filled with joy. *A lustiger dales geit iber ales* – a happy poverty overcomes everything. It is a most blessed *Yom Tov*, our last one in Yaneshik as we forget Colonel Alexandrovitch and his wife drowning their lust for Jew-baiting in toasts to the Czar, *zol er brenen afn fyer* – may he burn in hell.

The rules are relaxed for boys and girls and we chatter together. Morris and I gaze at each other from across the table as we finish *benshing* in our familiar way. Then he beckons me and we slip outside. Quickly he takes my hand. It is our last chance to talk for a long while, I know.

"Leah, my cousin Mordechai is safe in South Africa. So, my mind is made up. I will go to Libau, by train and on foot. Then I will take a boat. It goes to England first, Ben says and I've heard that the voyage is bad and I don't know how long it is, but think, Leah, a new world, a chance for a better life. For you too."

"Moshe, are you sure it's the right thing? Aren't you afraid? Will somebody go with you?"

"I am afraid to go but more afraid to stay. And I must go alone. Ben and I can't both leave Mama and Tati now. Anyway Ben is a Zionist. He prefers *Eretz Yisroel* and he thinks I'm running away. Maybe I am. How can we bring up our children here, Leah? Look at what happened tonight, what could have happened. And it won't be the last time." He draws himself up and breathes in deeply and says, "Will you come to me when I send for you?" and I know he does not take my feelings for granted. He pulls me close, kisses my eyelids. Then his mouth is hot and raw on mine.

But. How differently things have turned out. They are right – *zei zynen gerecht. A lecherdiken zak ken men nit ontfilen* – no one can fill a torn sack.

Mommy always brings too much stuff so Daddy struggles to fit it all in the boot: three large suitcases, her sewing bag, her book bag, her red vanity case, her tennis racket. Also his golf bag and my paints and crayons. He swears in a whisper but I still hear him. Mommy packs enough sandwiches so we never run out and there's always enough for 'in case.' Daddy stretches his arms on the steering wheel and I see the silky dark hairs. The hair on his head is stuck down with Brylcream. We sing non-stop to Scottburgh, he and me, and sometimes he winks at me in his mirror with his good green eye. The other eye has a scar through it from a wood chip and it looks greyish.

I went to the animal fair,
The birds and the beasts were there,
By the light of the moon,
The silly baboon was combing his auburn hair.

My toes press against the back of Daddy's seat and I can feel the vibration of the car and his rhythm as we sing according to themes: colours, seasons, place names. Each song reminds us of another one and another and we each have a chance to pick, jolly and loud, or soft and sad and slow.

I echo Daddy. Whatever he sings, I sing. Whatever the words, I learn them. I want to know everything he knows. We start with *There is a tavern in the town* as we leave Johannesburg, then *Sarie Marais* who lived in *die ou Transvaal* but went to *Mooi River*, *Vat jou goed en trek Ferreira* and *I stand in a land of roses and I dream of a land of snow* and songs that Zeida sang in Yiddish *shlof der Yiddele, shloff* and *Yiddel miten fiddel.* The languages mix together and each song has a story that I've heard before and that I ask Daddy to tell me again. Daddy is no poet. He only reads law books and the encyclopaedia. And Mommy is no beautiful princess. But I can hear the poems in his voice and in the melody when he sings to her, *We'll gather lilacs in the spring again.* It's the music that they danced to at

190

their wedding.

Mommy feeds us, fish sticks on Provita, hardboiled eggs dipped in salt, cold meat slices wrapped around a cucumber. We wash it down with cold orange squash from the red thermos flask. She pours it holding the cup between her legs as we drive. Daddy won't stop unless he wants a drink of icy water. It's in the canvas cooler bag tied onto the bumper of our black Citroen. Or if we have to, he'll make a pit stop on the side of the road where the grass tickles and wets my legs with early morning dew. Maybe there are scary snakes and spiders here but I can't hold back the hot stream another minute.

"Don't drink again. Not now. Not yet," Mommy says, but biltong is thirsty work and so is the duet of the century, so I drink more Oros and within ten minutes we have to stop again.

I left Bride at home in her floral, cardboard box. She has a rosebud mouth and auburn hair curls around her face that I comb and pin into her lacy Juliet's cap. She is elegant and I can't cuddle her because her arms stick up. I imagine my own wedding day, my groom, what he'll look like. I test out his name but I never give this doll a name. She is always just Bride, plain and simple.

Mommy sewed a dress by hand for my schoolgirl dolly, a dark green pleated skirt and matching top. She is small enough to go everywhere with me, in my suitcase if I can't hold her. She is smart, with neat shoes and level socks. I comb her straight blonde hair and tie it up in a ponytail.

My fairy doll is called *Monday's Child*. Her dress makes a full circle, spread out behind her as she lies in a starry pink box of tissue paper. She has hair like cotton wool so I can't brush it without spoiling it. She holds a wand with a silver star on top and is barefoot to show off her tiny painted toenails. Her body is made of delicate plastic and she has a turned up nose and grey eyes.

There is a poem written in gold on the lid of her box:

191

Monday's child is fair of face;
Tuesday's child is full of grace;
Wednesday's child is full of woe;
Thursday's child has far to go;
Friday's child is loving and giving;
Saturday's child must work for a living;
But the child that was born on the Sabbath day
Is bonny and bright and good and gay.

As we recite it, I think, I was born on a Monday, but I'm not pretty and it's unfair that everyone except Sunday's child has so few blessings. As for working on Saturdays, we aren't allowed to. Because look what happened when I painted. When I tell Mommy, she says,

"It's only a nursery rhyme, Hannah. Have a peanut butter sandwich."

Clementine is always next to me. I sing lullabies to her and give her hugs. Her face is round and her arms and legs bend at the joints. She fits into Elise's pink baby bath in my room. I have nappies and bottles for her. She makes wee-wee in her nappy and cries before I feed her. The only place she can't go with me is the sea because it will hurt her eyes. She's such a good baby I never have to give her a smack. When I hold her in my arms, I feel happy and warm. I promise her I will look after her always.

At the Coronation Hotel there is a raised stage with a microphone and piano in the games room. They are for the talent contest. I enter. I've never done it before but I make up my mind that I'm not too scared to sing *Blue Moon* in front of everyone.

"Hannah, should you be doing this?" I can hear that Mommy doesn't want me to. She says I should practise by myself in front of a mike first by myself. I've practised in my room in front of the mirror hundreds of times but Mommy and Daddy don't know because they've never watched me. Also I've sung in the car with Daddy and I sing when there's no one at home, in my bedroom and in the bath, the sad and slow *Lonely Ash Grove, Barbara Allen, Shenandoah, Poor Old Joe, Greensleeves* and *Golden Vanity.* That's Daddy's favourite. And I know all the words and the tunes of our school hymns off by heart. *All creatures of our God and King, Mine eyes have seen the Glory, Glorious things of Thee are spoken.* The melodies are not the same as the ones from *Shul,* like *Lecha Dodi, Einkaloheinu* and *Adon Olam* that I sing with Daddy as we stand next to each other and repeat as we walk home.

The only English songs Zeida knows are the ones I taught him. What would he and Bobba say if they knew I sing Christian songs in secret because I hear them going around in my head? And am I a *poyer,* a heathen, because I sing Christmas Carols that we learn at school? Will *Hashem* be angry with me? Mommy also knows *All things bright and beautiful* and she learnt the same hymns at the convent but I never hear her singing them aloud anymore. It's so long since we sang around the piano, maybe she's forgotten them. I love all the tunes. They make me feel not so sad.

Daddy says nothing and goes on doing his crossword puzzle, so maybe he thinks Mommy is wrong.

Maybe I'll win is what I think.

The first person to go up at the contest does juggling. The next one does magic tricks. He guesses the first card number wrongly so he's dox. Out. Still, everyone claps for him as he leaves the stage. After that, a girl in a clown suit tells *How the Camel got its Hump.* She curls her top lip so it looks like a dromedary camel. Every time she says 'hump,' it comes out as 'humph' and the audience are in fits of laughter right until the end. I think Daddy tells it much better. She bows and I know she thinks she has won because the audience liked her so much. Her family are standing up and shouting, more, more, even as I walk up to the stage. At last, the compère waves his hands and asks for silence so I can start.

My chest is a pump, my mouth like glue, my legs jelly. Even though I look straight out at the audience, I can see my parents in the front row. They shrink down into their seats as the announcement comes.

"And now, ladies and gents, Hannah is going to give you Billie Holiday's hit song." The pianist gives me the first notes, bloo-oo, so that I can get the key right and before I take a breath, she begins and I miss the beat. Daddy sinks down further in the front row and Mommy stares at the floor.

"Let Hannah have another try," instructs the announcer. "One, two three…" Everyone is looking at me. Somehow I get through it without another mistake although my face burns and my voice is a wind's whisper. I sit through the rest of the competition.

As we walk back to our hotel room, my parents are silent. Behind us is a gaggle of giggly girls laughing and pointing at me. The moon hangs brightly over the sea. If ever I need to see its face smiling at me, it's now. My father puts his arm on my mother's.

The warm air is filled with the saltiness of the sea breeze. I shudder. I've forgotten to bring a jersey and my skirt doesn't cover my legs below my knees. Bending down, I pick up a shell and put it into my pocket so I can listen to the sound of the sea when we are back in Johannesburg. In the bathroom, I lock the door and look at my face in the mirror in the bright light. My skin is Eno-white. Next time will be better, I tell myself. My voice wobbles but I go on singing softly, counting the beats. As soon as we get home I will ask Beatrice to play the piano and help me practise.

My husband strokes my head. To comfort me. But I don't want him on my bed. I don't want him in the room. I can't talk to him. Violet brings me my lunch. I hardly eat anything. My angina is bad. Hannah plays on the lawn with the dogs. I put out the cards for *Patience* on a tray on my bed. Stare out of the window. Stare at the photographs on my dressing table. Stare at Hannah with Elise in their swimming suits. Scottburgh beach. Hannahle laughing. Elise smacking the sand with her spade.

So. He was not sent to jail. The judge and assessors gave him a warning. How we all tried to smile when we left the court. But we will never be free.

"Perhaps we should go away?" he says. "Every time I come up the driveway it happens. Again and again. Other times also I see her in front of my eyes. The pain will be less if we go, perhaps. For Nathan and Susan too. Rabbi Perelman says we will feel better … with time."

I think how his mother wanted him to be a *rov*. She thought he had the qualities. Yet he is unable to help himself now. Or me. I think of when we called him Moshe. Such a long time ago. Things were so different then. So much has happened. We see how things are, yet we do not understand – *men zen ober men farshteit veinik*.

"There are opportunities for immigrants in Israel, Leah, like there were for Ben. We can make a new life. What do you think?"

My husband has an *ainredenish*. He talks himself into it that things will be better somewhere else. And it is what he wants me to believe. When it never can be better. Not there. Not as a stranger in a strange land again with no *landsleit* to give us soup or bread. Not here. Even though we have our comforts here. Everything we worked for. Everything we earned. How will I have the strength for another move? And Hannahle, *gezunt zol zie zyn*, may she be well, she needs me here and I want to be near her.

"It is a good time to sell my shares. The markets are high,

the right time to take the profits."

I don't talk. I take the inkbottle and my pen and dip. My hand shakes. I write,

Darkness brings another journey.
Der vint flit avek ober der kerpes blaibt –
the storm dies down but the driftwood remains.
Shtetl to city. City to city.
Vu bist main hoift? Where is my home?

But my Morris does not give in, wears me down. He talks about it as a done deed, brings passport forms to sign, then tickets for the *Union Castle*. He tells me which *ulpan* we will attend to learn the new language, on which *kibbutz* we will live with strangers. He buys new trunks, navy blue with gold corners. He stands them upright and shows me. One for him, one for me. So convenient with shelves for blouses and drawers for smalls. And hanging space for the queen, he tells me.

We pack.

I swing higher and higher and call to Zinkie underneath me. She is far away, smiling and saying, good girl Hannie, but when I look again she isn't there anymore. It is dark now so there isn't anyone else there either. I call Zinkie, Zinkie but still she doesn't come. The park is empty. My skirt is up around me and in front of my face and I can't see or breathe. It's cold. I want to call Mommy. I want to call Daddy but now my mouth can't open. I am shivering and shivering and I put my arms around myself to keep warm. I let go the chains and fly away and away and down and down and land on the ground with a crash and my knees and arms are all folded up. I call and call. Nobody comes.

Nathan lies wide-eyed in bed, then forces himself to get up. I linger, selecting my outfit for the day. I pull my new off-the-shoulders cream top over my head, holding my lips together so as not to smear my lipstick. The blouse tones perfectly with my navy skirt.

"Would you like to go to Zoo Lake Restaurant for dinner one evening?" Nathan asks as he leaves to take Hannah to school. He seems in no rush to get to his appointments. "I've heard that it's changed management and is excellent." Hannah blows me a kiss. "And we do need to finalise Hannah's school application. It's becoming urgent."

"I'll let you know later," but I have no intention of going. I give my presentation at the Women's Benevolent Society A G M. My suggestions for increased fund-raising are greeted with enthusiasm. The tea afterwards is lavish but I have no appetite. At home, I spoon a huge helping of mashed potatoes onto Nathan's plate next to two fried soles and push the French salad towards him. Hannah is chatting away and drawing in the tomato sauce with her fish sticks as I pick at my salad.

"Joe wants me to take over McKintyre's account. The old guy is driving him crazy, telephoning every other day, nagging for progress bulletins. Joe thinks I could handle him with my gentle steel."

"What did you tell him?"

"I accepted the challenge, of course, in spite of my excessive work load and he handed me the files straight away. McKintyre is difficult but I'm sure I can work with him. And it'll look great on my C V, a sizable account like that."

I look up, startled.

"Oh. Planning on moving?"

"Never know what crops up, do we? By the way, I met Stuart for lunch today. He and Viv have separated. He spent the entire time touching the webbing between his third and fourth fingers where his wedding band used to be, assuring me it was an allergy. I said I was really sorry to hear it and that he should come round and have dinner with us. I hope that's in order?" After this monologue, though he looks me in the eye. I wonder what he is really thinking.

"That's fine. I should think most of their friends were Vivienne's?"

"Yes, he said he's on his own most evenings and weekends."

Nathan pours himself a stiff whisky on the rocks and relaxes with the stereo playing softly. When the telephone rings I ignore it, hoping it isn't one of his clients. Violet answers,

"Hullo? Hullo?" She replaces the telephone receiver. When it rings once more, Nathan picks it up, speaks to Madge briefly and calls me. I mutter to myself when I finish.

"She goes on and on about how the ironing woman, Dorcas, isn't coping with the work." This is the way we interact, connected only through domestic conversation, avoiding what is really on our minds. Nathan reads to Hannah and is almost asleep himself when the telephone rings a third time. I pick up the receiver.

Felicity.

I can't look at him. These days he never mentions her at home.

"Mr Kramer, I'm sorry...." She starts talking before he has the telephone to his ear so I hear,

"It's alright. Don't worry...."

"Let me know...." He looks around to see where I am.

"Felicity's not coming in to work tomorrow, Sue. She has a crisis with her Mom so I'll have to work late again." I wonder what he expects me to say. I hear his footsteps as he goes back to Hannah to finish her story.

"Why don't you just go to her, just go to Felicity?"

I turn on my heel and disappear into the bathroom.

She appears again, out of the dark, out of nowhere, a little girl with long, dark hair in a long nightgown the colour of light, yellow and bright. Shiny it hangs to her feet. She is so small she can hardly see over the edge of the mattress as she stands quite still at the foot of my bed peering at me in the half-light. She is looking at me and through me, her pupils boring into me. She neither smiles nor frowns and she says nothing, stares without moving in the blackness. I can see right through her like one of my charms. Then she hovers over me and finally disappears, leaving me behind. I lie alone and wide awake, my heart pounding.

"Mmmm, that's so nice," Hannahle says, when I rub my fingers round and round her soft scalp, through her thick and heavy curls. "Look at your hair next to mine, Bobba." She holds her dark curls to my blonde waves, puts her arm with its olive skin to my peach. "Bobba, I want to grow my hair long like yours. But Mommy says no. Mommy says it would be wild. I want it wild, Bobba!"

Today she is at school, *a gezunt af ire kepele*, a blessing on her head. Violet hangs the washing and Frans finishes cleaning the house. I hear the lawn mower so I know. I stare at myself in the mirror and unplait my braids, let them fall down my back to my waist. Susan or Betty trim my hair for me, but only a little off the ends.

I pin it back up neatly.

When we were children, we all had lice. How the nits itched. My mother, may she rest in peace, *zol zi ligen in ru*, brought the kerosene tin. She took us all outside. "Mama, Mama," how we cried as the cold liquid burnt our scalps. But still it didn't help. Mama had to cut our hair anyway. That time was the last time mine was shorn off.

The colour of the wheat fields in harvest time, Morris calls my hair, touching the fine gold strands to his lips, all passion in his eyes. Before. Susan would be surprised, I think. Still I wonder how it is for her with Nathan. She never asked me about love – not even one question. I tried to give her Marie Stopes' book before she married, I was so worried that we had sent her to the convent.

"Ma, we won't need a book!"

"Only have a look. You don't need to tell Nathan but it will help you, maybe."

"We're fine, Ma."

I worry more now. They should be bound together. I watch them and I know that they are not. They don't touch. They don't clasp eyes. He looks at her. She turns away.

When Morris left Yaneshik, I cut a small lock of my hair. He

201

put it in his heart pocket and took my hand. He said, "Leah," and everything was in how he spoke my name, in the way he looked at me. Not since then have I taken scissors to my own head.

Again I untwist my hair, brush it, feel the softness of the skin of my neck and shoulders. My morning gown is open at the front and the hair lies on my breasts, curling up a little.

I think – they cut Nathan's shirt and Susan's dress. I think – Morris said *Kaddish* with Nathan. I think – they each put three shovels of earth on her grave for her blanket. I think – I did nothing.

I brush harder and harder, rough bristles sharp against my scalp, points pricking into my skin. My chin juts out. I shut my eyes tight, hold in tears, jab the spikes into my flesh. I bite my lips. Hard. Black dots rush inside my eyes as I shake my head this way and that. Faster. Faster.

Morris sharpens his razor on the strop, runs the blade across his fingers. Maybe I can use that razor myself. But instead I fetch Susan's pair of sewing scissors, brand new not to spoil her silk party dress. I run my thumb across the blades. There is the bitter taste of metal on my tongue as if I licked them. One by one I take the locks in my thumb and forefinger. Snip. Snip. Snip. Stabbing the scissors round my head. Then again. Hack, hack, until my hair is sawn off. All of it. Now it is short stubbles sticking up. Like feathers but with no tar. The hair lies all around me: cut wheatfields; the fields of the past.

I go down on my hands and knees, crawl around. Pick up the strands. Some stick to the fibre of the carpet, some to my fingers. I need a packet from the kitchen but I don't want to leave my room. So I let the hair fall into the dark of the dressing table drawer. When the drawer is full, I close it. Maybe one day I'll fill a pillow.

I need a shawl over my head. Maybe. Maybe not.

I put down my head on the cool dressing table.

When I wake up it is night. I tiptoe to the door. I can hear voices from the breakfast room. Good. I don't want to see anyone. I turn the key in the lock. Questions can wait for tomorrow. I lie down.

They hammer on my door. Slowly I get up, let Susan in.

"Ma, Ma? What have you done? What have you done?"

"Don't worry. Don't worry. It is nothing." No point to explain.

Then everyone is there. I have the taste of aloes in my mouth and my stomach burns.

"I must sleep now – *Ich muz gein shlofen.*"

I put up my hands. Touch my head. Touch the tender skin. I don't shrink away from it but caress it, naked and cold – *naket un kalt.* It feels soft. Like a baby's.

"What would you like to be in the concert?"

We are standing around Miss Blount in the icy Scout Hall with its brown, splintery floor at the end of the lesson. I fetch my pink crossover jersey from Mommy and come back to the circle.

"Stop that!" says Miss Blount to Vanessa who is sliding up and down in her socks on the polished stage floor. "And you," she turns to my friend Moira, "Don't talk!" We are all jiggling with excitement. For the production we are going to have tutus and costumes, red lipstick, pink stockings and pink satin slippers.

We wait to be given our parts: the Sleeping Princess or Briar Rose or the Queen of the Tulips, the Giant or the Giant Killer or Magic Merlin. We each have our chance to ask, some in little voices, some loudly, for a main role or a character part, for our own applause and our parents' pleasure as we whirl in the spotlight.

Moira wants to be the Big Bad Wolf and the part is exactly right for her, she is tough and athletic and can do somersaults and cartwheels across the stage. Dainty Bella will be the Sugar Plum Fairy in a silver tutu with a starry wand. She grins at me. It's the part she badly wanted.

My heart is pounding when my turn comes. Will Miss Blount hear me?

"Hannah?"

"Uh …a blue rose, please…." I clear my throat. "I want to be Blue Rose."

There is silence and then everyone is giggling.

"Really, Hannah. Whoever heard of such a thing? I really expected more of you. Ridiculous. You can be the Little Red Hen. Perfect, I think. I'm marking it on my list. Next?"

On the big night, I wear the feathery costume that Mommy makes me. It covers my arms, my legs and my back and scratches me all over. I also have a mask with a sharp beak and a red comb. I don't need any make up and nobody knows it's

204

me. When I look out from behind the curtain and see everyone watching. I waddle onto the stage and pretend to be clumsy but then I give the audience a surprise: I do quick cartwheels and somersaults without any mistakes and they all clap.

At the end, the chorus curtsey together and I have to come on with them. Bella comes on for her own curtain call. Laura gives Miss Blount a bouquet of roses and Miss Blount kisses her and blows lots of kisses to the audience.

I want to be a blue rose.

I want my Elly back.

Part 4
1960

Musical Chairs

Chairs are arranged in a circle, one fewer than the number of players who must keep moving while music plays. When it stops suddenly, each player must find a seat. The one who is left without one is eliminated. The game continues until only one player remains.

Nathan is involved with Felicity, to escape from me. Who else could it be? He spends hours with her at the office and I know he always liked her. They have a flat, a small place far away from the burdens of his life. A Spartan kitchen: a kettle, a couple of plates and knives and forks, a tiny fridge, perhaps a hotplate. He is only there for a few hours and he never needed much. She has chosen the floral eiderdown covers and pillowslips, the floral curtains that enhance their love nest and maintain their privacy.

When he arrives, he rushes up the stairs two at a time.

"Just washing up," he calls and splashes his ears and neck with cold water, slicks back his hair with his fingers, sails out. His dashing demeanour belies the dark rings around his eyes, his dulled complexion. Felicity is waiting for him on a yellowwood cottage chair reading last night's *Star*. She drops it onto the cream carpet and stands immediately he appears. Her youth energises him in a way I no longer can or want to. She moves into the circle of his arms so he can caress the bones of her shoulder blades. Their kisses are so hot and sweet I can almost taste them myself. They enjoy the peace that follows passion and he knows he is admired and loved.

Back at the office, his work is sharp and he makes no mistakes on the figures for McKintyre's merger. He walks past Felicity's office and beams, whereas at home he goes through the motions, putting one foot in front of the other, trying to keep his balance. As I do.

I hear the click as the front door opens and closes.

"Susan, I'm home." He hangs back his suit neatly in his wardrobe, throws his shirt and socks into the wash bin and has a quick shower, something he used to do in the morning, expounding on the virtues of ice water even in winter. It was this change of pattern that first alerted me.

He comes upstairs in a loose shirt and a casual pair of pants. Sometimes he still tries his old routines to make me laugh. Mostly he treads carefully around me and we are polite with

209

each other. Not tonight. He steps inside my sewing room and pulls me to him, putting his arms around me, smothering me. He kisses me with an open mouth and strokes my back. I know he wants to catch me off guard, wrest a reaction from my numbness but I cannot go along with it. It smacks of guilt, is a complete giveaway. He draws himself up.

"Speak to me, dammit! Where are you? I can't reach you. You aren't even trying. What is wrong with you? You're stuck in a hole and you won't come out and I'm going to go away from you because there is no one where Susan used to be." I start to argue with him but stop myself.

"Is it to be business as usual?" he chokes. "Will you never let down your guard, not even to me? Madge once told me that emotions are your enemies. What are you so afraid of?"

He has no understanding of me.

"What's the point? I can't be what I'm not. Nor can you."

"Who is it you won't forgive?" I know he is hoping to shock me into speaking, hopes that all will yet be well if he gives me time. But then I think he realises it is no use. I cannot feel the pain. I cannot feel the joy, not in our relationship, not from Hannah, not in anything I do.

"Is this how it's going to be from now on?" His eyes are moist as he leaves my sanctuary.

He has brought home a briefcase full of paperwork that needs attention and when he comes up to bed, I feign a deep sleep. He doesn't switch on the lights, but gently moves the blankets and crawls under them.

For me it is a night without a moon and without dreams.

Hannahle wears my gypsy costume, the black and yellow blouse, the skirt cut in a full circle, the long cummerband wound round and round her waist. All these years I kept it, a reminder of *der heim*. Of the *Purim-shpiel*. Of the celebration when we escaped from evil.

Oh, the festivities! The reading of the *Megillah*. The parade. Clowns. Musicians with their fiddles and accordions and drums. The *melamud*, the school teacher, with his pile of books. Jugglers. Fools. Biblical figures – Moses, Joshua, Aaron in his priestly robes; Mordecai – we knew that under the robe was Birka, the peddlar; Queen Esther – inside her fancy dress was Fruma, the *shneiderin*, the seamstress; King Ahashuerus with the cotton beard, who was really Yaakov, the water-carrier. No Haman. Not in our parade. But. He is always there.

Then after the parade, how we loved the play, the *shpiel*. A time we could laugh and dance without worrying – and our elders, our parents had fun too! And we'd sing *Purim ha-yom. Purim ha-yom. We thank the Lord above. For the miracle that He performed, He has our thanks and love.* Still I hear the beat of the cymbals and my own tapping feet. As if I had a gypsy fever, *a tsigainerishe hits*.

We ate *homentasen*, the triangular poppyseed cakes, and *lekach*, the honey cookies – and there was more than enough for everyone. On a day such as that, all of us were rich, happy. Our laughter was heard further than weeping – *unze gelechter hert men vaiter vi a gevein*.

But now.

Our clothes are packed. Morris closes and bolts our trunks. This time we have money and we will take the *Union Castle* from Cape Town. At Haifa dock we will be met. And on the *ulpan* we will learn Hebrew – with our Litvak accents.

How different from my trip when I left Yaneshik. Mama, *zol zi ligen in zain ru*, may she rest in peace, held onto me tightly with her rough hands, waved goodbye in her long black dress, her wrinkled face full of concern, if I would reach Morris safely.

Tati was not there – if he did not work there would be no money. My few bundles. The hay cart. The train. I was alone and afraid on the boat from Libau.

Then my birthday. A day of hope for the future, for a new life. A complete stranger gave me a gift – an orange. It was my first taste of this bright country. Never had I seen such a fruit – *az men trinkt ale mol esik, vais men nit az es iz do a zisere zach* – if all one has to drink is vinegar, how can one know that sweetness exists?

"It's like Africa *der goldene land*," she told me. "It's sweet and strong at once. Don't be surprised."

The mountain behind Cape Town, with the tablecloth cloud was just as they had told us. And the people! People everywhere! Two little boys on the ship hid in their mother's skirts, afraid of all the black faces. My hope was Morris and an easier life with him for the *kinder vi vet kumen*, for the children to come. Mine and his.

"Leah, time for the taxi."

I slide my gloves over my fingers and pull them down my wrists. But to tell the truth, I have no strength for what we must do now, after everything that's happened.

"Take our suitcases please, Frans." He is polishing the pine floor on his hands and knees but gets up to help Morris.

"Hannahle, *kum sheine meidele*. Come, darling. Come and kiss us goodbye." Terrible this. Leaving her, my shadow. She drags herself up the passage. Her skin is pale because she is indoors too much, like a Russian child in a land of a weak sun. How long since she skipped to me with her skirt whirling around her brown legs? Now her thumb is in her mouth. She pulls at her top lip with her little finger and holds her wrist with the other hand. The striped cummerband unravels and drags on the floor. She speaks but I can't hear her. I say,

"Mommy and Daddy can send you to us soon, perhaps? You can come by aeroplane. By yourself. What do you think?" She takes her thumb from her mouth and I wait for her to say, "Bobba, you mustn't say perrhaps. It's perhaps. Don't you know?"

From her pocket, she brings out the black and white photograph of me as a young girl wearing the same gypsy skirt, taken in the photographer's studio on the *shtetl* square. She holds it up to show me, then puts it back. I bend down and kiss her and hold her face.

Susan comes out of her room.

"Mom. Dad. The taxi is hooting already. Hurry." She kisses Morris first, then turns to me and takes my hand. She brushes my cheek with hers and turns away. To this day I have not seen her weep.

Who would have thought it would be like this? That we would be on our way once more? Johannesburg, this place of our South African history, is now just another place we leave. Morris and I are together this is true, but all our hopes are behind us.

Mommy never let me sleep over. Before. I used to say, "Please Mommy, I'll be good," but she said,

"No, Hannah, you must stay at home and sleep in your own bed."

So, when Rebecca and Rachel went in the school bus to Pretoria, I stayed behind. Only the naughty boys and me were not allowed to go. Mrs Roux gave us lots of work to do, sorting out her cupboards and dusting her books.

But now I am at my cousin Jenny for the week. I share her room. The two beds have a lamp in between that we can switch off ourselves whenever we want. We play *Scrabble* and listen to her record player. Later she wants to play *Spooky in the Dark* but I don't like it. Instead we talk, very softly so we don't wake Aunty Miriam and Uncle Alec. In the morning, we tiptoe out and eat raisins and nuts and fruit on the damp grass. There is a bird table where we put out paw-paw pips and breadcrumbs for the weavers and sparrows. Jenny has a puppy called Snowy. He is a cuddly Maltese poodle who yaps a lot. We put on his leash and take him for a long walk to the café to buy lucky packets. By the time we reach home, my pink sweets are finished but I keep the see-through Briar Rose charm to add to my collection.

Later, we go to watch the water skiing competition on the Vaal River and lie on blankets on the riverbank. Everyone walks around in swimming costumes with towels around their necks or waists, talking and laughing. I meet Jenny's friends. The smell of petrol from the boat engines is very strong as they start up the engines and the noise is so loud we can't hear ourselves speak. Aunty Miriam brought a picnic lunch of hard-boiled eggs, fish sticks and salad. There is trifle for dessert and we polish it all off.

We are tired from the fresh air and fall asleep early. I wake up sobbing in the middle of the night when the little girl in white flies in again. Aunty Miriam switches on the light and holds me and rocks me and brings me warm milk.

I say,

"I need to go home."

Next day Daddy fetches me. I lie on the back seat and watch the telephone poles flashing past. I try and count them but I can't. I fall asleep and when I wake up we are at home. Mommy telephones Aunty Miriam to say we are safe. She gives me the phone and I say,

"Thank you for a nice holiday."

In the middle of the night I creep out of bed. I tiptoe down the passage with my torch, holding my hand over the light and careful not to stand on the floorboards where I know they creak.

In Bobba and Zeida's room, the curtains are closed. Some of their furniture is still here. On the dressing table Bobba has left her glass ball with the pine trees inside. I turn it upside down to make a snowstorm. Bobba said it reminded her of *der heim* and how cold it was. In my torchlight, I see the marks on the walls where the photographs of Bobba and Zeida's family in Lithuania used to be, my uncles and aunts and cousins that I never met. There also used to be pictures of Elise and me. I've looked everywhere but never found them.

The only sound in the house is my breathing, so loud that I am sure Mommy will hear me. I open the drawers of Bobba's dressing table and wonder why she didn't take it with her. She used the mirror every day when I brushed her hair. I pull out each drawer as quietly as I can. One sticks and then jerks out. The torch flies from my hand and hits the wall. I hold my breath but nobody comes. There is nothing left in the drawers except the brown paper at the bottom. I flash the torchlight all the way round the room, making wavy lines of light through the blackness and onto the bed, the wardrobe and the walls.

In Bobba's cupboard are some of her dresses and shoes. So, they must be coming back, I think. Standing on the stool, I take down the dress with yellow flowers that she always wore around the house. I pull it over my head. I smell the scent of her skin and her Pears' glycerine soap that melts away so quickly that I was never allowed to touch it. I put on a pair of her low-heeled shoes and walk around. The bumps in the leather where her bunions were catch my toes. Mommy's shoes are much higher and tighter. I look at myself in the mirror and pull my hair back from my face so that I can pretend it's trailing down my back instead of sticking up in frizzy spikes around my face. I pull her fox fur off the hanger and wrap it around my shoulders, running my fingers over the sharp little teeth. The dead eyes stare back at me. I lift the dresses and look underneath. Bobba has left one of her hatboxes and inside is her large sunhat with bunches of cherries and grapes around the brim. I take it out of the tissue paper and put that on too.

Walking carefully so I don't trip over the long dress, I sit down on the stool in front of the mirror. I open the top drawer again. At the bottom there are a few strands of Bobba's hair. I collect them and wind them round my fingers so they shine in the torchlight. I put them in my gown pocket for later. Zeida's songs are going round my head but I have forgotten the words so I hum *ay li loo loo*. I hear Zinkie's voice, *a boetie Beatrisie*, and I wonder if she's alright. Violet told me that she went to work for the children down the road. There are a boy and a girl there and I wonder how she knows about looking after boys. I touch the bow in my hair that Violet made. It's crooked but I leave it. Maybe Zinkie will come and visit me soon, maybe on Sunday, and she can fix my hair properly. We can sit and have tea and gingerbread on the carpet. I want her to see my dolls' house with the new dolls in it that Bobba and Zeida gave me before they left. Also my flower girl dress for my cousin Marilyn's wedding. Maybe I'll ask her if Zinkie can come too. She can fit into our car on the back seat with me. Behind me in the mirror, I see Zeida's hats arranged in a row in the cupboard.

I put all Bobba's things away where I found them, even the dress though I struggle to get it back onto its hanger. I take my letter from my pocket. It says

Dear Fairy Isabelle,
Please bring Bobba and Zeida back.
With love from Hannah.

I open the dressing table drawer and put it in.

Back in my room, I'm wide awake. The dolls' house is in the corner. I turn the brass key and open the whole back wall like a door. I take out my smallest fairy doll. Her hair is golden and her dress stands out like a tutu. Her bedroom has a double brass four-poster bed and tiny carpets. There are tiny lamps on two little tables and a stand with an oval mirror made of silver paper. The house has six little rooms. There is a lounge with two sofas next to the kitchen with a stove, a fridge, an ironing board and a table with tiny pots, pans and teacups. In the bathroom are the china bath and the washbasin that Zeida took me to buy at Lilliputs, the toyshop in Jeppe Street.

I sit the fairy on the carpet and put out the little china dolls dressed in flower material and lace that matches Bobba's dresses. From my tin of charms I take out Alice and Cinderella and Sleeping Beauty who is awake. I put them in a circle around me.

When Mommy comes in she is surprised to find me asleep on the carpet, hugging Clementine.

"Hannah, come. Time for breakfast."

I pick up each little doll and put her back in her place in the doll's house, the fairy doll in the bedroom and the china dolls into the lounge on the sofas. Then I make sure to lock the door so they will still be there when I come back.

Violet keeps Nathan's dinner warm. When he gets home, I send Violet to her room, bring his food in and sit with him as he eats.

"I know, you know."

"What are you talking about?"

"Have you no conscience?"

"What do you mean?"

"Unbelievable. No wonder you make such a great lawyer. You give nothing away."

My accusations build into a tirade that goes on and on, but he remains impervious, thanks me for serving the meal and for waiting with him. He goes in to kiss Hannah good night.

I take his plates to the kitchen. He reads for a little while before going to sleep, as if nothing has changed and I wait for his light to go off. Only then do I switch off the sewing machine and go to bed. I wake as the sparrows cheep their dawn chorus, surprised that I have slept at all with the empty pit hollowed out inside me. I have no idea what I will do now. I don't cry.

I call Nathan at work and refuse to leave a message with Felicity.

"Meet me at Anstey's after work," I tell him and he is already in the tearoom in the store when I get there. Though I have dressed carefully I know I look awful. My complexion is grey and pallid. I order *Five Roses* for two. I shoot the question at him before he can start talking.

"What now?"

"You know I'll never leave you."

"Is it me or Hannah you won't leave?"

"Let's not get carried away here, Susan. You won't let me near you. It's been so hard since …and what exactly does our relationship mean to you anyway?"

"You have no idea what I go through every day…."

We sip in silence.

"I know you blame me for what happened. I struggle to get up in the morning, get through the day, run the house. And all the while, you're…. There's a price to pay for everything, but this is too high."

I am working myself up into a frenzy after being silent for months. All my pent-up anguish comes spilling out and when I finally stop, there are tears on my face, the first I have let him see. He looks as shattered as I feel.

"There's nothing more to say. I'm going. Don't come near me and don't try to stop me." I pull on my gloves, take my handbag, shove back my chair and, without a backward glance, leave him to pay the check. As I walk to the lift, I hold myself together with an iron will to prevent myself from sobbing out loud. I walk out to my car. I have forgotten to cover the steering wheel and it is too hot to touch. Play with fire you burn is what I am thinking when I see a parking ticket on my windscreen. I had forgotten to feed the meter.

I don't know where to go. At home Hannah will want me to play with her and answer endless and unanswerable questions. If I go to Beatrice or Madge I will have to explain. I drive around without direction for more than an hour and then go and sit at the Zoo Lake. The lapping of the water soothes me as I look beyond the surface reflection of sky to the greyish depths below. Bright yellow weavers fly back and forth finishing their nests and there are several kayaks rowing up and down. No one disturbs my thoughts. I understand the attraction water had for my father.

Nathan and I have never spoken about that day in any specific way. We still don't know exactly how it happened. And how would it help, such knowledge? We have staggered along dealing with essentials. Now I cannot stop weeping, one memory triggering another.

I go to a public telephone booth nearby. It smells of urine and damp but I have no choice. I hold my hand over my nose as I slide the shilling into the slot and hear the call connecting.

"Bea, please, can I come round?" I am shaky and afraid to drive, so I go slowly.

Beatrice is on the lawn watching her son and daughter playing badminton. I envy the cosy family scene in front of me, her peace of mind. She pours me a glass of orange juice and patiently waits for me to begin. Kevin and Melissa are occupied for the moment, but I know that soon they will demand attention. I picture myself at home sitting at my sewing machine, drinking a surfeit of coffee while Hannah chatters to me and I don't respond. As my story pours out, Beatrice listens, then puts out her hand and touches my shoulder.

"Oh, Sue, I'm so sorry. Would you like me to speak to him?"

"Perhaps it's better you don't get involved right now. But thanks."

"I'll fix you a snack, shall I?"

Back home I take down my suitcase from the top storage cupboard and pack, first underwear, then dresses, blouses, skirts, shoes. Nathan walks in while the case is still open.

"Why?"

"I told you I was going. I'm finished with all this. You can tell Hannah." I see from his expression that he doesn't believe what is happening. Or doesn't believe me.

"Why now?"

"*I'm* not the expert on emotions, Nathan. You are. So you must know why."

"Why like this? Surely we can work something out? We have so much going for us, so much to lose."

"Like what exactly? Elise is dead. So is our relationship. Our family is wrecked and so are you and I. We both need to move on while we're young enough to start over." I go on taking my dresses from their hangers one by one, smooth out the creases, fold them in. I collect my shoes from the wardrobe, wondering how to choose.

"I could overlook Felicity. I know that you don't get what you need from me, but I still can't give it to you. I don't know if I ever had it in me, but I thought, before, that it was worth a try. Not any more."

Nathan, determined not to give up without a struggle, sits down on my side of the bed.

"Maybe we could talk the issues through? Let's book a

weekend away, the two of us and we can try. After all that's happened, how can we begin all over again with someone else, someone who doesn't have our shared history?"

"It's not about us anymore, or about Hannah, for that matter. It's about me and my life and getting what I want. I'm tired of seeing blame in people's eyes. And the thing is, they are not wrong. I mean, what real mother would have been sewing an evening gown for herself while her children were in danger? A real mother would have anticipated and prevented it. No, Nathan, it's not about what you want anymore. It's about me having to make a life for myself in the only way I know how. And that's not here being a wife to you or a mother to Hannah. Can't you see?"

"Please, Sue, maybe if you give us time…?" He sounds lame, despite his fancy law qualifications and so-called abilities and I'm sure he recognises this himself.

"Alright then, but don't you think we should tell her together? It's another major loss for her."

"It'll be her gain. Don't pretend it's not what you need and want as well. She'll have you to herself and you'll both love that. You are all she wants. I mean, why do you think she needed to come home from Miriam's in such a hurry? And you don't have to worry: I'm not going to contest custody. You can say I walked out on you and you can have her to yourself. It's that simple," and I click my middle finger against my thumb, but my nail catches against my wedding band.

He watches as I fold my underwear. Suddenly I don't care about privacy. It's as if it's not me doing the packing, and my feelings belong to someone else. There is so much about me that he doesn't know, that he will never reach or touch. We have shared a home and a bed, yet we are as disconnected from each other as a couple of strangers passing each other in the street.

The clothes mount up. I go to my drawer to fetch my jewellery box, take out the cameo brooch, pin it on my lapel and hand him the box.

"Please keep this safely until I have my own place."

"Where are you going to stay? Can I bring Hannah to see you, Susan, tell me?"

"I'll let you know when I'm settled, but perhaps you should keep away from me for awhile. For your own good. And I'm not sure I want to see Hannah too soon either."

"Have you got money?" He opens his wallet and takes out a bundle of notes. "Here."

"I'm alright for now, thanks. You'll be hearing from my lawyers in due course and then we can make a settlement."

"Who are you going to use? Which of my friends?"

"You'll find out soon enough. But one thing is for sure, it'll be a good one." I allow myself a small grin as I snap the suitcase shut.

He moves to lift the case for me, but I brush his arm away.

"Don't worry. I'm fine. I'll call Frans to carry them and Beatrice will be here in a few minutes."

Violet visits me on her off day. What a surprise. We greet in our usual way, and sit in my room. She tells me about my family. The old people have gone away and Madam Susan is living somewhere else in a flat. In the house it is only Hannie and Master.

"Here in my place, everything is otherwise," I tell her. There is no one to help me. I work alone, make beds, dust and sweep. There is no machine, only a bath outside for making washing on the wooden board."

"Bending over and soaping the sheets against the zinc like on hard stones in the Pietersburg river?" Violet asks. I nod and show her the block of Reckett's Blue. It makes the clothes white. My skin on my hands is chapped even though I put on Vaseline every day.

"Yes, I remember how we put our clothes out on the grass to dry. I sent Temba to collect stones for each corner so the washing wouldn't blow away." We laugh a little, then I say,

"These children are bigger than Hannie and Elise; they don't need me to wash or dress them. They are not Jewish people and so there's no meat to soak for *koshering*, no silver to polish for Friday night. This Madam shows me how to make curry and rice, also lamb stew. The children shout and bang the doors. I want to go to my room for peace but I first have to bring supper."

"Do you remember how we would clear the table together?" I nod. I see how she is missing me too.

"After there are visitors, this Madam comes to the kitchen and shouts at me. She counts each fork and spoon before she locks them away. She tells me if she catches me pinching she'll call the police. I believe her."

I cook outside on a primus stove and eat alone. The gardener is a young Xhosa from Ixopo and he works in a different garden every day. We talk a little to each other, but he doesn't know Sotho, so mostly I keep to myself.

"Look Violet." I take my needles and filosheen cotton and show her the flowers sewn on white sheeting. "I do this in my

223

lunch time until I go inside again. I want a wireless like yours for music, but first I must pay for my Singer. I have already put down 2/6 at the bazaar in Twist Street near the hospital."

I don't tell her that the Madam pays me only enough for bus fare and for soap and toilet paper and that I only have a few shillings left over. One day when she gives me more, I will walk to the bazaar and put some more money towards the lay-by for the sewing machine.

I also don't tell her that when I go off the Madam checks my pockets and my brown packet before she'll lets me leave. One Sunday I dress for church in my green uniform. I rub Vaseline on my legs and pull on the stockings I bought with the money from Jan Smuts Avenue. I pin on the brooch that Bobba gave me when I left, the same one she pinned on her smart winter coat when she and Zeida went visiting. It has a round shiny stone with a silver pin at the back. This Madam asks me,

"Where did you get that, Zina?" I tell her but I know what she thinks.

Violet says,

"I only have to look after the Master and Hannah now."

"How's Hannie?"

"She asks all the time where you are. She'd like you to visit. Will you come, Sina?"

"Yes, Violet. Maybe I will visit you one of these days. Then I will see her."

Violet says,

"Hannah goes to school in a pinafore and a white panama hat like Bobba's when she went out. Like the one she put in her hat box, remember?"

Then I see Violet look at my belly. Flat.

"I'm well now," I say. "I will take my leave at Christmas. Then I can be with Matlina and Ma for New Year and be happy."

Sometimes I think about Jack. I don't go back to the church where he goes, but instead I walk to the small one near here. I pray that one day I'll see Jack again to make another baby for us and he will give Ma nine cows for *lobola*. Then we will be all together. Happy.

Nathan comes to my flat with Hannah. It is weeks since I have seen them. She clings to him as they arrive and sits on his lap while we talk, refusing my offer of tea. She takes one bite of finger biscuit and leaves it on her plate.

"Hannah's doing really well at school and she's gone back to the art class too, haven't you Hannah?" He looks from her to me. "Laura's Mom takes and fetches them. It's working out really well. She has brought a couple of her paintings. Show Mommy, Hannah," but she holds the folder tightly closed.

I don't want to hear how empty his house is with only Hannah there; how they talk; what goes on at school; that she sometimes brings a friend home in the lift scheme or that she goes from school to play with Rebecca or Rachel. I can picture it all for myself, Violet cooking supper while he reads the paper, him working at the dining room table while Hannah does her homework or draws in the kitchen, where every figure she paints is enclosed with a black outline.

I put my cup down with a clink on the glass coffee table. Hannah jumps and her eyes widen. I have chosen the name Bric-à-Brac for my new shop where already the shelves are filled with bolts of cloth, boxes of trimmings and buttons, tea and cigarette tins, war memorabilia and costume jewellery.

"How are you managing?"

"Well," I say, "Joe referred me to a brilliant divorce lawyer. I'll come and get my boxes when I can." I have everything I need for the moment and have only collected my sewing machine and some of my clothes.

"How are your parents?"

"They seem to have settled in, as much as I can tell when I call them. The connection is often crackly and my mother's voice was always soft." What I think is at least now I don't have to control myself not to scream, say anything hurtful to them, not to burst out at my father saying what I really think.

"I've submitted the forms to the motor vehicle insurance on Morris's behalf. It is going to be paid out soon." His voice is controlled. I wonder what made him decide to claim. It will be a lump sum but I don't ask what he intends to do with it.

"I need to get new books for Hannah, Susan. Do you have any suggestions? We keep reading the same ones, over and over."

"But you always enjoyed that. Why change it if she accepts your repertoire? And have you got the energy to look for new ones?"

"Yes, perhaps you are right. The words and the stories are safe for both of us. I still leave her light on, but now she reads to herself before she falls asleep. She has nightmares often though and calls me in the middle of the night." I don't comment. "I have not lifted a hand to her since that terrible night." He looks down. "I was overcome. It must have been a kind of dementia. You know I will always regret it?" I wonder what he wants from me. Absolution I can't give.

In the early days after the accident, Nathan tried to cajole me into going with him to *Shul*, but to whom would I pray? And for what? At the convent, the Catholic girls said a few Hail Marys as penance. Now I keep my rosary beads in my bedside pedestal. Would confession help me, I wonder and to what would I confess exactly?

"I suppose you'll always worry about her."

"At work, I go from one case to the other, applying my skills and dealing with clients' needs and demands. I meet deadlines and win difficult lawsuits. I am currently the senior consultant for motor accident cases and have to talk Joe through the fine details of the law. Yet I feel as if I'm living someone else's life." He pauses for breath, "How are you doing, Susan? Really?"

"I told you. Fine. Thank you."

I think about having to have a section in my shop for antique silver and bone china. At the moment I have only a few fine pieces from a deceased estate collection. Clarice, my assistant, has a wonderful eye for both the real thing and a bargain and we spur each other on.

Nathan looks at me as if to say, let's try again but instead says,

"Come Hannah. Let's go home and walk in the garden. Susan, we'll speak tomorrow." I let them out with relief. Hannah does not look at me and I do not bend down or try to kiss her. Her cardboard folder bumps against her legs as they walk down the passage. I am surprised Nathan doesn't suggest another meeting or that we go for counselling which he has so often said might be helpful.

Had the circumstances been different we could have blamed the driver, cursed the visibility, or the condition of the road, or of the vehicle. Had the perpetrator been a stranger to us, we would have had a target for our anger, been propelled to sue for damages, demanded compensation in financial terms, despite the fact that nothing could ever bring the victim back. We might have spoken freely to our friends, each of whom would have had an opinion or suggested how we could write to the press and air our views about the court's verdict. We might even have set up a support group.

Instead, we are condemned to collusion as we protect each other, trying not to make the situation any worse by laying blame, and the home that was filled with the joys of family life epitomises the silence and shame within us.

At night, alone here, I study the makers' marks and hallmarks of the china and silver pieces with wireless music for company, but no longer do I have to look at Hannah expecting to see two little girls where there is now only one.

227

Only the twisting road
leading no one knows where.
Vi blaibt? Who is left?

Morris went to meet Samuel Lederman for their weekly
chess game. He wore his grey flannels with his smart hound's
tooth jacket and black leather shoes, laces tied exactly. He
kissed me goodbye and touched my hair.

Then he filled his pockets with stones. He walked into
the lake. Lake Kinneret. My Morris. He ended his life in the
water. In the place he loved. How he must have struggled to
die, such a strong swimmer. But no one had to clean up. Not
his flesh and blood.

His papers are in order, as I would expect from him –
instructions how to finalise his will and divide his assets
between Susan and me. A fund for Hannah's education.
A legacy in memory of Elise to be donated to the Jewish
orphanage in Johannesburg.

Sitting here alone in the fading light, far from home, I do
nothing, write nothing. Sometimes I take out my poems and
read. About Morris. About my life. About my life with him.

I think about the past, how we cannot change anything. I
think – if you lie under the ground, you cannot fall – *as men likt*
unteren erd, ken men nit falen.

The house is empty now except for Daddy and me. We don't talk a lot. Sometimes I tell him what goes on at school. Sometimes I bring Laura home in the lift scheme or go home from school to play with Rebecca.

Violet cooks us supper while Daddy reads the paper. Afterwards he works at the dining room table and I do my homework. He tells me about being a lawyer and helping clients. On some nights, I paint in the kitchen. Daddy asks me to tell him about the people in my pictures. There is always one little girl standing and one lying on the ground. Also a man.

Daddy still reads to me on my bed even though I can read to myself now. I still call him in the middle of the night but he doesn't smack me and I know he is sorry for what he did. We telephone Mommy every day. Daddy says it's so we can help each other.

We go into the garden in the late afternoon, Daddy and I, and watch the birds at the birdbath and throw sticks for the dogs. We often hear the *Piet-my-Vrou* but we have not spotted him yet. Sometimes when we walk, I take his hand and hold on tight. I ask him where everyone has gone but he doesn't answer. We never talk about Elise and I don't ask him for her photographs anymore.

Then Bobba comes home and I go with Mommy to Cape Town fetch her. She brings back everything with her in the same two trunks that Frans carried down the stairs for them at the Stone House when they left, the samovar, the books that have been from Russia to South Africa, to Eretz Israel. She is alone as she pushes through the crowd at the harbour, down the gangplank towards us. In my mother's arms, she holds on and kisses her on both cheeks in the old way.

"I couldn't stay there…. I'm sorry."

Mommy doesn't reply. Bobba bends towards me and takes my hand and draws me towards her. She puts her mouth on my head and holds me for a long time. Her face powder is damp and it smears onto my collar, leaving a brownish blot against the white.

"Our train tickets are booked," says my mother. "We need to hurry." She beckons a porter who comes immediately and lifts the trunks onto his trolley. I cling onto Bobba's hand and we walk together, my small steps and her slow ones.

The journey back goes on and on. I lean into Bobba's body and smell Pears and also her eau de cologne. I read 4711 on the blue and gold label when she takes out the bottle and dabs the drops on her wrists. The bunions on her big toes stretch her shoes, and once she stops talking to take a tablet. She wears her white gloves with a white lace collar pinned to her dress. I keep looking her up and down to see if she has changed. Her face is thinner but her hair has grown long again and she wears it in a plaited bun. She seems the same as before but I can feel her bones next to my face through her clothes. I have grown and she is only a little taller than me.

First the two of them are silent, then they speak softly to each other. I understand some of what they say and I have so many questions of my own, but there is no space for them. Bobba doesn't look straight at Mommy and when she starts crying, her body goes up and down silently as if she is going to vomit. I wait for choking. My mother offers her a hanky but she waves it away and takes out her own big lace square from her handbag. She sniffs from a small bottle called smelling salts and leans back against the dark blue leather seat. Her eyes are closed and she sighs a lot and tears roll down her cheeks. First she blots them, then rubs them away with her fingers.

Now that she is back and living with my mother, I cannot decide where I want to be. I don't say anything to Daddy but I think he can see my wishing in my eyes because one day he asks,

"Hannah, do you want to go and stay with Mommy?"

"No, Daddy, I want to be here with you for always."

I think he believes me because he doesn't ask again. Then he starts taking other women out for lunch and dinner. Once or twice he takes me with, and once, Felicity goes with me to see *The Wizard of Oz* and buys me a packet of popcorn. I wish for a pair of shiny shoes like Dorothy's and hum *somewhere over the rainbow* when we drive home because I don't know all the words yet. Felicity wants to find out about my school and my friends. Her perfume is different from Bobba's, like jasmine, and she wears pale pink lipstick and her long nails are painted to match. I wonder how she keeps them like that when she types, but I don't ask.

Then we go on a game trip to the Kruger National Park. I am in the back of the car with Clementine. Her clothes for the trip are packed into the leather vanity case that was Bobba's before she left. It has a shelf on top for brushes and combs and slides and elastics. Underneath I have folded Clementine's summer dresses, shorts and tops and her white cape with a hood in case it's cold when we go for our dawn game drives. At the very bottom are Bobba and Zeida's letters from Israel. In the pocket of my shorts I have my special see-through blue Sleeping Beauty charm. I keep putting my hand in to check that she's still there.

The road winds up and around through the mountains and Daddy swings the wheel sharply this way and that. There are marks on the leather from his sweaty hands. He checks the rear view mirror and his arm snakes out of the car to straighten it.

"Close the window, Nate, please," Felicity says as she smoothes her flower scarf over her hair. It is really a doek but Felicity calls it a snood. She folds down the sunshade and checks her face in the mirror, takes out a gold compact and pats powder all over her face and puts more pink on her lips. The compact is exactly like the one Daddy gave Mommy for her birthday. I wonder if it has Felicity's initials engraved on it. This morning when we started out, she wanted me to leave some of Clementine's clothes at home. She said that it wasn't necessary to take everything with. I held onto the vanity case and got into the car.

It's completely dark inside the tunnel at Waterval Boven. The night goes on and on. I close my eyes tight, ram my hand in my mouth and hold my nose. It stops the scream coming out. Suddenly the sun is on my eyelids again. I open my eyes. Daddy's hand is resting on Felicity's neck.

"What's to eat, Fee?"

"What would you like? We have my speciality, delicious tomato and lettuce sandwiches on rye bread with Piccalilli or tasty snoek and sprouts on whole wheat." She hands him a rye sandwich and places a serviette on his lap to catch the crumbs and to wipe his mouth. Then she passes me my peanut butter and Rose's lime marmalade sandwich on ordinary white bread. She says,

"Use your napkin, Hannah dear," and that reminds me to change Clementine so I put my sandwich on the seat. I'm not hungry. Now Daddy drives with one hand on the steering wheel and one holding the bread. As he finishes eating, I can see his eyes in the driver's mirror, moving backwards and forwards but not looking at me.

"Nate, I do hope that the accommodation has air conditioning."

"It's a luxury bungalow. Don't worry, sweetheart."

She sneaks a peek at me and then faces forward. She whispers to Daddy but I hear her,

"I don't see *how* the three of us can share a room. It's just not right."

I don't think it's right either. Daddy doesn't answer but he takes his hand off the wheel again and squeezes her shoulder. He smiles and I know he is happy because he doesn't mind her seeing his crooked teeth. I lift Clementine and hold her on my lap to watch the scenery rushing by. I sing *one more river and that's the river to cross*, and Daddy joins in, but Felicity interrupts,

"Oh Hannah, just look at the windmills!" So when I come to the part where old Mrs Noah gets stuck in the door, I stick out my tongue. Nobody sees. Near Pietersburg, we pass by the hill at Moria.

"Look Daddy! There's Zinkie's white horse. Maybe she's here too."

"Hannah, it's not Zinkie," Felicity says. "You should call

232

her by her correct name, Zina. And it's not her horse. It belongs to *all* her tribe." I stare out of the window.

"We could do a detour to see Bourke's Potholes. Hannah, what do you think?" Daddy pretends he's asking my opinion. It's where someone found gold during the great rush so now it's called Bourke's Luck. Far below, the swirling water is deep green and the golden brown rocks twist and twine through it. I clutch onto the wooden fence and catch my breath, then step quickly away and grab for Daddy's hand. On the swinging bridge there are only ropes to hold onto as I look down into the huge holes. I tell Daddy I can't go, but he picks me up and swings me over his shoulder like a sack of potatoes and carries me across.

"There you are, safe as houses," and he bumps me down on the rock pathway. I bend and pick up a tiny gold stone and put it in my shorts pocket for Hannah's Luck. Then I check with my fingers all around the pocket, in the corners, in the stitching. Sleeping Beauty's gone.

I want to tell Daddy so he can help me look for her. I call "Daddy, Daddy," but he's walking ahead and his arm is on Felicity's.

At Numbi Gate, he goes into the office to pay. They give us a brown rubbish packet and a list of Don'ts. Don't leave your car anywhere in the park except in camp and in fenced areas. Don't feed the animals.

"And remember, Hannah, don't smoke near the lions!" Daddy jokes. He knows very well that in our family only he and Zeida smoke.

He's bought a new pair of binoculars and he gives me his old ones.

"Hang them round your neck. Now twist these knobs." I turn the middle one to adjust the binocs for my own eyes.

"First one to spot a lion gets 2/6," Daddy says as he puts on his spotting cap that is really plain green. "It's ages since I came to Punda Maria with my brothers. I can't wait."

"They say Skukuza is the best camp," says Felicity. "Will we make it before the gates close, do you think?"

Daddy checks his watch. "Plenty time. Unless we see a kill." I wonder what he means. It takes forever to get to Skukuza. The sun boils through the window but when I open it, the dust from passing cars flies into my face. I try to count a tangle of monkeys in the marula trees and the mass of fat buffalo that cross the road in front of us. The buffalo stand still and stare at us, slapping the flies away with their tails. Two giraffes are standing close together and Daddy says they are necking.

At Leeu Pan the water hole is all set around with fever trees just like Rudyard Kipling said in the elephant's child story. Felicity makes me smear my skin with stinky lemon verbena to keep the mosquitoes away.

"Thank you, Fee," Daddy says, and I say "fi, fo, fum" very softly inside my mouth and he looks at me crossly under his eyebrows in the rear view mirror.

In camp, we sleep in a *rondavel* with a grass roof. Daddy's bed is next to Felicity's and mine is by the curved wall. The curtains have bird pictures in green and red with lots of leaves and flowers and behind them is the wire mosquito netting. On the veranda are a small fridge and a hot plate but Daddy makes a fire for a braai using dried logs and coal. It doesn't light at first so he tears up *The Star* he brought with.

"So much for reading the news," he says but he doesn't seem very upset. He winks at me, "It all goes up in smoke anyway."

As she boils the potatoes, Felicity drips with sweat and she wipes her forehead with her apron so her rouge smears across her cheeks like mud. When the potatoes are nearly done, Daddy wraps them in silver foil, also three onions and puts them into the hot coals and then he wraps his arms around her. The sky is midnight blue and we can see the Milky Way clearly. The only sounds are the whispers of the other visitors and the call of a Scops Owl. Daddy fetches his big torch and we stroll round the camp after supper, checking in the trees. The owl is nowhere to be found but we do find a couple of *nagapies*. We call them bush babies but their name really means night monkeys. A pair of red eyes stares at us from the fence. It is a laughing hyena looking for dinner.

"We must keep the veranda door shut, Fee. Otherwise these blighters could help themselves. And the monkeys are equally cheeky."

"Even here in camp?"

"They are clever enough to lift the dustbin lid, if they can get to it!" Daddy calls me, "Come my little *nagapie*. It's time for bed. We need to make an early start. I don't want my chief spotter to be sleepy in the morning."

When Daddy touches my shoulder to wake me, the stars and moon are still floating in the sky. The morning air is cool and I bundle Clementine with me into my blanket. We drink tea, eat our rusks and are first at the gate to get out of camp.

"This is excellent timing," Daddy says. "We're bound to see great game." We cross the metal grid bumpbumpbump and Daddy turns onto the sand road. Felicity tucks her hair into her snood, then puts her hand on Daddy's leg and leaves it there.

"Let's hope it's worth the rush and the loss of sleep."

A hairy male lion with a huge mane is lying in the road. He grunts and yawns.

"He looks well-fed and satisfied. Probably just finished eating. I wonder where the kill is," Daddy says. A stripe of zebra trots across the sand road and we stop for a herd of brindled gnu and group of male kudu. Then we have a picnic at Tshokwane. Felicity spreads a red and white checked plastic tablecloth on the metal table. Daddy fetches boiling water in our thermos from a huge cooking pot with a tap like the one on Bobba's samovar.

"Thank you, Nate. You're a honey," Felicity says. Daddy beams. We eat our cornflakes with warm milk because she forgot to freeze the ice blocks last night to keep the milk cool. Horrible. I want to spit it out but Daddy's forehead crinkles so I swallow hard instead. As we eat he points to the hoopoes and hornbills and to a funny bird without a tail called a crombeck. The glossy starlings come marching towards us and peck up the breadcrumbs in the sand. Their eyes are teddy bear gold but their beaks are like daggers. I want to feed them my cereal but remember the sign at the gate.

When we drive off, I pretend to snooze on the back seat. The light is very bright so when I close my eyes there are bright red streaks on the inside of my lids, and when I open them, black spots float around in front of me. My skin sticks to the seat. Daddy and Felicity are whispering and I can feel her eyes checking on me. Daddy puts his arm out and takes her hand. She snuggles nearer to him.

Suddenly Daddy slams on brakes and I crash to the floor.

"Whoa! Sorry, Hannah! Are you alright? Look! Cheetah!"

I get back onto the seat and hug my knees where I banged them, but at least it's not at the general hospital. I rub my eyes hard to stop the tears. Standing on an anthill on the side of the road is a cheetah mother with her three cubs.

"They're going to cross right in front of us! Look quickly before they disappear into the bush," Daddy says.

"Such sweet babies, Hannah. Can you see?" Felicity tries to turn my head and I push her hand away. I want to say, "I'm not blind, you know!" but instead I go "mmmm" and open my window, stand up and lean out. There is a soft breeze and it cools my skin until a fat man in the car behind us shouts at me to put my head back inside. He yells at Daddy to get-the-car-the-hell-out-of-his-way.

"Hold your horses!" Daddy says and switches on the engine. We roll forward until we can see the cheetah family even better than before and Daddy switches off again. There is no shade. We stay watching them for a long time. Daddy tells me they are the smallest but fastest predators and can race up to a speed of 75 miles an hour. They can kill small buck like impala but these ones are very sleepy because their tummies are swollen full. They look after their babies until they are two. Then the babies can take care of themselves.

"Do you think we'll see leopard, Daddy?"

"I'll give you two quid if you can spot one for us."

After that, I stare carefully out of the window into the thick bush. I spot a kudu bull and a family of waterbuck who have white circles on their bums as if they sat in paint, but no leopard.

We braai that night too, and afterwards I scribble letters and patterns in the sand with a sharp piece of thatch. Daddy and Felicity are huddled close to each other on the bench and I hear words that sound like "tell her" and "what about Susan?" but I'm not sure. Daddy puts one hand on her tummy and looks into her eyes.

Later, Daddy tells me he is going to marry Felicity and she shows me her new initials engraved on her powder compact: L. K. I don't let them see me crying and I don't call Daddy in the night, even though the little girl in white comes again and again.

Then I say I want to go and live with Mommy and Bobba instead and he says yes. The drive home to Johannesburg seems longer than when we went. When we get to Mommy's place, Daddy helps me to take in all my stuff but I won't let him touch Clementine.

Part 5
1994

Jumping Jacks
(Also known as Jacks, Jack Bones, Five Stones or
Knucklebones)

This game was originally played with the knucklebones of a
sheep. The main bone, the jack, is tossed up. While it is in the
air, the other stones are picked up from the sand until all have
been gathered into the player's hand.

The traffic is heavy up Jan Smuts Avenue. At the corner of Empire Road, women on the pavement with babies blanketed to their backs hold out their hands for small change. Most of the drivers ignore them. Occasionally a window opens and a few coins drop out.

At the Sanctuary, the sharp bends and the jacarandas conceal the house from the road, set apart from the city because of its height. As it emerges out of the shadows, its exterior is unchanged, the austere stone structure echoing the rockeries from which the bricks are hewn, part of the landscape itself. I drive up the driveway where my parents must have imagined children cycling on the tar, running around outside on the lawns, hiding amongst the shrubs; imagined us growing up. I shiver as I emerge from the shadows into full sunlight.

Inside, the rooms have been changed to accommodate all their occupants. Bathrooms have been added and the kitchen extended. The bedrooms are now lined with bunks and cribs, the walls covered with brightly painted pictures. I am only here part time, but I laugh at the antics of the children with Sister Dorcas who is loud and loving, and Lerato who reminds me so much of Zinkie with her devotion to children not her own.

I shake away the thought as Lerato leads Nonthlala, Enrico, James, Marina and Xhosi out into the sun for Marie biscuits and Lecol, children whose mothers work as domestics and cannot look after them, whose grandmothers are unavailable. I lay out sheets of butcher paper on the grass and mix up powder paints so the children can watch the primary colours become green, orange and purple, squares become houses, triangles, sailing boats and circles the sun and the moon, as if by magic. As we paint, they chat happily to each other.

"Oh look, I've done it."

"Hannah, look," they crow with delight.

"Hannah, someone to see you," Dorcas calls, coming out to find me.

"Can they wait until we've finished here, perhaps?"

"Come see for yourself."

I don't recognise the figure sitting on the bench until she lifts her head.

"Zinkie?"

"Hannie!"

The voice is exactly as I remember. I rush towards her and circle her in my arms.

"Oh, oh…." We are heaving and remain locked together as we sit, our eyes never leaving each other's faces for a second. She is neatly dressed in a black skirt and white blouse, with her hair hidden under a pink doek knotted around her head and the brooch that Bobba Leah gave her pinned onto her collar. She takes my hand in hers and her fingers caress my skin as I remember that other bench in the park long ago.

"Why didn't you come back? I waited and waited."

"How's Bobba? How's Zeida?"

"How's Matlina? Jack? Where were you? Why didn't you come back?"

"What could I do? I sent messages to you with Violet…."

"Yes, she gave them to me. It was never the same afterwards."

"How did you find me now?"

"Violet told me you are at this place."

Slowly she recounts her struggle, to keep working, to educate Matlina, Jack's disappearance from her life. And then,

"I lost the baby, Hannie. My baby. Like your Ma. She lost her babies too."

I hear Zinkie's use of the plural but I don't interrupt.

"And on that very same day your Mummy said that I must leave."

"But it wasn't your fault!"

We sway together, crying, "Sorry, so sorry."

Too soon it is lunchtime. The children come inside covered in paint. Already I hear the hungry chorus from the nursery. Xhosi and Nonthlala feed themselves, but many of the children are too small or too sickly and need to be cradled and fed.

"Zinkie, could you help, please?"

While I spoon mashed pumpkin and potato into one of the baby's mouths, she holds ravenous Thabo. She looks over him at me but this is too much for both of us and we drop our eyes. She burps the baby, then I change his nappy. I lie him in his cot under the swinging mobile made by my daughter Tanya with spaghetti noodles and flower buttons from Granny Susan's winter coat.

It's music time. Outside on the lawn, Sister Josie and Sister Tandi hand out drums, triangles and homemade rattles, small boxes filled with dried beans and lentils. I take Zinkie by the hand and introduce her, then put on the record player. We sing and clap and dance. Little hands grab our dresses, wanting to hold our hands, to be the centre of attention. When we sit in a ring they calm down, panting and sweating. I sing *tula tu tula baba tula summa*, Zinkie's lullaby, and we rock peacefully in time to the music, arms around each other, eyes closed.

"Bye, Miss Hannah. Bye Zinkie," they wave as we leave. I drive Zinkie back to the house where she is employed now. At home at supper, I tell Michael and the children about it. The girls are jumping up and down.

"When can we see her Mommy? And Matlina? How old is she now, Mommy?" And Ella argues,

"It's Maggie, Tanya, get it right!"

"Michael, perhaps I can bring Zinkie to work for us? Maybe Matlina can visit? I want her grandchildren to spend the weekend with Tanya and Ella. I think it would be great, don't you?" He says nothing and as we finish eating our canned peaches and custard, I am lost in my own thoughts.

I take the twins off to do their homework. They are conscientious workers but very competitive: Tanya is happiest when she has a paintbrush or pencil in her hand; Ella works out her sums in a flash. Michael helps with their science project and the three heads bend together over their books.

The telephone rings. It's Lerato.

"Hannah, would you like to come to the conference in Durban at the end of the month? We think you would be the best representative for the Highveld group because you have

243

the Sanctuary's interests at heart. It was a unanimous vote! Say you will. Please."

"Thanks so much, Lerato. I'll get back to you," but as I put the telephone down I pre-empt the difficulties. The thought of standing up at the annual congress terrifies me. However, I could make a difference to the lives of those children. I begin planning my address in my head, the tactics I will use to cajole money out of big businesses for improving the orphanage system across the country.

Michael walks into my study, continuing our supper discussion.

"It's not that I don't want Zina or those kids here, Hannah, merely that I don't want you spending so much time on other people – or their children. Isn't it enough that you teach all day and go to the Sanctuary after that?" He sounds exactly like the logical, goal-orientated businessman he is. "And you're doing to Tanya and Ella exactly what Susan did to you."

"Michael, look how you have provided for them. Those children, Zinkie's, Matlina's, they have nothing. Please, it means so much to me to do it. I promise I'll try to keep it in reasonable limits."

He is thoughtful for a while, then nods.

"Also, they've invited me to represent them at the annual conference."

"That's amazing, Hannah. When is it? And where?" This he can relate to.

"October. In Durban. I'll need you to take care of the girls, check their homework, do the lift schemes. I know it's a lot to ask."

"I can try and get you some funding through the firm." Having braced myself for his resistance, he surprises me.

"After you get back, perhaps we can take the girls to Warmbaths?" I think how much Zinkie and her family would enjoy it too, but I hold my tongue. I'll wait for the right moment before I suggest it.

The next day, I stop at O K Bazaars to buy lucky packets for the bigger children. We spend the afternoon at the Sanctuary sucking scented pink sweets, exchanging the little whistles and clickers and cackling at how silly we look in the paper hats.

There are no little charms.

Zinkie's return into my life opens wounds that I thought long healed. They feel open and raw once more and I work up the courage to speak to Beatrice. Outside on her patio, the view of the lilac jacarandas is pretty but flat, lacking the majesty of the Stone House.

"You know what they say, when you finally have the questions, everyone who might be able to answer them is dead."

"You mean who will tell you the truth, or who is still alive?"

"There is no one else to talk to except you." I watch her face, the resemblance to my Bobba, who was her aunt, more marked with the years.

"I'll give you some background, shall I? It was partly because of the convent, you know."

"I don't understand how going to a private school can be difficult."

"Being sent away from home at such a young age was, to a cold place where the nuns forced us to walk up straight, keep our eyes modestly down, maintain our dignity at all times. But there was a lot more to it."

"What was so bad?"

"Enduring Sister Boniface's reign of terror because nothing was good enough and no one could protect Susan from her wrath. Morris believed she was getting the best education. He had been through so much himself and was so proud that he could afford to send her there. He expected her to get on with it."

"The Jewish version of the stiff upper lip! And my Bobba couldn't help because she was too sickly. I know."

"Susan was allowed home only once a month. At the end of the weekend, she would have to pack up her stuff, get back on the wagon, and leave again. We cousins waved her on her way, running down the sand road after her, then we'd whirl off to play while she had to face another week of torment. The

246

wrench never got easier but she learnt to conceal her feelings.

"Then I was sent off there too, and I had my own taste of the punishments that were out of all proportion to the so-called infractions. Did your mother ever show you the scar on her baby finger?"

I look blank.

"Susan pulled her embroidery stitches too tight, wrinkling the cloth. When she muttered in frustration, Boniface slammed her metal ruler down. The whole class jumped and your mother's gasp only provoked a diatribe. The next time she was punished, Susan bit down hard on her lip not to give that witch any satisfaction."

"How do you know all this? Did Susan tell you?"

"Not at the time. Remember I was much younger and she hated that people might find out her weaknesses, or just talk about her for that matter. When we were older, she did take me into her confidence a little as she realised that there was no danger of repercussions, that I didn't think any less of her."

"Was it as bad for you? I mean you at least can speak about it!"

"Well, by the time I got there, Boniface was only teaching the older girls so I had a lucky escape. Also, my own mother listened when I told her what was going on."

"Whereas Susan's didn't." It is a statement.

"Don't forget that while your grandparents were loving to *you* in every way, when Susan was growing up Morris and Leah were new immigrants, battling to make ends meet, to integrate themselves in an alien society. They assumed a private Catholic education would be an advantage but it was totally at loggerheads with what Susan experienced at home. Her accent distinguished her from her parents and her education widened the gap so she often felt unsure of herself."

I had the feeling that Beatrice was stalling, avoiding the topic of Elise and my parents' divorce, but I was afraid that if I hurried her she would lose her train of thought.

"And then there was the accident. But," Beatrice takes a deep breath. It is as if she were making some irrevocable choice, "that wasn't all." Her eyes glisten, "You were one of a twin."

"What? What do you mean?"

"Your sister was stillborn."

My mouth is dry and I feel winded. So there *was* more than one meaning to what Zinkie had said.

"The heartbeat disappeared and Susan knew she was going to deliver a dead baby. She only spoke about it once, described her monstrous labour."

"But she delivered a live baby too."

I see Beatrice's distress at my reaction.

"I tried to get her to tell you when you were little. At first she thought that you need never know, then she was always waiting for the ideal moment."

"Why did my father go along with her?"

"Perhaps he couldn't go against her."

"They separated anyway."

"Yes, but only long afterwards."

"Yes, after Elise."

A heavy silence hangs between us. My thoughts are confused and I have no idea how to process what I have just heard. Maybe it explains everything; maybe nothing.

"Susan wouldn't go to her funeral so your father went alone. There were only a few of us there. Susan withdrew after that. No one recognised then that she was suffering from post-natal depression. No such a diagnosis existed in those days."

"Then she had to bring me up, a task she carried out, as she did her other chores, where she made lists and followed through."

Beatrice says nothing. I tremble and hold my hands around my arms to steady myself and ward off the cold. What I want to say but can't, is how the burden I carried all the years is the belief that I never felt my mother's love. But even now it feels disloyal.

"And what happened to Elise…," I struggle for words to frame my thoughts, "she locked that away too."

"She could not allow such thoughts to surface."

"No wonder she was never at home for a minute. I remember when you telephoned to speak to her and I told you she was out, you'd say, 'where's your mother running?'"

"She couldn't afford to leave any gap for thinking, let alone speaking. She was always like that. Soldiering on. At the convent she would practise her tennis strokes over and over against the vegetable garden wall the whole afternoon, or race up and down the hockey field hitting the ball on her own. She never would ask for help."

I knew only too well that shut-down expression on my mother's face, and the shut-out feeling I experienced because of it.

"Yes, my mother's creed was business as usual. There was an unwritten agreement that whatever happened it must never be spoken of, that what goes on in a family must stay in the family."

"She never could see the point of confiding in people or of falling apart. Better to exercise self-control; better to have a plan, or an appointment no matter how trivial, to get you out of bed in the morning. Don't forget she was brought up not to be a nuisance, not to upset anyone."

"Yes, and so was I. Not to make it difficult for everyone else. My own feelings never mattered. I was just expected to get on with it. When I didn't cry, it meant I was coping well. We never mentioned the accident, nor Bobba and Zeida's disappearance, nor Zinkie's…. Where is she buried? My twin?"

"The cemetery has a special section for new-borns."

"Is there a tombstone?"

"No, only a marker because she was less than a week old."

"Not even our surname?"

"A number."

"What was her name?"

"She wasn't named."

"So that was that. You know, when I had Tanya and Ella, I asked my mother where Elise was buried. Even then she wouldn't speak about it. Nor did she respond to me when I tried to hug her." Silence falls between us again. Eventually

I break it.

"No wonder she would never let me out of her sight. Not even on school tours."

"I know. When you wanted to join Betar and go to their camp, she telephoned me in a panic."

"All I wanted was to be with my friends."

"She said, 'Beatrice, I can't. I know it would be good for her, but I can't. What if something happens?'"

"I was fourteen years old, ready to meet boys. But, obviously you couldn't dissuade her."

"It was a breakthrough in our relationship for her to confide in me at all. And then I thought, well, what if something did happen to you, heaven forbid?"

"I once blurted out that lightning doesn't strike twice in the same place. I couldn't have been more wrong. We could have done with some guidance, that's for sure."

"Grief counselling wasn't an acceptable option to her and there were no groups like Compassionate Friends in those days."

"Nor groups for siblings…. Are they buried close together? The two little girls?"

"No, in separate sections. I'll go with you to the cemetery if you like, and show you."

"I'll let you know. Thanks, Bea."

But I know I will go on my own. I had lost part of myself and hadn't known. How could my mother not have told me? What had she been afraid of? Who was she protecting? And what power did she have over my father that he never spoke of it either?

When I leave, Beatrice embraces me, wet-cheeked. I can barely see to drive home. Michael runs my bath. He doesn't ask me what the matter is and I'm relieved, not yet ready to share what I've heard.

The jacarandas are in full bloom as Elise's *yortseit* comes round once more. I telephone the local chapter of the *Chevrah Kadisha* who tell me the numbers of the numbers of the two little gravesites, of the milestones on my journey.

I find Elise's easily in the children's section as a pair of spotted dikkops with brown and black wings flailing, drive me away from their nest, fiercely protective of their babies.

The white marble book stands open, grey and cracked, with its inscription, once shiny silver, Elise Kramer, deeply mourned by her loving parents, Nathan and Susan, sister Hannah, grandparents and friends. There is no traditional mound of stones: there have been no visitors. I pick up a small pebble and place it as my personal mark and softly mouth *Yitgadal vi'yitkaddash shemei raba*....

The metal grave marker lies broken and rusted on the dark sand, a little way away from where my twin is buried. SB292. I brush away the debris from the weatherworn bricks marking out the small rectangle and pull up clumps of dry weeds and entangled veld grass. It is apparent that no one has ever been here. Once more, I place a stone, this time on the grave of the missing part of myself, the half that I never knew and never knew existed until now. A verse comes to me from Genesis, the words that refer to the Mizpah, the unbreakable bond: *May He watch between thee and me when we are absent one from another.*

I always imagined that my mother's eyes slid over me and I struggled to convince myself I was wrong. Now I understand: first there were twins, then there was only one baby. Later Elise was with me, but then, once more, there was only me.

Had Susan been more open with my father, perhaps she need never have left. Had she spoken of her pain to me, could our relationship been different? The tall pine trees cast heavy shadows in the cemetery, but these are not nearly as dense as those cast by the past.

"Bea, what happened to Elise's things?"

"I came to the house soon afterwards to find Susan packing up everything into cardboard boxes."

"She was the complete opposite of the bereaved parent who keep the child's room as a shrine. Do you know what she did with Elly's music box?"

"Gave it away with everything else. She thought it was the only way."

"What, that she could close away the past in a box and that would be that? Well, she may have managed it for herself, but it didn't work for me." I can't talk about how guilty I felt because of the number of times I wished Elise dead, how I coveted her locket, how I should have stopped her when she dashed behind the car.

Beatrice seems to know what I am thinking. She says gently, her green eyes bright,

"Children's wishes do not make things happen, Hannah."

"When people saw me, they asked how my mother was, never about me. I felt ignored, overlooked, as if my feelings didn't matter, that no one understood. So I was always the good little girl who didn't cause them any more pain than I had already."

"What do you mean?"

"Obviously my parents thought the whole thing was my fault. You must know that."

"Blame you, a child? Never!"

"Then you don't, didn't, know my mother as well as you thought." I hold my breath. Beatrice gets up and kneels by my chair. She covers my hands with hers.

"Hannah! You surely don't believe that?"

"No one ever told me otherwise."

"If only they would have spoken to you, this would never have happened. It was never your fault, for heaven's sake."

"You know, about the twin… it's the same. Maybe I caused her to die by sucking up all her air and devouring all the

252

nourishment first. So I could live."

"Hannah, you're not that powerful?"

"… If Susan or Nathan were to blame, it meant I couldn't depend on them or feel secure. Far better to blame myself. But then I also needed someone, an adult, one of them, to say they forgave me."

"And no one ever did because they each carried their own burden of self-blame."

"Susan didn't." The angry words are out before I can stop them, "And did my father really have an affair with Felicity?"

"He always denied it and Susan never had proof."

"Was she just looking for a way out? I could never believe that *he* would deliberately jeopardise what remained of his family, although in reality, who could have blamed him?"

"Well, the belief gave her the impetus to leave. She thought that was the right move so she could develop her own life and you yours, that her problems would have less impact on you if she left."

"Did *she* ever have another relationship?"

"Even if I knew, I wouldn't answer that." Beatrice purses her lips, "It would have been up to your mother to tell you if she'd wanted you to know. But, even after the divorce she only ever spoke of one man in her life. Your father."

"Then why…?"

I do not expect a reply as I look out over the Johannesburg vista in the summer morning, talking to Beatrice as my mother never spoke to me, my mother who was so private she could never divulge her secrets, not even to her only daughter. It is easy to see now how her own lack of mothering, coupled with the abuse she endured at the hands of the nuns, eroded my mother's sense of herself; and how this was then exacerbated by the loss of my sisters. In those days there was a dark taboo attached to bereavement counselling, even had Susan been willing to seek it out, to acknowledge the necessity to mourn her lost babies. That I suffered the havoc of post-traumatic stress syndrome is clear now and no less so my parents, my grandparents or Zinkie. But it had no name then and so instead, Susan asserted that she was fine, that we were fine and did not need any help, thank you very much.

"Why did Zeida and Bobba have to leave?"

"Well, the Jewish belief is that if you change your location, you can change your fate. They would even change a sick person's name to confuse the Angel of Death."

"When there is a tragedy, people believe anything."

"Your Zeida even believed that changing his name from Yiddish to English would bring good luck."

"You know, I found Bobba's poems and letters, what she wrote about how they met, about Zeida's suicide. There are so many crossings out and smudges, I can barely read them."

"She used to find a little comfort in writing."

When Leah returned from Israel, broken in spirit after my Zeida's death, in a poor state of health herself, she once again lived with Susan. They forged a new bond as they spent time together, as my mother assisted my Bobba in her ablutions, her finances, and her medical needs. Still, they never referred to what happened.

"Was she relieved, do you think, that Zeida…? Were they…?"

Beatrice stands up and goes inside so I cannot see her expression. She comes back carrying a tray of tea and biscuits, tactics similar to Susan's when she wanted to avoid a topic of conversation.

"Don't forget there were no miracle drugs like Valium then that might have dimmed their pain."

"Even if there had been, there would be no removing it. Nor could we ever have 'closure.' That's just modern psychological jargon. All one can hope for is an ability to function in the normal world, to get through another day, for the ability to hide behind a mask which eventually becomes a permanent fixture on one's face."

I have carried my burden for so long I can't imagine what it might be like to be free of it. The meaning of my whole existence revolves around what happened that November day. To stop blaming myself, to give that role away, leaves me feeling bereft, though I should be only too happy to leave it behind.

But everyone has a story and this one is mine. I am possessive of it still, the secret I hold so close to me while pretending to be the same as everyone else.

Beatrice is totally accepting of me. We feel comfortable with each other, as our conversation continues over the weeks when smog blankets the roof tops as it never did in the days when I looked out from my mother's veranda and believed that, if I wished hard enough I could transport myself away on Pegasus' back.

"When I had Tanya and Ella my nightmares began again but this time of babies sliding out of reach." I hold my head in my hands, suffocated by my inability to prevent the inevitable. "I was so well-behaved that for twenty years I did not even think about the accident, buried it away so deeply that the dreams were the only way it could manifest itself. The pervasive silence that surrounded it was an inflammation that even Michael knew nothing about. So I was my mother's best pupil. She achieved her goal and maintained her honour code: no one ever knew what was really going on."

"Hannah…? Hannah darling…?" Beatrice is stroking my hair.

"Once the photographs were gone, so was that part of our lives. The only snap that survived was the one my father kept by his bedside when my mother left. It was as if Elise never existed and as if nothing I did was ever good enough. She never told anyone about my achievements."

"Perhaps she was afraid that the Evil Eye would take them away? It had happened before."

"She said that others would begrudge the success. She also thought that girls should never, ever show their intelligence."

"You mean be seen as a blue stocking?" We both giggle at how old fashioned this sounds.

"Oh yes! Never appear to be more intelligent than a man. So she hid her own light under the proverbial bushel too. What a waste." Beatrice serves us each another cup of tea and I breathe in my Zeida's concoction, as Beatrice asks,

"Do you remember when Zeida stood in your freezing kitchen, swilling out the teapot with boiling water, soaking the tea leaves for a precise number of minutes? Once poured into the glass, he added honey and a thickly sliced lemon wedge to the potion and sucked it through the sugar lump he'd popped into his cheek."

"Now all we do is dunk in a tea bag and add a teaspoon of refined sugar for a quick sugar-lift."

"It used to be a ritual of comfort and safety...."

"... as well as a fix. I still have Bobba's silver glass holders and her long handled spoons that reach the bottom to stir the honey properly."

"Those holders and the samovar were some of the things Leah brought with her as part of her *nadan*."

I look quizzical.

"Her dowry. Not that she had much. You and I never experienced such grinding poverty."

"When I asked Bobba why she came here and wasn't she afraid, she said there was no choice, all they had to eat *in der heim* was bread and brine."

"Even once they were here, they often didn't know if there'd be enough food for a nourishing meal. But there were also great possibilities if they were hardy enough and had the vision. Will you stay for supper, Hannah? There is *gefilte* fish and I have *chrein* made to your Bobba's recipe."

The more Beatrice and I speak about the past, the more we intersperse our conversation with Yiddish. What began as explanation has become reminiscence enhanced by the rituals of drinking tea and savouring the red horseradish that brings tears to our eyes.

"Was it a love match, Susan and Nathan's?"

"Your Zeida arranged it, but still we all thought so. After the accident...."

"Blackie, that was Zeida's nickname for me – he told me my eyes were like coals and my hair the colour of pitch – in the days before the dark."

"And then?"

"For a long time he didn't say my name at all. In fact he didn't speak much to anyone. None of them did. The house was silent. After Zinkie left, even Violet wasn't very talkative and the kitchen door was kept closed. I sometimes heard her singing the same songs that Zinkie had taught me. My parents sat in the breakfast room, my father doing the crossword, my mother darning.

"Only after she left did my father listen to his record collection again. I didn't enjoy his selection much. I should have told him that just his choice of music could keep her away. Everything sounded like a requiem as I sat with him night after night and stared out of the window or plodded through my homework. I wanted them to get back together so badly."

Over supper, suddenly I put down my fork.

"Sorry, Bea. I can't eat. It's like immediately afterwards, when all everyone knew was to offer me food, as if by concentrating on my mouth and stomach I could forget my heart. Instead I hid away in books, anything I could lay my hands on, my library books, hers, or newspapers that my father gave me that she thought unsuitable."

"And if anyone tried to speak to you, you stuck your thumb in your mouth, turned away, held onto Clementine for dear life."

"I was certain no one really wanted me there. Even that day when you said you wanted to watch Rag with me, I was surprised."

"And look what happened then."

"Or when I thought I'd lost Clementine. I sobbed and sobbed, the way we all should have done for the real little girl but couldn't."

It is not only the meal that takes time to digest when I leave Beatrice's place that night. Though her affection and loyalty to Susan are unshakeable, they do not prevent Beatrice from confronting the impact of Susan's choices. She helps me to see my mother's reality as well as my own, but how can anyone

257

else ever truly understand? Those were not her babies, not her siblings.

My twin sister was stillborn but Susan never spoke about it, going on with the day-to-day business of living as she always had. When we were shattered by the loss of Elise, she used the self-same rescue methods, tactics for survival that operated at the expense of her family on the silent battlefield of her marriage.

My father referred to the accident only once, after Tanya had stitches for a cut in her finger. Then he said that all wounds heal but if there is subsequent tragedy, the old scars reopen. The best one can hope for is that such scabs are not apparent on the surface of one's life all the time.

What he never did acknowledge was what happens when what is so deeply buried explodes and the resulting lava incinerates everything in its path.

Epilogue
2000

Cat's Cradle

Place a knotted piece of string over the hands and hook the strands between the fingers. Create new patterns by lifting these strands up, re-fashioning them into a diamond, a clock or a cradle.

Zinkie remains behind when we go on holiday, to feed the dogs and turn on the lights in the evening. We lock the main part of the house where the telephone is but give her a key to the kitchen to allow her access to the refrigerator.

We rollick through the gate on our return, Michael, Tanya, Ella and I, raucously singing *She'll be coming round the mountain* just as Nathan and I did when we climbed the last hill to the Stone House. Michael winks at the girls in the rear view mirror and the dogs leap at the car doors, peeing on the tyres and jumping on us as we get out.

"Down, boys, down!" Shoving them away, I turn back to the car to pick up my handbag and the rubbish packets in front of my seat. The house is in darkness. Michael goes to the kitchen door. It isn't locked and he pushes it open with a puzzled expression. He says nothing as he turns on the lights, always one to make sure of his facts before voicing them.

The girls bounce inside, carrying their backpacks and dolls. Tanya dumps Bride onto the table and she plonks onto the linoleum. Without comment, I lift her up and brush off her wedding dress. Returning to the kitchen door, I push open the fly screen.

"Zinkie! Zinkie?"

There is no answer. The dogs are still barking and I follow them to Zinkie's room. There is a bar of light beneath the door and I hear low moaning. I knock.

"Hannie…? Hannie?"

Zinkie is lying on her side under a mound of blankets, her hair uncovered and entangled, black and silver strands standing up in points. Her arms cradle her head and her eyes are closed. Sweat beads her face. Her glass of water is empty. Quickly I refill it at the outside tap, raise her head gently and let her wet her lips. She falls back onto the cushions, breathing heavily. Under her bed is an unemptied chamber pot. There is a nightdress pushed under the cushion, half wrapped in newspaper but I can see the crimson splatters. On her pine

261

pedestal is an empty bottle of aspirin.

"Zinkie? What is it? What's happening?"

"Sorry, Hannie, so sorry. The bleeding won't stop." Her nostrils are scabbed and her cheeks smeared. As she speaks, the bleeding begins again. On the floor is a bowl to catch the blood and a towel covered with brown stains.

"Michael! Michael!"

"Coming...what is it?" He assesses the situation straight away. "She needs a doctor, the hospital. And fast."

"Zinkie, can we move you? We need to move you."

"Mommy, what's happening?"

"Zinkie, what's the matter?"

Tanya and Ella have come to find us.

"I don't know, my darlings. Zinkie's sick. We need to take her to the hospital. Will you be big girls and go inside and get ready for bed while Daddy and I help her into the car?" Docilely they leave, but Ella, exhausted, puts her thumb into her mouth and starts pulling at her upper lip.

"Have you eaten anything today?" I ask. Zinkie shakes her head, no. "Can I give you bread and jam before we go?" Again the slight headshake. She is weak from the loss of blood. I hunt in her wooden drawers for a clean nightdress and a pair of bloomers but then realise that changing her is impossible. A big woman, she is unable to help herself but I am reluctant to ask Michael to help. She tries to lift herself but falls back onto the pillows with a sigh, her head lolling to one side. That the foot of the bed is raised on bricks doesn't help matters as she keeps sliding back down. I manage to heave her into a sitting position, turn her so her legs hang over the side of the metal bed and help her into her bloomers. Her skin is clammy to my touch. She points to the drawer where I find socks and once they're on, I take the top blanket off the bed and wrap her up. She holds the edges together, shuddering as I pin it closed around her neck with a large safety pin.

Michael meanwhile has finished emptying the boot of the car and taken our suitcases inside. The back seat is covered with the debris of our journey. He dumps it all on the kitchen table and floor, then drives the car as close as he can to Zinkie's room. Between us we half-carry, half-walk her and, puffing with the exertion, lie her down on the back seat. I tamp her nose with a cloth which becomes drenched with blood even as I watch. Back inside the house, I fetch extra towels and fill a hot water bottle to tuck in on her swollen stomach.

Which of us should take her and which stay with the girls? Michael decides that I will put the girls to bed, but when it comes to it, and although I have already said goodbye to Zinkie, I change my mind. He hugs me as I get back into the car. I can't think about how tired I am. The night is not yet over.

I look left, right, left and ignore the red robots. Zinkie groans, her body a leaden hump under the blanket. She tries to speak to me but I can't make out the words. Up Twist Street and Hospital Hill. The journey is the same, the same lampposts, the same streets. I whisper the names of the streets to myself like a mantra, as if this time things will be different.

I race straight into the parking lot and up to the emergency entrance where the sign is now in English, Afrikaans, Zulu, Sesotho and Xhosa. I put on my emergency flickers and speed through a line of backed up ambulances, jump out of the car and beckon an attendant who saunters towards me, flicking a cigarette stompie into the driving and grinding it out with his heel.

"Hurry," I said, "Please. Hurry."

"Here everybody needs to hurry." He peers into the car window and turns away. I call, "Please, can you bring someone else to help us?"

He mouths something and gives a mock-yawn. I see another guard and charge off to convince him of the urgency of my mission. Rapidly, he fetches a stretcher and his crew and together they lift Zinkie out of the car. By this time, she is too feeble to hold up her head herself.

I run after the stretcher and fill in the necessary forms, while all around is a hubbub of the sick, injured, old and young as waves of patients, doctors and nurses scurry about giving or carrying out orders. Patients lie in the passages and lean against the walls, with drips dangling from their wrists, bandaged, crying, smoking. I am assailed by the sounds of weeping as a mother brings in her son with a knife sticking out of his chest, blood pumping from the wound. A nurse whizzes in and removes him to be stitched and bandaged up. I try desperately not to faint away. There is no place to fall.

Zinkie is taken up to the ward. I place my hand on her as we trundle along.

"Will you be alright, Zinkie? Will you?"

For the first time, she gives me the smallest smile. Her eyes are yellow and bloodshot and she gasps for breath through a parched mouth. In the emergency ward, she is one of twenty, perhaps thirty patients where the beds are packed together with no curtains between. Notices proclaim hospital hours but visitors loll around on the floor, sharing the patients' soft porridge, wiping their hands on their clothes. The smell of rancid food, Dettol, stale urine and excrement makes me bilious and I try to hold my breath.

Once Zinkie is settled, I give her the sandwiches, her clean nighties in a brown paper packet and her toothbrush and soap in a purse. I slip a few coins into her hanky and she puts it under her pillow, changes her mind and indicates that I should pin it to her nightdress, under her blanket. She tries to thank me but I hold my finger to my lips and shake my head. For a while I sit hunched on her bed, squashed up, feeling conspicuous and in the way.

"Zinkie, what happened? How long have you been like this?" She tries to answer me but all I can make out is "Aspro" and "cold, so cold." She is still shivering. I ask the matron where I can refill the hot bottle. When I come back, Zinkie is sleeping, despite the noise and the incessant bumping against her bed. How will I leave her here? In this havoc, who will look after her properly? I must wait for the doctor. I must.

"Later," the matron says, "he comes later." She flaps her arms at me to leave.

"Will you make sure that he looks at Mrs Lekganyane

tonight, please? It's an emergency. She's bleeding all the time and it won't stop." The matron gives me a weary look.

"Here, everything is life and death. See for yourself." It is true. I am surrounded by the sick and the wounded, the results of family battles and township violence.

I try not to look at my watch. There is no bench. I could fall asleep like a stork. Eventually, I bump down onto the floor, leaning against the sick green wall over which yellow bulbs cast ghastly shadows. It is past midnight when the doctor arrives. He shoos the visitors out impatiently and I watch from the door as he checks pulses and blood pressure, tut-tutting all the while. Finally he emerges.

"Please, can I speak to you for a moment?" He pauses and swivels, his eyes sunk into his face with exhaustion.

"How can I help you?" At least he is prepared to talk to me. "The woman in the emergency ward, the one bleeding through her nose...."

"An overdose of aspirin. They never read the labels."

"Why...?"

"It thins the blood. Should never be taken for more than ten days."

"Will she...?"

"I can't answer you. Tonight. Tomorrow. Then we'll know."

"Can't you do something? Anything? Please?"

He looks at me as if to say, where were you when it was happening? and walks away. I trudge back to Zinkie's bed, knowing I can't stay there the whole night and that already Michael will be worried as it is after two o'clock.

I telephone the hospital the next day to find out how Zinkie is doing but no one knows who I'm talking about. By the time I get back there in the afternoon, someone else occupies her bed. The matron hands me Zinkie's personal belongings wrapped in yesterday's newsprint.

Susan visited my father regularly before she died, even though by the time Nathan was admitted to this care facility, they had lived apart for many years. His colleagues are too busy to do so, or else cannot endure being witness to his decline from the sharp-tongued, smart and insightful lawyer he was to the way he is now, to be reminded of their own vulnerability.

I find him alone. Beneath his taut skin with its red and broken blood vessels, the fine bone structure remains, the Roman nose slightly too large, the thin lips shaped like a bow, the imperfect front teeth. I search for a smidgeon of recognition but his grey-green eyes are veiled. Occasionally, I think he knows who I am, but then he speaks and I know I am only a stranger who brings him his tea and biscuits and fetches his washcloth.

Next to his bed is the framed picture of Susan, Nathan, Elise and I, the only photograph of Elise that he managed to salvage after Susan tried to eradicate our history. I don't need it to remind me of Elise's dribbly smile or the sores on her fingers where she broke the skin with her teeth.

"Dad? Daddy?" I rest my hand on his arm and settle down on the edge of his bed. "Would you like me to read to you?" I brush the fringe of grey hair from his forehead, uncertain which is the more devastating side of senile dementia: when he is passive as if he has already vacated his body, or when he fights aggressively for something that is still important to him.

I have more questions than ever now, having spoken to Beatrice, but realise that she would not have confided in me so freely had my father been well, that he might regard her disclosures as disloyal. Certainly my mother would have found them unforgivable, the supreme breech of trust.

The matron helps me to wheel my father outside into the garden. In the beginning, I read wherever the pages fell open but these days I choose subject matter that interests me – to him it no longer makes any difference. He doesn't react, interact or remember.

Today, I select a passage in the Britannica about the life of Rudyard Kipling, named for the lake in Staffordshire where his parents courted, brought up by a governess in England while his parents lived in Bombay, a child who lived in his imagination, concocting tales to explain his universe. Although my father does not know me now, and did not recognise who I was then, the tales continue to bind us together, as does our shared history.

The matron comes towards us,

"Alright Mr Kramer?" but he doesn't answer. Above us, two nests are under construction. The sparrow's is muddled, an irregular, hairy ball of dry twigs on which the male builder twitters gleefully. The weaver's is an architectural creation of criss-crossed grasses hanging neatly from a thin branch. The sparrow seems to leave the final outcome to chance, while the weaver strives for perfection. In each nest, babies will struggle to adulthood.

"I have to go, Daddy." I close the book, lean down and hug him. There is no response, no touch, not even of fingertips. I blow him a kiss. Whether because of the angle of his body or because there is a tiny window of clarity for him, I fancy that he raises his head slightly and that his lips sliver a smile.

As I unlock my car, a middle-aged woman strides towards the entrance and disappears behind the frosted glass, sliding doors, followed by a lanky young man: Felicity with Anthony, my half-brother.

When I get home, the twins are waiting for me at the front door.

"Mommy, we need to go to the library. Why are you so late?"

"Sorry girls. We'll go tomorrow, straight after school, I promise. Wednesday is your early day, remember?"

Michael returns home to find us on the couch reading.

My father's favourites were the Kipling stories that bring victory to the underdog: to Rikki Tikki Tavi, the mongoose who defeated the cobra couple, Nag and Nagaina, against all odds; to the elephant's child, full of insatiable curiosity who eventually got his own back on his spanking relatives; tales that my father knew by heart and that he recounted to me while perched on my bed. Each time, I held my breath at the exciting bits, laughed in the same places and joined in the chorus, just as Tanya and Ella do now.

But what I always loved most was when he cleared his throat and, in his deep, warm voice he called me his Best Beloved.

Sleep eludes me just as it always did in the Stone House on the hill where the flagstones in the kitchen and the bathrooms were impossible to warm, though a fire burned in the coal stove; the house that could be reached only by the twisting driveway that became steeper the higher up it went; where none of us ever complained because that was just how it was. I fetch a hot water bottle for my toes as Michael sleeps on, unaware of how night slices open the memories encased in silence, the defence my family erected against what happened to us.

In the lounge, on the mantelshelf is a pair of bronze shoes, children's size 4D, shiny reddish-gold, scratched at the little toe and scuffed along the fronts, the narrow heels and wide fronts turned up and inwards. The buttons are safely stitched on with a loop, pushed through the tightly bound buttonholes. Inside, revealing the original red kid leather in places, the bronze is now a mottled green and crackles under my fingers. There are no holes in the soles – I outgrew the shoes long before I wore them out but they still preserve the shape of my journey.

There should be a second pair, Elise's ankle boots, slightly smaller, scratched and battered from when she walked and then ran; the day when I called and called and nobody came.

Did our lives unravel with a neglected shoelace? None of us ever knew.

Spotted Dikkops

Lethal-billed,
Mom and Dad stand guard,
luring me away from their young;
the price I'll pay if I intrude,
a pecking, not a kiss on the cheek.
I give them a wide berth
in wonder
at how they keep their babies
out of my reach.

In the cemetery.
Alone in veld-green icy-heat,
transfixed by the hissing song,
I stand out, my pain breaking
my human camouflage.
The dikkops merge,
black and brown,
into the background.

Head bowed,
I place a stone on each little grave
far away from Mom and Dad.
Separated in life,
they are together in death.

Is there some message
on the inside of stones:
love's declarations or
the secret of life?
Those that I place are small
insignificant cairns to memory,
as the trees dance,
and the jasmine surprises me
on the fence.

GLOSSARY

Yiddish
Afrika, der goldene land: Africa, the land of gold
alef: the letter a
bagel: round roll with a hole through the centre
bashert: destiny, fate, one true love.
beis: the letter b
bensh; benshing: to make the blessing after eating
bensh licht: light candles
Bikkur Cholem: organisation that helps the poor and sick
bima: raised platform from which the Torah reading is given
bissele: small piece
brocha: blessing; festive meal
burikes: beetroot
bulves: potatoes
challah: plaited, special bread; kitke
Chanukah: festival of celebration
Chevrah Kaddisha: Jewish burial society
cholent: special dish prepared before Shabbos to be eaten on
    Shabbos
chrein: horse radish sauce
fardroes: worry; sadness
frum: orthodox and observant
gehakte: chopped
gemorrahs: Gemarra; part of the Talmud
glezele tei: tea in a glass

greisen dank: thank you very much
hotinke maizele: darling little mouse
immigranten: immigrants
in der heim: at home in the old country
Kaddish: prayer for the dead
kale: bride
kasher: to make kosher food according to correct process
kein ainhora: lit. no evil eye; fig. amazement at
    accomplishment
kitke: special plaited bread for the Sabbath
klezmer: music
kosher: food fulfilling requirements of Jewish law
kreplach: meat pies
landsman (pl. landsleit): those who came from the same
    place in the old country (Lithuania, Latvia, White
    Russia, Poland)
latkes: potato pancakes
l'chaim: a toast to life
lesheiv basuccah: to sit in the succah
Litvak: of Lithuanian descent
Magen David: Jewish Star of David
Mama-loshen: mother tongue
matza: unleavened cake
maven: expert
Megillah: The story read on Purim of how Queen Esther
    saved the Jewish people from Haman.
mehitsa: curtain separating men from women in synagogue
mishpoche: family
mitzvah: good deed
niggunim: songs
Oifn pripertchile brent a fyerel: a fire burns in the coal stove
parnose: livelihood
perena: eiderdown
perogen: meat pies
pripertchik: coal stove
Purim: festival of celebration
rov: rabbi

schachat: ritual slaughterer
schadchen: matchmaker
Shabbos: Sabbath
Shema: holy prayer said twice a day
sheine meidele: beautiful girl
shmattes: lit. rags; clothes
shochet: man who kills fowls, sheep and cows according to
    ritual law
shpiel: play
shtetl: little village in the old country
shtiebele: small prayer house
shtum: quiet
Shul: Synagogue
shvaig: keep quiet
siddur: prayer book
simcha: joyous occasion
succah: flimsy house with three sides and a roof of leaves
tallis: prayer shawl
Talmud: Jewish civil and ceremonial law
tate-mame: parents
teiglach: small cakes boiled in honey
treif: non-kosher
tryer: itinerant salesman who tried to peddle all manner of
    transportable goods.
Tsena Rena: Yiddish Bible for women
tsoris: trouble
tsurissen: torn
tumel: loud noise and confusion
vei is mir: expression of distress (lit. I am hurting)
yeshiva: place of religious study
yicchus: of noble descent
Yit gadal vi'yitkaddash shemai raba: opening line of mourner's
    Kaddish
Yom Tov; Yom Teivim: holy day; holy days
yortseit: anniversary of the day of death
yortseit candle: the flame lit every year on the anniversary

Sesotho

boloko: cow dung

diketo: game played with one hole and 26 stones

kobo: blanket

lelwala: stone mortar

lobola: bride price paid by the tribal groom to his future wife's family

morabaraba: game played with six holes and stones in the sand

pepa: to carry a baby on the back in a blanket or towel

setlatla: stupid fool

tshetlo: pestle

wena: you